OXFORD WORLD'S CLASSICS

FRANZ KAFKA

The Metamorphosis
and Other Stories

Translated by
JOYCE CRICK

With an Introduction and Notes by
RITCHIE ROBERTSON

OXFORD
UNIVERSITY PRESS

OXFORD
UNIVERSITY PRESS

Great Clarendon Street, Oxford OX2 6DP

Oxford University Press is a department of the University of Oxford.
It furthers the University's objective of excellence in research, scholarship,
and education by publishing worldwide in

Oxford New York

Auckland Cape Town Dar es Salaam Hong Kong Karachi
Kuala Lumpur Madrid Melbourne Mexico City Nairobi
New Delhi Shanghai Taipei Toronto

With offices in

Argentina Austria Brazil Chile Czech Republic France Greece
Guatemala Hungary Italy Japan Poland Portugal Singapore
South Korea Switzerland Thailand Turkey Ukraine Vietnam

Oxford is a registered trade mark of Oxford University Press
in the UK and in certain other countries

Published in the United States
by Oxford University Press Inc., New York

Translation © Joyce Crick 2009
Editorial matter © Ritchie Robertson 2009

First published as an Oxford World's Classics paperback 2009

British Library Cataloguing in Publication Data

Data available

Library of Congress Cataloging-in-Publication Data

Kafka, Franz, 1883–1924.
[Short stories. English. Selections]
The Metamorphosis and Other Stories / Franz Kafka;
translated by Joyce Crick ; with an introduction and notes by Ritchie Robertson.
p. cm. — (Oxford world's classics)
Includes bibliographical references.
ISBN 978-0-19-923855-2 (pbk. : acid-free paper)
1. Kafka, Franz, 1883–1924—Translations into English. I. Crick, Joyce. II. Title.
PT2621.A26A6 2009
833'.912—dc22
2009005387

Typeset by Cepha Imaging Private Ltd., Bangalore, India
Printed in Great Britain
on acid-free paper by
Clays Ltd., St Ives plc

ISBN 978-0-19-923855-2

9

CONTENTS

BIOGRAPHICAL PREFACE

FRANZ KAFKA is one of the iconic figures of modern world literature. His biography is still obscured by myth and misinformation,
yet the plain facts of his life are very ordinary. He was born on 3 July
1883 in Prague, where his parents, Hermann and Julie Kafka, kept a
small shop selling fancy goods, umbrellas, and the like. He was the
eldest of six children, including two brothers who died in infancy
and three sisters who all outlived him. He studied law at university,
and after a year of practice started work, first for his local branch of
an insurance firm based in Trieste, then after a year for the state-run
Workers' Accident Insurance Institute, where his job was not only to
handle claims for injury at work but to forestall such accidents by
visiting factories and examining their equipment and their safety pre-
cautions. In his spare time he was writing prose sketches and stories,
which were published in magazines and as small books, beginning
with *Meditation* in 1912.

In August 1912 Kafka met Felice Bauer, four years his junior, who
was visiting from Berlin, where she worked in a firm making office
equipment. Their relationship, including two engagements, was carried
on largely by letter (they met only on seventeen occasions, far the longest
being a ten-day stay in a hotel in July 1916), and finally ended when in
August 1917 Kafka had a haemorrhage which proved tubercular; he
had to convalesce in the country, uncertain how much longer he could
expect to live. Thereafter brief returns to work alternated with stays
in sanatoria until he took early retirement in 1922. In 1919 he was
briefly engaged to Julie Wohryzek, a twenty-eight-year-old clerk, but
that relationship dissolved after Kafka met the married Milena Polak
(née Jesenská), a spirited journalist, unhappy with her neglectful husband. Milena translated some of Kafka's work into Czech. As she lived
in Vienna, their meetings were few, and the relationship ended early in
1921. Two years later Kafka at last left Prague and settled in Berlin
with Dora Diamant, a young woman who had broken away from her
ultra-orthodox Jewish family in Poland (and who later became a noted
actress and communist activist). However, the winter of 1923–4, when
hyperinflation was at its height, was a bad time to be in Berlin. Kafka's
health declined so sharply that, after moving through several clinics and
sanatoria around Vienna, he died on 3 June 1924.

The emotional hinterland of these events finds expression in Kafka's letters and diaries, and also—though less directly than is sometimes thought—in his literary work. His difficult relationship with his domineering father has a bearing especially on his early fiction, as well as on the *Letter to his Father*, which should be seen as a literary document rather than a factual record. He suffered also from his mother's emotional remoteness and from the excessive hopes which his parents invested in their only surviving son. His innumerable letters to the highly intelligent, well-read, and capable Felice Bauer bespeak emotional neediness, and a wish to prove himself by marrying, rather than any strong attraction to her as an individual, and he was acutely aware of the conflict between the demands of marriage and the solitude which he required for writing. He records also much self-doubt, feelings of guilt, morbid fantasies of punishment, and concern about his own health. But it is clear from his friends' testimony that he was a charming and witty companion, a sportsman keen on hiking and rowing, and a thoroughly competent and valued colleague at work. He also had a keen social conscience and advanced social views: during the First World War he worked to help refugees and shell-shocked soldiers, and he advocated progressive educational methods which would save children from the stifling influence of their parents.

Kafka's family were Jews with little more than a conventional attachment to Jewish belief and practice. A turning-point in Kafka's life was his encounter with Yiddish-speaking actors from Galicia from whom he learned about the traditional Jewish culture of Eastern Europe. Gradually he drew closer to the Zionist movement: not to its politics, however, but to its vision of a new social and cultural life for Jews in Palestine. He learnt Hebrew and acquired practical skills such as gardening and carpentry which might be useful if, as they planned, he and Dora Diamant should emigrate to Palestine.

A concern with religious questions runs through Kafka's life and work, but his thought does not correspond closely to any established faith. He had an extensive knowledge of both Judaism and Christianity, and knew also the philosophies of Nietzsche and Schopenhauer. Late in life, especially after the diagnosis of his illness, he read eclectically and often critically in religious classics: the Old and New Testaments, Kierkegaard, St Augustine, Pascal, the late diaries of the convert Tolstoy, works by Martin Buber, and also extracts from the Talmud.

His religious thought, which finds expression in concise and profound aphorisms, is highly individual, and the religious allusions which haunt his fiction tend to make it more rather than less enigmatic.

During his lifetime Kafka published seven small books, but he left three unfinished novels and a huge mass of notebooks and diaries, which we only possess because his friend Max Brod ignored Kafka's instructions to burn them. They are all written in German, his native language; his Czech was fluent but not flawless. It used to be claimed that Kafka wrote in a version of German called 'Prague German', but in fact, although he uses some expressions characteristic of the South German language area, his style is modelled on that of such classic German writers as Goethe, Kleist, and Stifter.

Though limpid, Kafka's style is also puzzling. He was sharply conscious of the problems of perception, and of the new forms of attention made possible by media such as the photograph and cinema. When he engages in fantasy, his descriptions are often designed to perplex the reader: thus it is difficult to make out what the insect in *The Metamorphosis* actually looks like. He was also fascinated by ambiguity, and often includes in his fiction long arguments in which various interpretations of some puzzling phenomenon are canvassed, or in which the speaker, by faulty logic, contrives to stand an argument on its head. In such passages he favours elaborate sentences, often in indirect speech. Yet Kafka's German, though often complex, is never clumsy. In his fiction, his letters, and his diaries he writes with unfailing grace and economy.

In his lifetime Kafka was not yet a famous author, but neither was he obscure. His books received many complimentary reviews. Prominent writers, such as Robert Musil and Rainer Maria Rilke, admired his work and sought him out. He was also part of a group of Prague writers, including Max Brod, an extremely prolific novelist and essayist, and Franz Werfel, who first attained fame as avant-garde poet and later became an international celebrity through his best-selling novels. During the Third Reich his work was known mainly in the English-speaking world through translations, and, as little was then known about his life or social context, he was seen as the author of universal parables.

Kafka's novels about individuals confronting a powerful but opaque organization—the court or the castle—seemed in the West to be fables of existential uncertainty. In the Eastern bloc, when they became accessible, they seemed to be prescient explorations of the fate of the individual within a bureaucratic tyranny. Neither approach can be set aside. Both were responding to elements in Kafka's fiction. Kafka worries at universal moral problems of guilt, responsibility, and freedom; and he also examines the mechanisms of power by which authorities can subtly coerce and subjugate the individual, as well as the individual's scope for resisting authority.

Placing Kafka in his historical context brings limited returns. The appeal of his work rests on its universal, parable-like character, and also on its presentation of puzzles without solutions. A narrative presence is generally kept to a minimum. We largely experience what Kafka's protagonist does, without a narrator to guide us. When there is a distinct narrative voice, as sometimes in the later stories, the narrator is himself puzzled by the phenomena he recounts. Kafka's fiction is thus characteristic of modernism in demanding an active reading. The reader is not invited to consume the text passively, but to join actively in the task of puzzling it out, in resisting simple interpretations, and in working, not towards a solution, but towards a fuller experience of the text on each reading.

INTRODUCTION

THIS collection includes four of the seven books that Kafka published during—or just after—his lifetime.[1] Even if Kafka's three novels had remained unpublished, in keeping with his professed wish, his short fiction would have given him a secure place in the modernist canon. During his life they brought him, if not fame, at least the respect of many fellow-writers. Robert Musil invited him to write for the *Neue Rundschau* (*New Review*), the leading literary magazine in Germany, though Kafka was unable to accept the invitation; Rainer Maria Rilke attended the public reading of *In the Penal Colony* that Kafka gave in Munich, and revealed in conversation that he knew and admired Kafka's previous stories. Kafka was not as obscure an author as is sometimes imagined.

Yet Kafka's literary output is small, and was produced under difficult conditions. He held down a day job as an extremely able and valued employee in a state-run workers' accident insurance firm. Officially his working hours were from 8 a.m. to 2 p.m. without a break, but of course he often had to stay in the office for longer, and after the outbreak of war in 1914 the absence of many staff serving in the army increased the workload for those who, like Kafka, were exempted from military service on the grounds that they were indispensable. In his early years Kafka also paid many visits to factories in the industrial zone of northern Bohemia to report on the safety standards of the machinery in use. On leaving work he would walk, swim, or rest. Since he lived with his parents in their flat until he was 30, he could not find peace to write until everyone else had gone to bed.

Having such limited writing time, Kafka tended to favour short fiction. Even his novels, especially *The Trial*, are very much series of episodes. The mood-pictures which make up *Meditation* are very short; eight of them appeared in the Munich periodical *Hyperion* in 1908, marking Kafka's debut as a published author. Brevity had the advantage that the initial impulse could be sustained throughout the text. With longer texts, Kafka, who never planned his work, found

---

[1] The others are *The Stoker* (1913), which also forms the first chapter of the unfinished, posthumously published novel *The Man Who Disappeared*; *A Country Doctor: Little Tales* (1919; actually published in May 1920); and *A Hunger Artist: Four Stories* (published in August 1924, two months after Kafka's death).

that his original inspiration tended to flag. The great exception was *The Judgement*, written in a single night, but he never again achieved such a unified, coherent piece of writing; he was dissatisfied with the end of *The Metamorphosis*, perhaps because of the change of perspective required by the protagonist's death.

As an author, Kafka was not only self-critical, but as perplexed by his own works as his readers have subsequently been. He wrote to Felice Bauer: 'Can you discover any meaning in *The Judgement*—some straightforward, coherent meaning that one could follow? I can't find any, nor can I explain anything in it.'[2] His writing is sharp, precise, and beautifully paced, yet his descriptions become enigmatic and bewildering on close scrutiny, and he packs into his narratives a wealth of suggestions and implications which refuse to yield any simple or single interpretation. The philosopher Adorno wrote of Kafka: 'Each sentence says "Interpret me", and none will permit it.'[3] At the same time, Kafka's narratives and images are frighteningly direct. A father condemns his son to death. A commercial traveller is turned into an insect. Colonial justice is administered by an elaborate machine. Themes of power and violence are given palpable form. Yet the messages of the stories are complex, ambivalent, and inexhaustible.

Kafka's literary skill is apparent also in the long autobiographical letter he wrote to his father (but fortunately never delivered) in November 1919. The ability to argue a case that Kafka had developed as a lawyer is exercised with eloquence, passion, cunning, and a precise and vivid recall of crucial episodes from his childhood. How far the *Letter to his Father* should be seen as literature is still undecided, but as a text on the borders of autobiography and imaginative fiction it remains a painful masterpiece.

Meditation

Kafka's first book was a collection of impressionist sketches of urban life, whimsical, wistful, and gently humorous. This genre was popular at the turn of the century. Its main exponents included the Viennese Peter Altenberg, whose book of sketches, *Wie ich es sehe*

---

[2] Letter of 2 June 1913 in Kafka, *Letters to Felice*, tr. by James Stern and Elizabeth Duckworth (London: Vintage, 1992), 265.

[3] Theodor W. Adorno, 'Notes on Kafka', in *Prisms*, tr. Samuel and Shierry Weber (London: Spearman, 1967), 243–71 (p. 246).

(*As I see it*) aroused great attention when published in 1897, and the Swiss Robert Walser (himself an important author for Kafka). One reader imagined that *Meditation* had been written by Walser under a strange pseudonym, and had to be told: 'Kafka isn't Walser but really a young man in Prague with that name.'[4]

These sketches begin with the relative happiness of childhood and end with the unhappiness of an adult persona. Childhood in 'Children on the Highway' is above all a fluid state of being. The boundaries between inside and outside are easily crossed. Sitting on a swing in his parents' garden, the boy narrator is aware of people going past outside. Passers-by touch the curtains; a friend leaps through the window to fetch the narrator. Emotions are fluid too: the boy sighs for no apparent reason; later the children are suddenly 'ready to cry'. And the individual easily merges into a group, in contrast to the isolation which dominates adult life in other sketches.

The children lead a vivid life of sensations: 'We rushed off, butting through the evening with our heads.' Their energetic activity is an end in itself, as purposeless as the wind they feel on their skins, in contrast to the predetermined movement of a mail-coach and a train. The motif of escape, however, is suggested by the Indian war-whoop one of them utters, and taken further at the end, when the narrator, instead of returning home, runs into the wood, in search of the legendary city of fools.

The sketches with an adult speaker often turn on his wavering self-confidence. While the child on the swing was not disturbed by his unsteady perch, the speaker in 'The Passenger', on the juddering platform of an electric tram, feels uncertain about his place in the world, in the city, in his family. In 'Unmasking a Confidence-Man' the speaker, who seems to have moved to the city only a few months earlier, feels unable to shake off an unwanted companion and enter a house to which he has been invited; finally he recognizes his companion as a confidence-man, one of many who haunt the city and prey on people from the country, and though he is ashamed of his gullibility, the exposure of the confidence-man gives him the assurance to enter the house. In 'The Sudden Stroll' the opposite happens: the speaker suddenly gains the confidence to go out after supper, and feels 'absolutely solid'. In 'The Way Home' the atmosphere after a thunderstorm

[4] Quoted in Mark Anderson, *Kafka's Clothes: Ornament and Aestheticism in the Habsburg Fin de Siècle* (Oxford: Clarendon Press, 1992), 25.

imparts a feeling of self-confidence: the speaker feels responsible for everyone, especially lovers. This introduces the mild erotic theme that runs through the later sketches.

Isolation is a recurrent theme. In 'Decisions' the speaker, feeling miserable, decides not to assume a forced sociability and prefers to sink into his misery, descending to an animal level ('with a brutish gaze'), even a death-like state ('the final tomb-like stillness'). In 'The Trip to the Mountains' the speaker is so isolated that even speaking to himself he speaks soundlessly. Feeling that 'No-one-at-all' will help him, he imagines going on a trip with a group of nobodies. The loneliness of an elderly bachelor is vividly anticipated in 'The Bachelor's Distress'. Isolation is expressed by the window, which is the border between home and the street (as in 'Gazing Out Idly') but which also offers the possibility of escaping isolation: thus in 'The Window on to the Street' the lonely person staring out is at last swept off 'in the direction of human concord'—at least to imagine, if not experience, contact with other people.

The speaker in 'The Small Businessman' feels his isolation with particular acuteness. Living in a world of abstract commercial dealings, he is linked only by monetary transactions to the people who buy his wares. He imagines them travelling, to Paris, to a city full of processions, to a place where sailors can be heard cheering on a battleship, while he himself is a victim, ignored or even robbed. These fantasies occur in the lift, a liminal place between the street and his flat, and in the evening, a liminal period between work and sleep, where several of the sketches are located. In the context of this theme of isolation, the short 'Trees' looks less like the universal parable as which it has often been read, and more like a reflection on the individual's relation to society: superficially one seems unconnected to society; on a closer look, one is rooted there; but even that is an illusion compared to the undisclosed ultimate truth. Rootedness in the soil was a standard metaphor in conservative discourse, and Kafka, as his early letters show, was inclined to regard the countryside and its soil as the site of valuable aesthetic experience;[5] but this aphorism also shows his distance from such ideas.

As the antithesis to the lonely, timid 'I', we meet a succession of virile masculine figures. They include the man with a (phallic) walking-stick for whom girls step aside ('Children on the Highway'), the man

[5] Anderson, *Kafka's Clothes*, 56.

in 'Gazing Out Idly' who seems momentarily to threaten a little girl, and the imagined male heroes in 'The Rebuff'. Their chief exemplars are the 'Gentleman-Riders' (*Herrenreiter*), amateur jockeys who may be supposed to own their own horses, and who are admonished with veiled humour that winning a race actually brings all sorts of disadvantages. In the fantasy of escape headed 'Wish to Become a Red Indian', the speaker imagines being both a horseman, like the gentleman-riders, and an Indian, as in the games of the children on the highway. He thus combines the strength of the adult male with the freedom of the child and the appeal of the exotic, transforming them into pure onward movement.

A curious kind of integration into society is suggested by the recurrent image of clothes. The small businessman deals in fashionable garments. The nobodies who are to accompany the 'I' into the mountains must all be dressed smartly in tail-coats. The taffeta dress of the girl in 'The Rebuff' and the blouse, skirt, and collar of the girl on the tram in 'The Passenger' are described with fascinated precision. 'Dresses' evokes smart, ornate garments, which will soon become old and worn, and equates them with the natural but transient beauty of young women. 'We are suddenly in the world of baroque allegory,' comments Mark Anderson, 'confronting now a beautiful woman's face, now her old and decaying clothing.'[6] Clothes, for the wearer, are a form of self-presentation; for the viewer, they are a social code which is not necessarily easy to read.

From 'The Passenger' onwards, relations with women become a prominent theme, treated with a quietly wistful air. The 'I' may look at them without venturing to address them; if he does speak to them, he will get (or imagine) a gentle rebuff. In the final sketch, 'Unhappiness', the 'I' is isolated in his room, exploring further dimensions of inner space. One such is the reflection in the mirror, which seems to offer a further goal for his restless pacing. Another is the ghostly shadow-self who appears in the form of a young girl. By saying 'Your nature is mine', he admits that she is a projection of himself. He seems unsure whether he wants her presence or not. After she has gone, he has a conversation with a very solid neighbour who he thinks wants to take his ghost away from him. He goes forlornly to bed—unhappy with the ghost, or without it.

---

[6] Ibid. 31.

The Judgement

The Judgement marked Kafka's literary breakthrough. For over a year he had been working intermittently at his novel set in America, _The Man who Disappeared_, but felt that it was shapeless and rambling. He wanted to produce a story which had the tautness and precision of the classic German novellas by Kleist and Grillparzer that he so much admired. On the evening of 22 September 1912 he sat down at his desk at ten o'clock and wrote continuously until six in the morning. 'That is the _only_ way to write,' he told his diary afterwards, 'with such coherence, with such a complete opening of body and soul' (23 September 1912). He would never again achieve such a satisfying experience of writing, nor produce a work which he could approve with so little reservation.

The story crystallized many of Kafka's preoccupations. Its father–son conflict expressed his own difficult relationship with his father. The fiancée, Frieda Brandenfeld, has the same initials as Felice Bauer, whom Kafka had met a month earlier and to whom he would get engaged twice. Kafka wrote the story just after Yom Kippur, on which he had failed to attend the synagogue. The previous year he had attended the Kol Nidre evening service, preceding Yom Kippur, in the orthodox Altneu Synagogue, and been unimpressed by the 'low Stock-Exchange muttering' and by seeing the family of a brothel-keeper whose establishment he had himself recently patronized (diary, 1 October 1911). But while he felt that Western Jewry was in decline, he had learnt much about the comparatively vibrant Jewish life of Eastern Europe from his enthusiastic attendance at the plays performed by Yiddish actors from Galicia.[7] His relation to Judaism, as well as to his family, feeds into the story.

The emotional conflict turns on ambivalence. Kafka recorded in his diary that while writing the story he had 'thoughts of Freud, naturally'. But an acquaintance with psychoanalysis could only reinforce Kafka's sharp awareness of the deceptive duality of emotions. Georg Bendemann—very unlike his creator—is a successful and self-satisfied young businessman. Towards his friend in Russia he feels a patronizing mixture of compassion and exasperation. His reluctance to tell his friend about his engagement may stem from a

[7] On these matters, see now Iris Bruce, _Kafka and Cultural Zionism: Dates in Palestine_ (Madison, Wis.: University of Wisconsin Press, 2007).

wish to spare his friend's feelings, or from an unexplained inhibition, a feeling that in getting engaged he has somehow betrayed his friend. His fiancée's words, 'If you have friends like that, Georg, you shouldn't have become engaged at all' (p. 21), suggest that having such a friend is incompatible with marriage, and has invited critics to see this conflict as a version of the conflict Kafka felt between marriage and writing. Georg's evident fear of solitude implies that for him, bachelorhood is to be dreaded, as in the sketch 'The Bachelor's Distress' in *Meditation*. In expressing concern for his friend, he may only be projecting onto his friend his worries about his own possible future.

Towards his father, Georg appears to be a dutiful son. We learn, in information coloured by Georg's perspective, that they 'mostly' spend their evenings together, but this is promptly undermined (in a typical Kafka technique) by the information that Georg 'most often' visits friends or his fiancée. That they have lunch 'at the same time' (not 'together') may also be suspicious (p. 22). When Georg enters his father's room, some unease, attributed to his father's stature, is apparent, but the division between father and son opens up only when the friend in St Petersburg is mentioned. Inexplicably, the father questions whether Georg has any such friend, and Georg replies with apparent irrelevance: 'A thousand friends wouldn't replace my father' (p. 24)—as though his father had in fact cast doubt on his filial love. A great display of filial concern follows, in which we learn that Georg had in fact given no thought to what his father would do after Georg's marriage; his unctuous reassurances centre on the ambiguous phrase 'covered over', implying his wish both to protect and to bury his father.

The father, however, refuses to be covered over. Leaping upright, he towers over his son and wrong-foots him with incomprehensible accusations. Georg has in some unexplained way dishonoured his mother's memory and betrayed his friend and his father by falling for a young woman's cheap blandishments. His father ends by charging Georg with absolute egotism and by describing him in a way that amounts literally to nonsense but has a powerful emotional impact: 'After all, you were an innocent child really—but more really you were a diabolical human being!' (p. 28). This is the key sentence of the story, yet it is linguistically malformed ('really—but more really'), and hence doubly enigmatic.

A possible interpretation is that Georg (like all of us) lives simultaneously in two dimensions. In one, he is a natural, self-centred being,

endowed with energy and appetite. He is amoral, and hence innocent, like a child. His unacknowledged desires to replace his father,
triumph over his friend, and enjoy Frieda Brandenfeld (it is hinted
that he is a passionate lover) are natural expressions of the will to
power which reigns in an amoral world. Kafka was familiar with the
philosophy of Nietzsche, and this conception of amoral and hence
innocent appetite can be called Nietzschean.

The other dimension is one of moral absolutes, recalling in their
rigour the ethical absolutism of Kant. In this dimension Georg is
judged and condemned as a diabolical human being. The two cannot
be reconciled. In the judgement which his father passes on Georg,
the latter's Nietzschean will to power is defeated by an absolute,
unforgiving justice which requires him to annihilate himself.

Yet there is a further twist. If we take the father as the spokesman
of an inflexible morality, we have to admit also that he regards
himself as engaged in a power-struggle with his son, and that after
years of apparent submission he is now asserting his victory. In this
light, the language of moral absolutes looks like a mere instrument
which the father uses to overcome his son. So-called absolute justice
is only a tool in the service of the will to power, and the father turns
out to be a more determined and more successful Nietzschean than
Georg.

The story thus presents us with two sets of values—Nietzschean
amoral naturalism and Kantian moral rigorism—and shows us first
one, then the other, without allowing us to decide which is preferable.
Like the famous picture which can be seen either as a duck or as a
rabbit, but never as both at once, the world Kafka shows us may
equally well be Nietzschean or Kantian, but not both. To pursue
one's desires may be natural and innocent, or it may be wicked and
diabolical. To balance such alternatives, Kafka needed an art of
uncertainty and ambiguity.

The world of *The Judgement* is haunted by other, older value
systems. Allusions to Judaism and Christianity are uneasily present,
but refuse to shake down into any clear meaning or message. The
Christian allusions are associated with betrayal: as Peter denied
Jesus, it may be hinted, so Georg betrays his friend in St Petersburg.
The father neglected by his successful son recalls the relationship
between Judaism and Christianity. Judaism is the parent religion from
which Christianity developed. Much Christian theology assumes that

Christianity supersedes and replaces Judaism, as a son supersedes his father. But the painful history of Christian–Jewish relations, in which Jews have suffered ostracism and often persecution, implies a guilty unease with a parent religion which refuses to be covered over. The father's return to vigour can be read as a fantasy of the vengeful return of the undead older religion which sweeps away its would-be successor.

The duality of the story, its simultaneous presentation of two incompatible value-systems, is mirrored in its narrative method. The first part presents Georg's situation from a perspective close to his own and with no departure from realism. We learn much factual detail about his world, even about the fivefold increase in his firm's turnover; the prominence of money in Georg's thoughts implies that for him the world can be counted, measured, and manipulated. When Georg goes to the back room where his father lives, however, the atmosphere changes. The room is badly lit; Georg is uneasy in his father's presence; the conversation becomes ominous and enigmatic; finally the father leaps upright and browbeats his son in a manner which is realistically impossible. The story's mode has changed from a realistic mode to an Expressionist one, in which events that would otherwise be absurd serve to express the deeper forces animating the world. Kafka thus breaks his narrative contract with the reader. Ordinarily we would expect that when a work of fiction presents its world in a certain way, it will continue to do so consistently: a realist novel like *War and Peace* will not feature ghosts or miracles. Kafka, however, first introduces us to a realist fictional world which seems predictable and calculable, then replaces it with a fictional world which is governed by unpredictable, irrational, and emotional forces. Which of the two is the better image of the world we live in? The story offers us both and refuses to help us choose.

The Metamorphosis

In this story, as in *The Judgement*, Kafka has combined a realist with an Expressionist narrative. But he has done so in a different way. In *The Judgement*, the realist narrative moved seamlessly but bewilderingly into the Expressionist narrative. In *The Metamorphosis*, one is superimposed onto the other. The insect is as extraordinary and as impossible as the savage god who in Georg Heym's poem 'The God of the City' (1910) squats on a tower-block and shakes his fist at the modern urban cityscape. But, like Heym's god, the insect appears in a modern and mundane setting. The humdrum life of the Samsa family, Gregor's dreary job as a travelling salesman, the family's financial problems and its dealings with servants, are all evoked in the 'style of scrupulous meanness' with which Kafka's contemporary James Joyce claimed to have written his first book, *Dubliners* (1914).[8] Gregor's transformation is, as it were, an Expressionist bombshell thrown into a realist setting. It cannot be explained away as a dream, for Kafka is at pains to tell us: 'It was not a dream.'

When we look closely at Kafka's apparent realism, however, we find elements of caricature, exaggeration, and mystification. Take the insect. The opening description seems precise, but the 'arch-shaped ridges' are not found in real insects, and if the abdomen forms such a high dome, how are the 'many' (insects have six) little legs able to reach the ground? Vladimir Nabokov, who was an entomologist as well as a novelist, does his best to identify Gregor's species: he cannot be a cockroach, because cockroaches have flat bodies and large legs, whereas both Gregor's back and belly are convex; his hard back suggests a beetle's wing-case, but if so, Gregor never realizes that he has wings. Nabokov concludes, surely rightly, that Kafka did not envisage the insect very distinctly.[9] Gregor's size seems also to vary according to the requirements of the story: if he can rear up and open a door with his jaws he must be several feet long, but when his father pursues him we have to believe that he can be squashed by his father's shoes, and when his mother and sister are clearing out his room, Gregor, clinging to the wall, at first looks like a brown stain which the women fail to notice. Kafka did not specify what kind of creature Gregor became, using the word 'Ungeziefer', which suggests 'vermin' or 'pest', and he insisted that the cover illustration should not depict the insect. The physical appearance of the insect is far less important than its emotional connotations. There is no need to imagine far-fetched symbolism. Transformation into an insect is a readily intelligible expression of self-disgust. In a novel that Kafka had read, Dostoevsky's *The Brothers Karamazov*, Dmitri Karamazov

    [8] James Joyce, letter to Grant Richards, 5 May 1906, quoted in Richard Ellmann, *James Joyce* (London: Oxford University Press, 1959), 218.

    [9] Vladimir Nabokov, 'Franz Kafka, "The Metamorphosis"', in his *Lectures on Literature*, ed. Fredson Bowers (London: Weidenfeld & Nicolson, 1980), 251–83 (pp. 258–60).

calls himself an 'insect' and a 'bedbug', and urges his brother Alyosha to 'crush me like a cockroach'.[10] Kafka turns such metaphor into literal reality.

The behaviour of Kafka's human characters is often grotesquely exaggerated, especially since Kafka relies heavily on gesture to convey their feelings. Thus, when the chief clerk leaves the flat, his shoulder twitches, he retreats gradually then suddenly withdraws his leg from the threshold of the living-room, stretches out his right hand, clings to the banisters on the landing, and then leaps down the stairs. These minutely choreographed movements suggest the silent cinema, of which Kafka was a devotee. Kafka also read Dickens—he described *The Man who Disappeared* as an imitation of *David Copperfield*—and one can see Dickensian caricature in such a figure as the door-slamming charwoman, the three indistinguishable lodgers, or Gregor's boss who addresses employees while perched on his desk. With the latter, we also approach the Expressionist technique of representing figures of authority as monstrous, like the insane Father in Reinhard Johannes Sorge's play *The Beggar* (1912) or the dictatorial Engineer in Georg Kaiser's *Gas I* (1918). Gregor's father, when he appears reinvigorated in the second section, is such a figure, and his action in bombarding Gregor with apples, one of which lodges in his back and helps to kill him, is an absurd yet terrifying example of paternal violence, a counterpart to the father who pronounces a death sentence in *The Judgement*.

Clearly Kafka's own family tensions have gone into the story. His overbearing father, affectionate but ineffectual mother, and his favourite sister Ottla, an independent-minded young woman—against the wishes of her parents, she later married a Gentile and obtained professional training in farm management—are all present as ingredients of the story. But the fictional characters differ considerably from their real-life originals. Rather than try to reduce the story to its presumed biographical origins, we should read it as a reflection on family life in general.

Kafka had strong views about the family as an institution. He spoke of parental love as smothering, and of family life as a battleground. 'I have always looked upon my parents as persecutors,' he told Felice on 21 November 1912. 'All parents want to do is drag one down to

[10] Fyodor Dostoevsky, *The Brothers Karamazov*, tr. Richard Pevear and Larissa Volokhonsky (London: Quartet Books, 1990), 108, 113, 153.

them, back to the old days from which one longs to free oneself and escape; they do it out of love, of course, and that's what makes it so horrible.'[11] Eight years later he described to Milena Jesenská, with significant imagery, the awfulness of 'sinking into this circle of kindness, of love—you don't know my letter to my father—the buzzing of the fly on the lime-twig'. But, he added, even this had its good side: 'One man fights at Marathon, the other in the dining room, while the god of war and the goddess of victory are omnipresent.'[12] Kafka is not here complaining about parental unkindness or abuse. For him, it is the sticky bond created by parental affection that is so hard to resist.

In his critique of the family, Kafka was close to the radical psychoanalyst Otto Gross. Writing in a leading Expressionist journal, Gross upheld Nietzsche's individualism and Freud's concept of the unconscious. Both, he wrote, revealed the rich human potential that was normally frustrated by the authoritarian family: 'Only now can we realize that the source of all authority lies in the family, that the combination of sexuality and authority, shown in the family by the rights still assigned to the father, puts all individuality in fetters.'[13] Gross soon felt the truth of his words. His father, a prominent professor of criminal law whose lectures Kafka had attended at Prague University, used his influence to have Otto arrested and confined in a mental institution on grounds of irresponsible behaviour, shown in his drug-taking, active commitment to free love, and radical social views. Gross's confinement produced an outcry among intellectuals, which Kafka and his friends followed in the avantgarde journals. Kafka met Gross personally in 1917 and discussed with him the idea of founding a journal called 'Pages on Combating the Will to Power'.

The representation of the family in *The Metamorphosis* anticipates Gross by showing that the family resembles other institutions in being based ultimately not on love but on violence. The monopoly of violence belongs to the father. When Gregor 'breaks out' for the second time, his father drives him back into his room, and, as Gregor gets stuck in the doorway, his father sends him in with a powerful kick.

---

[11] *Letters to Felice*, 55.

[12] Letter of 31 July 1920, in Kafka, *Letters to Milena*, expanded edn., tr. Philip Boehm (New York: Schocken, 1990), 123.

[13] Otto Gross, 'Zur Überwindung der kulturellen Krise', *Die Aktion*, 2 Apr. 1913, pp. 385–7 (p. 386).

Kafka also anticipates Gross in stressing the monopoly of sexual power possessed by the father. At the end of Part II of the story, Gregor almost sees his mother naked as her petticoats fall to the floor. Naked or nearly naked, she embraces her husband, 'in total union with him', begging him to spare Gregor's life (p. 59). What Gregor sees—and the failing of his eyesight suggests that this is something taboo—is what Freud called a primal scene, a sexual encounter between his parents, which, in allowing him to go on living, repeats and re-enacts the encounter which gave him life in the first place. The secret on which the family is founded—the parental sex which brings children into being—is thus exposed. But only momentarily, for the taboo on knowledge of parental sex is promptly reimposed. Gregor involuntarily obeys this taboo: as something becomes visible which he ought not to see, he becomes unable to see it—'Gregor's sight was already failing' (p. 59). Moreover, his mother uses sex as a means of cajoling his father into sparing his life. Kafka reveals a constellation of sex, power, and violence at the heart of the family.

By contrast with his father's sexual power, Gregor suffers sexual deprivation. He recalls a few sexual contacts—'a chambermaid in a hotel in the provinces, a sweet, fleeting memory, a girl, cashier in a millinery shop, he had been seriously courting, but too slowly' (p. 62)—but before his transformation his sexual life is confined to the lady in furs whose picture hangs as a pin-up opposite his bed.[14] Furs, which were fashionable in 1912, suggest animality, and hence the physical side of Gregor which cannot find expression is his arid life as a commercial traveller. They also recall the notorious novel *Venus in Furs* (1870) by Leopold von Sacher-Masoch, which left traces not only here but in *The Man who Disappeared*. The fur-clad dominatrix in Sacher-Masoch's novel exerts her power over a sexual thrall, Severin, whom she obliges to change his name to Gregor. The picture of the fur-clad lady is so important to Kafka's Gregor that when his mother and sister are clearing out his room he does his best to save it by covering it with his body. His blocked sexuality also finds expression in a fantasy of union with his sister. As the only person who appreciates her violin-playing, he will keep her in his room; he will never let her leave, but she will stay there voluntarily—a fine example of the

---

[14] A picture such as Gregor might have had, from a fashion magazine of December 1912, is reproduced in Frank Möbus, *Sünden-Fälle: Die Geschlechtlichkeit in Erzählungen Franz Kafkas* (Göttingen: Wallstein, 1994), 85.

self-serving illogic in which Kafka's figures indulge; and he imagines rearing up, in his insect form, and kissing her on the throat (as Josef K. kisses Fräulein Bürstner in *The Trial*).

Gregor's attachment to his sister makes it all the more poignant that she is chiefly responsible for his death. After his appearance has frightened away the lodgers on whom the family think their income depends, his sister, who now emerges as the real head of the family, insists that the insect must go (without saying how), and that in any case it cannot really be Gregor. This illogical argument serves to exert moral pressure on Gregor, who takes the hint and obediently dies during the following night. 'His own opinion that he should vanish was, if possible, even more determined than his sister's' (p. 71).

Gregor is not only the victim of his family's neglect; he also sacrifices himself for their sake. Kafka repeatedly reminds us of the Samsas' Christian piety. When his sister enters his room, Gregor hears her invoking the saints. After his death, his father says: 'Now we can thank God,' and all three cross themselves. Yet this piety asks to be read as self-serving hypocrisy which matches a Nietzschean will to power. The need to earn their own living, forced on them by Gregor's incapacitation, seems to do them all good. After his death, they gain the self-assurance to throw out their lodgers, and find that their jobs are much more promising than they had realized; they take a day off work and go for a trip to the country. Appropriately, the damp and dreary weather that has prevailed so far is now over, and spring has arrived. Vitality asserts itself. The parents notice that their daughter is 'full of life', and has 'blossomed of late into a handsome, full-figured girl' who should soon get married (p. 74). Grete herself stretches her young body with physical ease and grace. The surviving Samsas are healthy animals such as Nietzsche wanted to see, and they have the capacity for forgetting the past which Nietzsche thought as important as the ability to digest one's food. We can recognize the Nietzschean world-view which was presented to us already in *The Judgement*.

The alternative, however, is no longer the Kantian moral rigorism evoked there, but something more mysterious and even mystical. Gregor's descent into solitude, squalor, and self-disgust can also be seen as the way to a new realm of experience. That realm is represented by music. Previously unmusical, Gregor is the only member of the audience who actually appreciates his sister's violin-playing.

At the same time, after a phase in which he enjoyed such things as mouldy cheese, Gregor has long since lost his appetite for earthly food. Food seems to have been replaced by music as a potential source of nourishment. The violin-playing makes him reflect: 'Was he a beast, that music should move him like this? He felt as if the way to the unknown nourishment he longed for was being revealed' (p. 66). This enigmatic passage has a key position in the story, corresponding to the father's cryptic sentence ('An innocent child . . .') in *The Judgement*.

Why music? Kafka, who himself professed to be extremely unmusical, knew the philosophy of Schopenhauer, for whom music is the supreme art because it is the direct expression of the Will, which in turn is the impersonal force that drives on all life. Schopenhauer's Will is a quite different concept from Nietzsche's will to power. Nietzsche conceives the will to power as a force that motivates individuals, albeit unconsciously, and enables strong and ruthless individuals to attain happiness. Schopenhauer, by contrast, thinks that the concept of the individual is itself illusory, and that, while under this illusion, we cannot be happy, because life consists of suffering; the Will has no interest in our happiness, merely in the continuation of existence. '[N]othing is more suitable than to accustom ourselves to regard this world as a place of penance and hence a penal colony,' he says.[15] Art affords a temporary relief from suffering. Music may afford something more—an insight into the nature of the world, such as Gregor glimpses. But the only way to escape the tyranny of the Will is to renounce life, to die to this world. Such pessimism and self-negation are also, according to Schopenhauer, the doctrine of New Testament Christianity if rightly understood, and also of the Greek pre-Socratics and of Hinduism and Buddhism. He quotes the Buddhist scriptures to support his case:

Nothing can be more conducive to patience in life and to a placid endurance of men and evils than a *Buddhist* reminder of this kind: '*This is Samsara*, the world of lust and craving and thus of birth, disease, old age and death; it is a world that ought not to be. And this is here the population of *Samsara*. Therefore what better things can you expect?' I would

---

[15] Arthur Schopenhauer, *Parerga and Paralipomena: Short Philosophical Essays*, tr. E. F. J. Payne, 2 vols. (Oxford: Clarendon Press, 1974), ii. 302. The phrase 'penal colony' is in English in the original.

like to prescribe that everyone repeat this four times a day, fully conscious of what he is saying.[16]

Samsara, the world of suffering to which we are condemned, may even have contributed to Gregor's surname Samsa.[17] In this light, Gregor may be seen as undergoing a mystical development away from the physical world. He loses his bodily appetite, his eyesight weakens, and he finds that family affection is fragile; he gains a tentative glimpse of another reality through music, and finally dies in a 'state of vacant and peaceful reflection' (p. 71). The word 'deliverance' (*Erlösung*), which recurs throughout the text, may be interpreted as foreshadowing this conclusion.

As in *The Judgement*, Kafka in this story holds in suspension two incompatible sets of values. Alongside the life-denying Schopenhauerian asceticism which is inexplicably forced on Gregor, there is the life-affirming Nietzschean vitalism, sustained by hypocrisy, to which his family resort. Not surprisingly, since Kafka was a dedicated vegetarian, the contrast between the two is focused by the image of food. Gregor ceases to eat, so that after his death his body is found to be flat and empty. As the defeated lodgers trail down the stairs, they pass a butcher's boy coming up with a tray of meat on his head. With Gregor's death, that is, the ruthless vitality symbolized by meat-eating has been restored.

In the Penal Colony

Schopenhauer's description of the world as a 'penal colony' provides one point of access to this story, especially as the word translated as 'place of penance', *Strafanstalt*, resembles the word *Strafkolonie* in Kafka's title. But while in some ways the story approaches allegory, in others it is a disturbingly detailed evocation of torture in a colonial setting, and thus relevant to contemporary events in the non-European world. Like the earlier stories, it places two views of the world in stark opposition. One is the officer's fanatical, quasi-religious

[16] Schopenhauer, *Parerga and Paralipomena*. (footnote). See Moira Nicholls, 'The influences of Eastern thought on Schopenhauer's Doctrine of the Thing-in-itself', in Christopher Janaway (ed.), *The Cambridge Companion to Schopenhauer* (Cambridge: Cambridge University Press, 1999), 171–212.

[17] See Michael Ryan, 'Samsa and *Samsara*: Suffering, Death and Rebirth in *The Metamorphosis*', *German Quarterly*, 72 (1999), 133–52, where further possible sources are suggested for Kafka's knowledge of Eastern religions.

dedication to the torture-machine; the other is the liberal, humanitarian outlook of the European traveller. But while in the previous stories the two world-views were evenly balanced, here the narrator comes down in favour of the traveller's liberal outlook, albeit with qualifications.

In the story, set in a French-speaking colony, an officer shows a European visitor an 'apparatus' (a word used not only for machinery but also for the apparatus of administration) designed for punishment. A prisoner inserted into it has his crime inscribed on his skin by needles during a twelve-hour period which ends with his death. The prisoner is not otherwise told his sentence: he learns it 'in his flesh' or 'on his body' ('an seinem Leibe'), an idiomatic phrase which is here made literal.

In the minute description of how the torture-machine works, one can see Kafka's own morbid preoccupation with torture. His diaries contain many gruesome fantasies about throwing himself through a window and being cut by the glass, or having a meat-slicing machine cutting into his side. These fantasies were particularly intense in October 1914, when he paused from working on *The Trial* to write the story. About the same time he wrote the chapter of *The Trial* headed 'The Thrasher', in which one of the guards who arrested Josef K. is punished for minor misdemeanours by being stripped naked and flogged so mercilessly that he screams with pain. A few months earlier Felice Bauer had broken off her engagement to Kafka in a painful confrontation which made him feel intense guilt. His preoccupation with torture was strengthened by his reading, which included not only *Venus in Furs*, as we have seen, but also the novel *The Torture Garden* (1899) by the French decadent writer Octave Mirbeau. In the novel, European visitors tour a Chinese prison in whose magnificent garden prisoners undergo a variety of ingenious tortures; it seems also to have suggested the vaguely Oriental setting of the story. Finally, the story also reflects Kafka's work in a state-run insurance office. Part of his job was to inspect safety standards in factories and try to prevent accidents being caused by dangerous machinery. His annual reports include technically precise descriptions of industrial machines and illustrated accounts of the different mutilations caused by their malfunctioning.

The officer is the last devotee of the machine for administering justice invented by the old commandant, now dead, who formerly ruled the colony. As 'soldier, judge, engineer, chemist, draughtsman all in one' (p. 79), this commandant sounds like a superhuman being, possibly like the God of the Old Testament, as Malcolm Pasley suggested in an influential interpretation: 'We are reminded of Jahve as He is portrayed in the Book of Exodus, fighting for the Jews against the Egyptians, setting out a code of laws, and giving detailed specifications for the construction of the tabernacle, and even for the mixing of the holy unguent.'[18] The old commandant's conception of justice, shared by the officer, is that guilt is always certain. Anyone who is charged is automatically guilty. Justice is therefore synonymous with punishment; punishment is always capital; and its purpose is that the tortured victim should finally attain insight through his wounds. The contrast between the old and new commandants might tempt us to see this again as alluding to the jealous God of the Old Testament, but that would be only a partial interpretation. The story seems to imply a more general critique of religion as a system of organized cruelty in which, nevertheless, a kind of illumination may be possible, and in which people can believe that absolute justice is being enacted before their eyes. Nietzsche, in *On the Genealogy of Morals*, asserts that 'the Christian . . . has interpreted a whole secret machinery of salvation into suffering'.[19] This religious system belongs to the past, and the old commandant is buried in an old building which conveys 'the force of earlier times' (p. 98), but the inscription on his tombstone foretells that he will rise from the dead and reconquer the island.

This warning tells us not to be too confident that the values of the new commandant and the European traveller have superseded those of the old commandant and the officer. Nevertheless, the new values are more attractive. The traveller feels the punishment-machine to be barbarous. When urged by the officer to support its use, he struggles with the usual scruples: what business has he to interfere with a foreign culture? However, the narrator assures us that he is basically honourable and courageous, and he frankly tells the officer that he is an opponent of this procedure and cannot advocate it. On the other hand, the liberalism of the new commandant seems a little half-hearted, since he has not abolished the punishment-machine outright but merely

---

[18] 'Introduction', Franz Kafka, *Der Heizer, In der Strafkolonie, Der Bau*, ed. J. M. S. Pasley (Cambridge: Cambridge University Press, 1966), 1–33 (p. 21).

[19] Friedrich Nietzsche, *On the Genealogy of Morals*, tr. Douglas Smith, Oxford World's Classics (Oxford: Oxford University Press, 1996), 49.

banned it to a remote valley. The traveller himself is only too glad to escape from the colony, and prevents the soldier and the ex-prisoner from following him by threatening them with a heavy knotted rope.

Although Kafka never left Europe, he knew a certain amount about conditions in the European colonies. One of his uncles, Joseph Löwy, worked from 1891 to 1902 in the Congo as administrator on a railway which was built by forced labour; his experiences seem to have inspired a fragment in Kafka's notebook about 'building the railway in the interior of the Congo', and to have shaped *In the Penal Colony* by coalescing with reports of Captain Dreyfus's unjust imprisonment in the French penal settlement of Devil's Island.[20] Kafka would also have known from the press about the genocidal suppression by the German colonial authorities of the Herero uprising in South-West Africa (now Namibia). The key phrase about 'feeling [his crime] in his own flesh' also features in German discussions of how to treat the surviving Hereros: they were to feel the consequences of their rebellion 'in their own flesh'. The prisoner has been struck across the face with a horsewhip for a small infraction of duty; in 1894 the Socialist leader August Bebel shocked the German Reichstag by displaying the hippopotamus-hide whips that were used, despite official denials, in the German colonies.[21] Finally, Mirbeau's *The Torture Garden* also denounces, through its leading character, the sadistic Englishwoman Clara, the wanton murder and torture practised by colonial powers in the name of civilization.[22]

One may feel that this story is aesthetically less satisfactory than its predecessors. Although it turns on a dramatic confrontation between the representatives of two opposed outlooks, it lacks the tautness of *The Judgement* and *The Metamorphosis*, and such suggestions of deeper significance as the contrast between the old and new commandants are so scantily scattered that one may attempt a simple allegorical reading (e.g. Old versus New Testament) which the story, however, will not sustain. The description of the punishment-machine may also be thought excessive. But if one wants to criticize the story as too

[20] See Anthony Northey, *Kafka's Relatives: Their Lives and His Writing* (New Haven and London: Yale University Press, 1991); Sander L. Gilman, *Franz Kafka, the Jewish Patient* (London and New York: Routledge, 1995).

[21] See Paul Peters, 'Witness To the Execution: Kafka and Colonialism', *Monatshefte*, 93 (2001), 401–25.

[22] See Octave Mirbeau, *Le Jardin des supplices*, ed. Michel Delon (Paris: Gallimard, 1988), esp. 193.

painful, one has to consider the reply Kafka made to his publisher, who had raised this objection: 'To explain this last story I only add that not only it is painful; rather, the time in which all of us live, and myself in particular, is painful.'[23]

Letter to his Father

According to Max Brod, Kafka wrote this letter while staying in the resort of Schelesen in November 1919, in order to explore his troubled relationship with his father and to clear the air between them. He fully intended to give it to his father, but was dissuaded by his mother. It is difficult to imagine what Hermann Kafka would have made of this letter, but impossible to believe that it could have achieved the desired effect of reconciliation; it could only have convinced Hermann Kafka that his son was a hopeless eccentric.

How far should the *Letter* be regarded as a work of autobiographical fiction? There is no need to suppose that anything in it is actually fabricated.[24] It is of course one-sided: Kafka himself described it, in a letter to Milena Jesenská, as a 'lawyer's letter', and hence an exercise in self-justification.[25] He explains to his father how the latter is responsible for his own sense of being a failure. His father's bullying personality, his physical bulk, his authoritarian behaviour at the family dinner-table, are all described resentfully in order to explain how Kafka himself became a lanky, hypochondriac, permanently worried young man who was unable to satisfy his family's expectations by getting married. This of course is a very one-sided and stylized self-portrait. Perhaps its most remarkable feature is how Kafka, then aged 36, represents himself as dependent on his father, in what seems like an attempt to deny responsibility for his own life. Kafka is saying in effect: 'You may not approve of me, and I don't approve of myself, but you have made me what I am.' He particularly blames his father for not teaching him to take Judaism seriously; at this time Kafka was learning Hebrew and contemplating eventual emigration to Palestine.

---

[23] Kafka, letter to Kurt Wolff, 11 Oct. 1916.

[24] The biographical value of the *Letter* is robustly defended by Kafka's latest biographer, Reiner Stach, in *Kafka: Die Jahre der Erkenntnis* (Frankfurt a.M.: Fischer, 2008), 322–4.

[25] Letter of 4/5 July 1920, *Letters to Milena*, 63.

It is illuminating to read the *Letter* alongside the sensitive analysis of Kafka's character given by the psychiatrist Anthony Storr.[26] Kafka suffered, as Storr plausibly argues, from a deficient sense of identity. He was not firmly established in his own body; he often felt his body as something external, alien, even hostile to him. He never quite overcame the sense of helplessness felt by the child who is dependent on other people. In his early childhood, he probably did not receive adequate parental care. He had too little contact with his mother, who worked in the family shop. Altogether he saw little of his parents and spent much time alone. He had two younger brothers who died in infancy, and presumably took up most of the attention their parents could give; and his first sibling to survive infancy, his sister Elli, was not born till Kafka was six. The young Kafka felt helpless, exposed to injury by others, and, above all, neglected and treated as if he did not matter. And since children tend to blame themselves, the motif of guilt in Kafka's writing may originate here. It is notable that Kafka says little about his mother and places all the blame on his father, reconstructing his childhood primarily as an unsatisfactory relationship between the two of them.

In two respects Kafka tries to alleviate the intense focus on family conflicts by placing his relationship with his father in a larger framework. The first is that of the Löwy and Kafka families. Kafka was sharply conscious of the different temperaments that predominated in his father's and his mother's families. The Kafkas were physically powerful and energetic. Kafka's paternal grandfather, Jakob Kafka, a butcher, is described as giant-like in stature.[27] Kafka recalled how his cousin Robert, son of his uncle Philipp, used to go swimming after work and would 'plunge about with the strength of a beautiful wild animal'.[28] Hermann Kafka and his three brothers had worked their way up from rural poverty to become self-employed businessmen. The relatives of Kafka's mother, Julie Löwy, on the other hand, were rabbis, scholars, and often mildly eccentric bachelors. Kafka was particularly interested in his great-grandfather, the rabbi Adam Porias, whom his mother could just remember as a devout old man with a

[26] Anthony Storr, 'Kafka's Sense of Identity', in *Churchill's Black Dog and Other Phenomena of the Human Mind* (London: Collins, 1989), 52–82.

[27] Klaus Wagenbach, *Franz Kafka: Eine Biographie seiner Jugend, 1883–1912* (Bern: Francke, 1958), 16; a photograph of Jakob Kafka, who does indeed seem huge, is reproduced opposite p. 17.

[28] Quoted in Max Brod, *Über Franz Kafka* (Frankfurt a.M.: Fischer, 1974), 180.

long white beard. He liked his paternal uncles much less than his maternal ones, and especially liked his uncle Siegfried Löwy, a country doctor whom he often visited as a child. Kafka tended to stylize this temperamental difference into a contrast between ruthless go-getters and eccentric losers that often structures his fiction, for example as the contrast between Georg Bendemann and his unsuccessful friend in *The Judgement*. In using it to define himself as against his father, he is using a fictional structure, even an element of myth-making, to shape his *Letter*.

The other framework in which Kafka places his family is a sociological one. He attributes Hermann Kafka's lack of interest in Judaism to his membership of 'this transitional generation of Jews who migrated from the countryside, which was still relatively devout, to the cities' (p. 125). Hermann Kafka was indeed an upwardly mobile immigrant for whom the synagogue (the temple, as Kafka calls it) was above all a place to display one's social status and to make contacts. Iris Bruce has recently described how he first joined a relatively modest reform synagogue, then transferred to the second oldest synagogue in Prague, the Pinkas Synagogue, and finally to the very oldest, the orthodox Altneu Synagogue.[29] Kafka complains that his father was so worldly as to point out to him the sons of a millionaire in the synagogue. The problems created by Hermann Kafka's social mobility, however, pervade the *Letter* more widely. Focused on the struggle for commercial success, he wanted his only surviving son to take the next step into a successful professional career. Cousin Robert, the lawyer, was one role model; another was the more distant cousin Bruno Kafka, also a lawyer, who became a professor at Prague University and a notable politician. Franz Kafka, by contrast, had an undistinguished job as a civil servant and showed an obsessive interest in literature with which his father could not sympathize; even worse, he took up what his father thought worthless fads, such as vegetarianism and Zionism, and brought back to the family flat such unsuitable friends as the shabby Yiddish actor Isaak Löwy and the writer Max Brod, whom Hermann Kafka called a 'meshuggener ritoch' (crazy hothead).

It is, of course, common for the children of successful parents not to pursue the careers which their parents have mapped out for them, but to take up cultural pursuits and radical politics with which their

[29] Bruce, *Kafka and Cultural Zionism*, 13.

parents cannot sympathize. A well-known literary example occurs in Thomas Mann's *Buddenbrooks* (1901), in which the businessman Thomas Buddenbrook, secretly frustrated in his career, is estranged from his frail son Hanno who is obsessed exclusively with music. From the viewpoint of the parents, it is naturally sad that their children, with apparent ingratitude, take for granted their parents' sacrifices and adopt what seem eccentric values. It is salutary to imagine Hermann Kafka's viewpoint, as Nadine Gordimer has done in her brilliant story 'Letter from his Father', where Hermann, writing from beyond the grave, not only deplores his son's injustice but regrets that Franz, triumphing in the power-struggle between them, has given posterity a one-sided image of his father as an unfeeling tyrant.[30] Gordimer's 'Letter' is of course a piece of self-justification; but so was Kafka's.

[30] Nadine Gordimer, 'Letter from His Father', in *Something Out There* (London: Cape, 1984), 39–56.

NOTE ON THE TEXT

Meditation, *The Judgement*, *The Metamorphosis*, and *In the Penal Colony* were published during Kafka's lifetime. The texts here translated are those of the first published editions, as reproduced in the volume of the Critical Edition of Kafka's works entitled *Drucke zu Lebzeiten*, edited by Wolf Kittler, Hans-Gerd Koch, and Gerhard Neumann (Frankfurt a.M.: Fischer, 1996). The critical apparatus, published as a separate volume, includes the—not extensive—variants in Kafka's surviving manuscripts. The manuscripts of *The Judgement*, *The Metamorphosis*, and some of the sketches in *Meditation* survive, but not that of *In the Penal Colony*.

The *Letter to his Father* was made available by Max Brod in the volume *Wedding Preparations in the Country*, published in 1953. This translation follows the manuscript as presented in the volume of the Critical Edition, *Nachgelassene Schriften und Fragmente II*, edited by Jost Schillemeit (Frankfurt a.M.: Fischer, 1992), 143–217.

NOTE ON THE TRANSLATION

FOR readers of a classic written in a language not their own, the translator has always got there before them, filtering, selecting, dithering, finally having to decide—because deciding is what the job consists in—between seemingly fine options, when better judgement tells one that none of them, in principle and by the facts of the case, will be the right, true one. What the reader is getting has passed for a second time through Celan's 'language-grid', which has both held something back and let something through; it is already by its choices to some degree an interpretation. Nowhere does this become more apparent than in translating Kafka. His texts above all challenge the reader to a search for meaning, but at the same time are so constructed as to frustrate any single interpretation, inviting several, often incompatible, often only briefly sustainable readings, while the translator's decision for one fixed option can close off the possibility of all the others. So a note on the translation in this case turns into a note on the attempt to deal with indeterminacies, mutually exclusive alternatives,[1] intractabilities.

But I made one decision very early: to try to render Kafka's exceedingly complex syntax as closely as possible. This often meant going further than English syntax can naturally accommodate. Kafka's virtuoso syntax is in any case unnatural, with its endless sentences proliferating with qualificatory sub-clauses, themselves impeded by dense clusters of adverbs; with his headlong sequences of appositions, with no pause for breath in between from a merciful 'and'—all devices for suspending any final resolution to a statement. They are a vehicle for the way his figures think, as these conduct their seeming-rational arguments with themselves, which so often, after great expenditure of mental energy, conclude a paragraph or even a page later with the proposition they began with, as Georg Bendemann does when considering whether to summon back his far-away friend, or in Gregor's panic-stricken attempts to explain his delayed departure to

---

[1] For example, in *Meditation* are the ('stark durchbrochene') curtains where the boy is eating his supper full of holes because they are torn or because they are made of lace? There is nothing in the context or the (child's? or narrator's?) language to guide one conclusively to one or the other. I have opted for the latter, but without certainty.

the chief clerk. These symptoms of the figures' bad faith (Georg is deceiving himself, Gregor deceiving himself as much as the chief clerk) already strain the German syntax, and ask to be conveyed comparably in the English translation too. Some compromises are unavoidable, though I have tried to keep them to a minimum: for example, having to break up a group of obstructing adverbs, when the obstruction was the point; or slipping in an 'and' or a present participle to ease the tense strings of appositions, when the tension was the point. These are normal tactics in translating from relatively dense German into looser modern English syntax. Only, with Kafka one has a bad conscience about it.

Kafka also conveys the zigzag movement of this pseudo-argumentation by deploying a number of shifty qualifiers: 'allerdings', 'doch', 'übrigens', 'aber', 'wohl', 'vielleicht', 'als ob', and so on. The problem here is to catch the elusive tone, the location of emphasis. The range of English resources is every bit as nuanced as the German: 'although', 'besides', 'anyhow', 'after all', 'still', 'nevertheless', 'on the other hand'—and 'if and perhaps and but'. Still, to get them in the right place and qualifying the right word... The problem is especially tricky in those cases where the same qualifier could indicate either understatement or extremity, duck or rabbit: from 'fast' and 'beinahe' to 'ganz' and 'geradezu' and the intractable 'förmlich'; and equally, from 'quite', 'almost', or 'pretty well', to 'outright', 'positively', 'practically', those qualifiers, especially 'literally', that qualify themselves and really mean 'not really'.

Where Kafka's syntax is elaborate and complex, his vocabulary is as restricted as the world his figures inhabit, confined to the language of family, office, and business, as colourless as the drained lives his figures lead. It is all of a piece with this narrowness of range that the same words should get repeated: again and again the officer in *In the Penal Colony* reiterates the objects of his obsession: the 'apparatus' and the 'procedure' of its functioning, the 'new', the 'old' commandant. The problem for the translator here is one of self-abnegation, of having to choose the neutral word and resist the temptation of gratuitous colour, especially when Kafka's situations are often so absurd as to seem to invite it: the family hullabaloo when Gregor breaks out is more properly just a commotion, and the literary pleasure not one of expressiveness but of ironical contrast between sober style and wild event. It is telling that the most vivid language is put into the fathers' mouths, as coarse and energetic as they are themselves, in the fictions as well as in the *Letter to his Father*, where it most probably had its model.[2] The style of the early *Meditation* pieces, on the other hand, is far more mannered, even playful, more self-consciously literary. One suspects that the first of Kafka's bonfires contained texts of this kind.

The *Letter* differs in many ways from the other pieces in the present collection. Many of its paragraphs are shaped by the rhetoric of forensic attack: Kafka the lawyer makes out the case for the prosecution in rapid triple sequences of parallel clauses or sentences, climaxing in a brief and painful punchline. They are compositions every bit as literary as the winding sentences of the stories, but what is distinctive about this text is the visible personal anger and hurt. Just as Gregor broke out, so, in this text, does an 'I'. But by no means throughout. Where Kafka generalizes, he will frequently resort to the impersonal German *man*, which one renders by the English equivalent 'one'; more significantly, where the pain is too great, or his own responsibility too close to admit, he will muffle it with a '*man*/one'.[3] His fictional figures use much the same tactic to hide their own particular in the general; indeed, the impersonality of Kafka's storytelling itself is only seeming: the introductory sentence to *The Judgement* may sound at first as if it were in the manner of the traditional nineteenth-century narrative with its distanced who, where, and what, but all unawares we soon find ourselves thinking along with Georg's reflections, as he turns his disavowals into apparent concern for his friend with a sustained sequence of muffling impersonal '*man*'s/one's'. 'What could *one* write to such a man who... Should *one* advise him...', and so on. And on. It is in their sheer quantity, so close together, that the problem lies in English. To have Georg sound like royalty would scarcely produce the right effect, and in this passage, and elsewhere (though not everywhere), this translator has had to admit defeat and has resorted to using the English colloquial-impersonal 'you'—which is, strictly, too natural a rendering.

[2] On the whole it is in their speech that his writing shows traces of distinctively Austrian usage, as it does occasionally in the course of the narration: for example, in the same sentence the ceiling Gregor crawls over is not only a German 'Decke', but is also elegantly varied to an Austrian 'Plafond'. Here the translator is stuck with mere repetition.

[3] A passage from an early work, *Wedding Preparations in the Country*, may be illuminating here. The (personalized) narrator observes to himself of his place in the story he is about to tell: 'as long as you say "one" instead of "I", it's nothing, and one is able to begin this story; but as soon as you admit to yourself that it is you, then the knife literally goes through you and you are horrified . . .'

The issue is endemic in all the pieces here, but most disturbing in the *Letter* because of its tendentiously confessional nature.

Kafka also takes advantage of another impersonal trick possible in German usage and next to impossible to carry over naturally into English, one which also provides an instance of how translation can hardly avoid affecting interpretation: it is his adoption of the impersonal definite article to designate family members: the mother, the sister, above all the father. He uses the possessives, which at the very least express a personal relationship, only sparingly: in *The Judgement*, indeed, Georg refers to 'mein Vater/my father' only once, and in the course of the narrating, 'sein Vater/his father' also occurs only once. The effect is to turn the figures into functions, and in the case of the father, to bring immediately to the surface the possibilities of a giant father-imago, or a punishing God-the-Father, both of which have been influential readings of *The Judgement* and *The Metamorphosis*. English idiom does not use the definite article so easily, and when it occurs it draws attention to itself. So although I have used the unobtrusive possessives very frequently, I have made a point of using the definite article where such archetypal resonances are most apparent, as they are in the third part of *The Metamorphosis*.

There are also single words where the problem is one of semantics rather than idiom. 'Schuld' and its cognates in Kafka's writings are obviously the most crucial. In German, a language with a relatively limited lexis, such words have a range of connotations, tolling like a single great bell with many overtones and undertones. English, with a far wider and more differentiated lexis, rings the changes on the prime 'guilt' with 'blame' and 'fault' and 'debt', together with all their cognates, including 'blameless' and 'indebted', with variations played on 'owing'. They all occur in the present translation of course—English usage requires the differentiation—but the reader should be alert to the single shared word behind them and the overlap of connotation.

'Schuld-as-debt' is one associated meaning to 'Schuld-as-guilt' that lends itself to treatment in literal terms which are capable, in Kafka's hands, of elaborate narrative development (we begin to wonder what kind of debt it is which his parents have incurred and Gregor has to pay). It is an instance of what is perhaps the most distinctive aspect of Kafka's writing, 'literalization', to use Michael Wood's term: the way he takes the latent concrete meanings of words and phrases and daily sayings, and exploits their lost metaphorical meaning by representing them quite literally. 'Am eigenen Leib erfahren', literally, 'to experience in one's own body', is a faded metaphor used mainly in the weak sense of 'to experience for oneself', but Kafka not only restores it to full strength in the officer's terrible apparatus, but has already hidden it in Gregor's litany of his miseries as a travelling salesman, 'when it is only once he is at home that he can feel in his own flesh the serious consequences they entail'; the phrase itself suggests some of the causes for his literal transformation into something subhuman. The translator has to find a phrase with a physical reference that will do this, and will also work in both stories. A more teasing kind of interplay between literal and abstract is to be found in *The Judgement*, where, in a kind of partial allegory, one with no stable referent, the concrete 'Russia' gradually slides into variations of 'fremd', which in English is differentiated into 'strange', 'foreign', 'alien', remote', and related words: here, in the space of one paragraph, 'Russia' modulates into 'remote as he [the friend] was' and 'in that remote place of his', reinforced by 'estranged'. The translator has to find a sequence of phrases which makes these unobtrusive transitions just about visible. Similarly, the apparently solid exchange of uneasy letters between Georg and the friend becomes a 'curious corresponding relationship'. One begins to see the depths in the father's question: 'Do you really have this friend in Russia?', and to wonder what dimension of reality he might more really inhabit.

If there is one word that signals this characteristic literalization, it is 'förmlich', a qualifier that belongs with 'geradezu', 'positively', and 'practically'. Their function is to emphasize, but also, as Kafka uses them, to suggest that they are overdoing it, and a little scepticism might be in order. 'Förmlich' does the same, but in addition it also seems to act as a Platonic marker for some particularly strong verbal form, a metaphor, a little allegory, correlative to the feeling expressed, a ghostly trace of something lived. A passage from a letter from Kafka, written at much the same time as that letter intended for his father, to the sister of his second, unhappy sometime fiancée may clarify his peculiar use of it. He is referring to the lingering traces of pain from his unhappy first engagement, in a possibly Platonic sense: 'the pain is over, but the form (*das Formelle*) of the pain has remained, literally (*förmlich*) the channel made by old wounds where every new pain sails up and down.' For such instances I have used 'literally'. It may sound like an impermissible solecism. Did disputes in the family really wear furrows in Kafka's brain (*Letter*)? Not really, perhaps, but more really; not in life, but in literature, 'literally'.

My warmest thanks are due to my editors for their careful reading of my many, many revisions: to Judith Luna for her fine sense of English style—and for her patience; to Jeff New for his meticulous copy-editing; and above all to Ritchie Robertson for his great expertise in the literature of the Dual Monarchy and after, including his knowledge of distinctively Austrian turns of phrase, for his help in reading many intractable passages, and for saving me from many errors. Those remaining are my own. Finally—but how to thank Kafka when the debt is so great?

J. C.

SELECT BIBLIOGRAPHY

(CONFINED TO WORKS IN ENGLISH)

Translations of Kafka's Non-Fictional Works

The Collected Aphorisms, tr. Malcolm Pasley (London: Penguin, 1994).

The Diaries, tr. Joseph Kresh (Harmondsworth: Penguin, 1972).

Letters to Friends, Family and Editors, tr. Richard and Clara Winston (New York: Schocken, 1988).

Letters to Felice, tr. James Stern and Elizabeth Duckworth (London: Vintage, 1992).

Letters to Milena, expanded edn., tr. Philip Boehm (New York: Schocken, 1990).

Letters to Ottla and the Family, tr. Richard and Clara Winston (New York: Schocken, 1988).

Biographies

Adler, Jeremy, *Franz Kafka* (London: Penguin, 2001).

Brod, Max, *Franz Kafka: A Biography*, tr. G. Humphreys Roberts and Richard Winston (New York: Schocken, 1960).

Diamant, Kathi, *Kafka's Last Love: The Mystery of Dora Diamant* (London: Secker & Warburg, 2003).

Hayman, Ronald, *K: A Biography of Kafka* (London: Weidenfeld & Nicolson, 1981).

Hockaday, Mary, *Kafka, Love and Courage: The Life of Milena Jesenská* (London: Deutsch, 1995).

Murray, Nicholas, *Kafka* (London: Little, Brown, 2004).

Northey, Anthony, *Kafka's Relatives: Their Lives and His Writing* (New Haven and London: Yale University Press, 1991).

Storr, Anthony, 'Kafka's Sense of Identity', in *Churchill's Black Dog and Other Phenomena of the Human Mind* (London: Collins, 1989), 52–82.

Unseld, Joachim, *Franz Kafka: A Writer's Life*, tr. Paul F. Dvorak (Riverside, Calif.: Ariadne Press, 1997).

Introductions

Preece, Julian (ed.), *The Cambridge Companion to Kafka* (Cambridge: Cambridge University Press, 2002).

Robertson, Ritchie, *Kafka: A Very Short Introduction* (Oxford: Oxford University Press, 2004).

Rolleston, James (ed.), *A Companion to the Works of Franz Kafka* (Rochester, NY: Camden House, 2002).

Speirs, Ronald, and Beatrice Sandberg, *Franz Kafka*, Macmillan Modern Novelists (London: Macmillan, 1997).

Critical Studies

Alter, Robert, *Necessary Angels: Tradition and Modernity in Kafka, Benjamin and Scholem* (Cambridge, Mass.: Harvard University Press, 1991).

Anderson, Mark, *Kafka's Clothes: Ornament and Aestheticism in the Habsburg Fin de Siècle* (Oxford: Clarendon Press, 1992).

——'Kafka, Homosexuality and the Aesthetics of "Male Culture"', *Austrian Studies*, 7 (1996), 79–99.

Boa, Elizabeth, *Kafka: Gender, Class and Race in the Letters and Fictions* (Oxford: Clarendon Press, 1996).

Corngold, Stanley, *Lambent Traces: Franz Kafka* (Princeton: Princeton University Press, 2004).

Dodd, W. J., *Kafka and Dostoyevsky: The Shaping of Influence* (London: Macmillan, 1992).

——(ed.), *Kafka: The Metamorphosis, The Trial and The Castle*, Modern Literatures in Perspective (London and New York: Longman, 1995).

Duttlinger, Carolin, *Kafka and Photography* (Oxford: Oxford University Press, 2007).

Flores, Angel (ed.), *The Kafka Debate* (New York: Gordian Press, 1977).

Gilman, Sander L., *Franz Kafka, the Jewish Patient* (London and New York: Routledge, 1995).

Goebel, Rolf J., *Constructing China: Kafka's Orientalist Discourse* (Columbia, SC: Camden House, 1997).

Heidsieck, Arnold, *The Intellectual Contexts of Kafka's Fiction: Philosophy, Law, Religion* (Columbia, SC: Camden House, 1994).

Koelb, Clayton, *Kafka's Rhetoric: The Passion of Reading* (Ithaca and London: Cornell University Press, 1989).

Politzer, Heinz, *Franz Kafka: Parable and Paradox* (Ithaca, NY: Cornell University Press, 1962).

Robertson, Ritchie, *Kafka: Judaism, Politics and Literature* (Oxford: Clarendon Press, 1985).

Sokel, Walter H., *The Myth of Power and the Self: Essays on Franz Kafka* (Detroit: Wayne State University Press, 2002).

Zilcosky, John, *Kafka's Travels: Exoticism, Colonialism, and the Traffic of Writing* (Basingstoke and New York: Palgrave Macmillan, 2003).

Zischler, Hanns, *Kafka Goes To the Movies*, tr. Susan H. Gillespie (Chicago and London: University of Chicago Press, 2003).

Historical Context

Anderson, Mark (ed.), *Reading Kafka: Prague, Politics, and the Fin de Siècle* (New York: Schocken, 1989).

Beck, Evelyn Torton, *Kafka and the Yiddish Theater* (Madison, Wisc.: University of Wisconsin Press, 1971).

Bruce, Iris, *Kafka and Cultural Zionism: Dates in Palestine* (Madison, Wisc.: University of Wisconsin Press, 2007).

Gelber, Mark H. (ed.), *Kafka, Zionism, and Beyond* (Tübingen: Niemeyer, 2004).

Kieval, Hillel J., *The Making of Czech Jewry: National Conflict and Jewish Society in Bohemia, 1870–1918* (New York: Oxford University Press, 1988).

Robertson, Ritchie, *The 'Jewish Question' in German Literature, 1749–1939* (Oxford: Oxford University Press, 1999).

Spector, Scott, *Prague Territories: National Conflict and Cultural Innovation in Franz Kafka's Fin de Siècle* (Berkeley, Los Angeles, and London: University of California Press, 2000).

The Short Fiction in General

Eilittä, Leena, *Approaches to Personal Identity in Kafka's Short Fiction: Freud, Darwin, Kierkegaard* (Helsinki: Academia Scientiarum Fennica, 1999).

Gross, Ruth V., 'Kafka's Short Fiction', in Julian Preece (ed.), *The Cambridge Companion to Kafka* (Cambridge: Cambridge University Press, 2002), 80–94.

Kempf, Franz, *Everyone's Darling: Kafka and the Critics of His Short Fiction* (Columbia, SC: Camden House, 1994).

Pascal, Roy, *Kafka's Narrators: A Study of His Stories and Sketches* (Cambridge: Cambridge University Press, 1982).

White, J. J., 'Endings and Non-endings in Kafka's Fiction', in Franz Kuna (ed.), *Franz Kafka: Semi-Centenary Perspectives* (London: Elek, 1976), 146–66.

Meditation

Rolleston, James, 'Temporal Space: A Reading of Kafka's *Betrachtung*', *Modern Austrian Literature*, 11 (1978), iii–iv. 123–38.

Ryan, Judith, 'Kafka Before Kafka: The Early Stories', in James Rolleston (ed.), *A Companion to the Works of Franz Kafka* (Rochester, NY: Camden House, 2002), 61–83.

Sandbank, Shimon, 'Uncertainty in Style: Kafka's *Betrachtung*', *German Life and Letters*, 34 (1981), 385–97.

The Judgement

Berman, Russell A., 'Tradition and Betrayal in *Das Urteil*', in James Rolleston (ed.), *A Companion to the Works of Franz Kafka* (Rochester, NY: Camden House, 2002), 85–99.

Ellis, John M., 'Kafka: *Das Urteil*', in *Narration in the German Novelle* (Cambridge: Cambridge University Press, 1974), 188–211.

Robertson, Ritchie, 'Kafka as anti-Christian: *Das Urteil, Die Verwandlung*, and the Aphorisms', in James Rolleston (ed.), *A Companion to the Works of Franz Kafka* (Rochester, NY: Camden House, 2002), 101–22.

Swales, Martin, 'Why Read Kafka?', *Modern Language Review*, 76 (1981), 357–82.

White, J. J., 'Franz Kafka's *Das Urteil*—An Interpretation', *Deutsche Vierteljahresschrift*, 28 (1964), 208–29.

The Metamorphosis

Corngold, Stanley, *The Commentators' Despair: The Interpretation of Kafka's 'Metamorphosis'* (Port Washington: Kennikat Press, 1973).

——(ed.), *The Metamorphosis: Translation, Backgrounds and Contexts, Criticism* (New York: Norton, 1996).

Luke, F. D., 'Kafka's *Die Verwandlung*', *Modern Language Review*, 46 (1951), 232–45.

Nabokov, Vladimir, 'Franz Kafka, "The Metamorphosis"', in *Lectures on Literature*, ed. Fredson Bowers (London: Weidenfeld & Nicolson, 1980), 251–83.

Ryan, Michael P., 'Samsa and *Samsara*: Suffering, Death and Rebirth in *The Metamorphosis*', *German Quarterly*, 72 (1999), 133–52.

Straus, Nina Pelikan, 'Transforming Franz Kafka's *Metamorphosis*', *Signs: Journal of Women in Culture and Society*, 14 (1989), 651–67.

Waldeck, Peter B., 'Kafka's *Die Verwandlung* and *Ein Hungerkünstler* as Influenced by Leopold von Sacher-Masoch', *Monatshefte*, 64 (1972), 147–52.

In the Penal Colony

Burns, Wayne, '*In the Penal Colony*: Variations on a Theme by Octave Mirbeau', *accent*, 17 (1957), 45–51.

Davey, E. R., 'The Broken Engine: A Study of Franz Kafka's *In der Strafkolonie*', *Journal of European Studies*, 14 (1984), 271–83.

Dodd, W. J., 'Dostoevskian Elements in Kafka's *Penal Colony*', *German Life and Letters*, 37 (1983–4), 11–23.

Gray, Richard T., 'Disjunctive Signs: Semiotics, Aesthetics, and Failed Mediation in *In der Strafkolonie*', in James Rolleston (ed.), *A Companion to the Works of Franz Kafka* (Rochester, NY: Camden House, 2002), 213–45.

Pasley, J. M. S., 'Introduction', Franz Kafka, *Der Heizer, In der Strafkolonie, Der Bau* (Cambridge: Cambridge University Press, 1966), 14–22.

Peters, Paul, 'Witness to the Execution: Kafka and Colonialism', *Monatshefte*, 93 (2001), 401–25.

Letter to his Father

Bruce, Iris, '"A Frosty Hall of Mirrors": Father Knows Best in Franz Kafka and Nadine Gordimer', in Linda E. Feldman and Diana Orendi (eds.), *Evolving Jewish Identities in German Culture: Borders and Crossings* (Westport, Conn.: Praeger, 2000), 95–116.

Neumann, Gerhard, '*The Judgment*, *Letter to his Father*, and the Bourgeois Family', in Mark Anderson (ed.), *Reading Kafka: Prague, Politics, and the Fin de Siècle* (New York: Schocken, 1989), 215–28.

Politzer, Heinz, 'Franz Kafka's *Letter to his Father*', *Germanic Review*, 28 (1953), 165–79.

Further Reading in Oxford World's Classics

Kafka, Franz, *The Castle*, tr. Anthea Bell, ed. Ritchie Robertson.
——*The Trial*, tr. Mike Mitchell, ed. Ritchie Robertson.

A CHRONOLOGY OF FRANZ KAFKA

1883　3 July: Franz Kafka born in Prague, son of Hermann Kafka (1852–1931) and his wife Julie, née Löwy (1856–1934).

1885　Birth of FK's brother Georg, who died at the age of fifteen months.

1887　Birth of FK's brother Heinrich, who died at the age of six months.

1889　Birth of FK's sister Gabriele ('Elli') (d. 1941).

1890　Birth of FK's sister Valerie ('Valli') (d. 1942).

1892　Birth of FK's sister Ottilie ('Ottla') (d. 1943).

1901　FK begins studying law in the German-language section of the Charles University, Prague.

1906　Gains his doctorate in law and begins a year of professional experience in the Prague courts.

1907　Begins working for the Prague branch of the insurance company Assicurazioni Generali, based in Trieste.

1908　Moves to the state-run Workers' Accident Insurance Company for the Kingdom of Bohemia. First publication: eight prose pieces (later included in the volume *Meditation*) appear in the Munich journal *Hyperion*.

1909　Holiday with Max and Otto Brod at Riva on Lake Garda; they attend a display of aircraft, about which FK writes 'The Aeroplanes at Brescia'.

1910　Holiday with Max and Otto Brod in Paris.

1911　Holiday with Max Brod in northern Italy, Switzerland, and Paris. Attends many performances by Yiddish actors visiting Prague, and becomes friendly with the actor Isaak Löwy (Yitskhok Levi).

1912　Holiday with Max Brod in Weimar, after which FK spends three weeks in the nudist sanatorium 'Jungborn' in the Harz Mountains. Works on *The Man who Disappeared*. 13 August: first meeting with Felice Bauer (1887–1960) from Berlin. 22–3 September: writes *The Judgement* in a single night. November–December: works on *The Metamorphosis*. December: *Meditation*, a collection of short prose pieces, published by Kurt Wolff in Leipzig.

1913　Visits Felice Bauer three times in Berlin. September: attends a conference on accident prevention in Vienna, where he also looks in on the Eleventh Zionist Congress. Stays in a sanatorium in Riva. Publishes *The Stoker* (=the first chapter of *The Man who*

Disappeared) in Wolff's series of avant-garde prose texts 'The Last Judgement'.

1914 1 June: officially engaged to Felice Bauer in Berlin. 12 July: engagement dissolved. Holiday with the Prague novelist Ernst Weiss in the Danish resort of Marielyst. August–December: writes most of *The Trial*; October: *In the Penal Colony*.

1915 The dramatist Carl Sternheim, awarded the Fontane Prize for literature, transfers the prize money to Kafka. *The Metamorphosis* published by Wolff.

1916 Reconciliation with Felice Bauer; they spend ten days together in the Bohemian resort of Marienbad (Mariánské Lázně). *The Judgement* published by Wolff. FK works on the stories later collected in *A Country Doctor*.

1917 July: FK and Felice visit the latter's sister in Budapest, and become engaged again. 9–10 August: FK suffers a haemorrhage which is diagnosed as tubercular. To convalesce, he stays with his sister Ottla on a farm at Zürau (Siřem) in the Bohemian countryside. December: visit from Felice Bauer; engagement dissolved.

1918 March: FK resumes work. November: given health leave, stays till March 1919 in a hotel in Schelesen (Železná).

1919 Back in Prague, briefly engaged to Julie Wohryzek (1891–1944). *In the Penal Colony* published by Wolff.

1920 Intense relationship with his Czech translator Milena Polak, née Jesenská (1896–1944). July: ends relationship with Julie Wohryzek. Publication of *A Country Doctor: Little Stories*. December: again granted health leave, FK stays in a sanatorium in Matliary, in the Tatra Mountains, till August 1921.

1921 September: returns to work, but his worsening health requires him to take three months' further leave from October.

1922 January: has his leave extended till April; stays in mountain hotel in Spindlermühle (Špindlerův Mlýn). January–August: writes most of *The Castle*. 1 July: retires from the Insurance Company on a pension.

1923 July: visits Müritz on the Baltic and meets Dora Diamant (1898–1952). September: moves to Berlin and lives with Dora.

1924 March: his declining health obliges FK to return to Prague and, in April, to enter a sanatorium outside Vienna. Writes and publishes 'Josefine, the Singer or The Mouse-People'. 3 June: dies. August: *A Hunger Artist: Four Stories* published by Die Schmiede.

1925 *The Trial*, edited by Max Brod, published by Die Schmiede.

1926 *The Castle*, edited by Max Brod, published by Wolff.

1927 *Amerika* (now known by Kafka's title, *The Man who Disappeared*), edited by Max Brod, published by Wolff.

1930 *The Castle*, translated by Willa and Edwin Muir, published by Martin Secker (London), the first English translation of Kafka.

1939 Max Brod leaves Prague just before the German invasion, taking Kafka's manuscripts in a suitcase, and reaches Palestine.

1956 Brod transfers the manuscripts (except that of *The Trial*) to Switzerland for safe keeping.

1961 The Oxford scholar Malcolm Pasley, with the permission of Kafka's heirs, transports the manuscripts to the Bodleian Library.

THE METAMORPHOSIS
AND OTHER STORIES

Meditation

CHILDREN ON THE HIGHWAY

I HEARD the wagons passing the garden fence; sometimes I caught sight of them through the gaps made by the gentle stirring of the leaves. How the wood of their spokes and shafts creaked in the summer heat! Workmen were coming from the fields, laughing quite disgracefully.

I was sitting on our little swing, just resting for a spell among the trees in my parents' garden.

Beyond the fence there was no end to it: children trotted past and vanished in a moment; wagons carrying corn with men and women sitting on the sheaves and round about made the flower-beds dark; towards evening I saw a man with a walking-stick taking a leisurely stroll, and some girls, coming towards him arm in arm, stepped aside onto the grass as they greeted him.

Then birds were flying up like sparks; I followed them with my eyes and saw how they rose in one breath, until I began to believe not that they were rising, but that I was falling; and holding on tight to the ropes, from mere weakness I began to swing gently. Soon I was swinging more strongly as the breeze blew cooler, and instead of the soaring birds the trembling stars appeared.

I had my supper by candlelight. Quite often I had both arms on the wooden table-top as I took a bite of my bread and butter, already tired. The wide-meshed curtains billowed in the warm wind, and some-times, if someone passing by outside wanted to see me better and talk to me, he would hold them fast in his hands. Most times the candle would go out, and for a while still the gathering of midges would dance around in the dark candle-smoke. If someone asked me a question from the window, I would look at him as if I were gazing at the mountains or into the empty air—and a reply from me wouldn't matter very much to him either.

But if one of them leapt over the windowsill and told me that the others were already outside, I would get up, though it was with a sigh.

'Go on, why are you sighing like that? What's happened? Is it something especially bad that can't ever be put right? Won't we be able to get over it, ever? Is all really lost?'

Nothing was lost. We ran out in front of the house. 'Thank heavens, there you are at last.' 'You always come so late.'—'What, me?'—'Especially you; stay at home if you don't want to come with us.'—'No quarter!'—'What do you mean, no quarter? What a way to talk!'

We rushed off, butting through the evening with our heads. There was no daytime and no night-time. One moment the buttons of our waistcoats were rattling close together like teeth, the next we were each running at the same distance from one another, our mouths breathing fire, like beasts in the tropics. Like cuirassiers in ancient wars, stamping and rearing high in the air, we drove one another down the short lane, and with this run-up to give us a start, we pelted on up the highway. Some rushed wildly into the roadside ditches; they had hardly vanished against the dark embankment before they were standing like strangers up on the track along the field, looking down.

'Come back down!'—'You come up first!'—'So that you can push us down—not a chance; we're not that stupid.'—'You're that frit, you mean. Come on, come on.'—'Really? You lot? You lot push us down? I'd like to see you try!' We attacked, and got shoved in the chest, and lay down in the grass of the ditch, falling of our own free will. It all had the same warmth from the sun. We didn't feel warm or cold in the grass; we just got tired.

When you turned on your right side and put your hand under your head, you wanted to fall asleep so badly. Of course, you wanted to rouse yourself again with chin held high, but you wanted to fall into a deeper ditch instead. Then, holding your arm across your body and with bent legs flying, you tried to fling yourself into the air—and fall again for certain into an even deeper ditch. And you wanted it to go on and on.

You hardly thought about how you might stretch out straight in the last ditch, your knees especially, to sleep properly; ready to cry, you lay on your back as if you were ill. You blinked when at one point a boy jumped over us from the embankment on to the road, on silent feet, his elbows bent to his thighs.

The moon was already to be seen quite high in the sky; a mail-coach went driving past in its light. A gentle wind rose everywhere; even in the ditch we could feel it, and nearby the forest began to murmur. It wasn't so important to you any longer then to be alone.

'Where are you?'—'Come here!'—'All together!'—'Where are you hiding? Stop fooling about!'—Don't you know, the post has already gone by?'—'No—already?'—'Of course, it went by while you were asleep.' I've been asleep? No, really?'—'Shut up! You still look sleepy.'—'Surely not.'—'Come on!'

We ran closer together; some stretched out their hands to one another, we couldn't hold our heads high enough because the road ran downhill. Someone gave an Indian war-whoop; our legs fell into a gallop as never before; as we leapt the wind lifted our thighs. Nothing could have stopped us; we kept up so easily that even when we were passing each other we could fold our arms and look around us calmly.

We stopped on the bridge; the ones who had run ahead turned back. The water below was pounding against stones and roots as if it weren't already late evening. There was no reason why one of us shouldn't jump onto the parapet of the bridge.

A railway train emerged from behind low trees in the distance; all the carriages were lit up, the glass windows certainly lowered. One of us started to sing a popular song, but we all wanted to sing. We were singing faster than the train was travelling, we swung our arms because our voices were not enough; our voices all tumbled out together, which made us feel good. When your voice joins in with others, it's like being drawn along by a fish-hook.

So that's how we sang, with the forest behind us, for the distant travellers to hear us. The grown-ups were still awake in the village, mothers making the beds ready for the night.

It was time. I kissed the one standing next to me, just gave my hand to the three nearest, and began to run back; nobody called me. At the first crossroads where they could no longer see me, I turned off and ran along the field paths into the forest once more. I was aiming for the city in the south which they told of in our village:

'The people there! Think of it, they just don't sleep.'

'Why not?'

'Because they don't get tired.'

'And why not, then?'

'Because they're fools.'*

'Don't fools get tired?'

'How could fools get tired?'

UNMASKING A CONFIDENCE-MAN

At last, towards ten in the evening, in the company of a man I knew slightly from some earlier occasion, who had latched on to me once again out of the blue and dragged me round the alleys for two whole hours, I arrived at the grand house where I had been invited for a social gathering.

'Well now!' I said, clapping my hands as a sign that it was now absolutely necessary that we should part. I had already made several less resolute attempts, and by now I was quite tired.

'Are you going up right now?' he asked. I heard a sound in his mouth like teeth snapping together.

'Yes.'

After all, I was invited. I'd told him straight away. But I was invited to go up into the house, where I had for so long wanted to be, not to stand here in front of the gates looking past the ears of my opposite number, and now, on top of that, to fall silent with him, as if we were determined to stay on this spot for a long time. At the same time all the houses round about promptly took part in this silence, and so did the darkness above them, reaching as far as the stars. And the footsteps of invisible passers-by, whose course I had no wish to guess at, the wind that kept on driving against the other side of the street, the gramophone singing behind closed windows in some room—they made themselves heard in this silence, as if they had owned it for ever and ever.

And my companion acquiesced to this in his own name and—with a smile—also in mine, stretched his right arm upwards along the wall, and closing his eyes, rested his cheek against it.

But before this smile had ended, I turned away filled with sudden shame. For it was only by this smile, nothing more, that I had recognized he was a confidence-man. And yet I had already been in this city for months and believed I knew these confidence-men through and through, how they come out of side-streets towards us at night like some innkeeper, stretching out their hands; how they dodge around the advertising pillars where we're standing as if they are playing hide-and-seek, spying at us from behind the pillar with at least one eye; how if we hesitate at a crossroads they dance out all of a sudden in front of us on the edge of the pavement! After all, I understood them so well because they had been my first city acquaintances in the little taverns, and it was to them I owed my first glimpse of a ruthlessness which now I cannot imagine the earth to be without, so much so that I was already beginning to feel it in myself. How they would persist in confronting you, even if you had long ago run away from them, even if there was nothing more to con! How they kept at it, not giving in, but on the contrary looking at you with eyes that were still persuasive, even from a distance! And their methods were always the same. They would plant themselves in front of us, straddling as broad as they could, trying to keep us away from where we were aiming for, preparing instead a lodging for us in their own breast; and if in the end our pent-up feelings would rebel, they took it as an embrace which they would eagerly accept, face to the fore.

And it was only after being in his company for so long that I recognized those old tricks again. I rubbed my fingertips together in an attempt to undo the shame.

But my fellow was still leaning here as before; he still regarded himself as a successful confidence-man, and his free cheek grew pink with satisfaction at his destiny.

'Unmasked!' I said, tapping him lightly on the shoulder. Then I rushed up the steps, where such blind loyalty on the faces of the servants gave me as much pleasure as a delightful surprise. I looked at them all, one after the other, as they relieved me of my overcoat and brushed the dust from my boots. Then, with a sigh of relief and walking tall, I entered the drawing-room.

THE SUDDEN STROLL

If in the evening you seem to have decided once and for all to stay at home, having donned your dressing-gown, sitting after dinner at the lamp-lit table and intending to take up this bit of work or that game, after which you will go to bed as usual; if the weather outside is unkind, which makes staying at home the natural thing to do; if by now you have already been sitting silent at table for so long that going out would be bound to provoke general amazement; if the main staircase is already dark and the front door locked, and if despite all this you get to your feet in sudden unease; if you change your dressing-gown and appear fully clad for outdoors, declare that you have to go out, and after a brief goodbye actually do so; if you think you have left behind you a greater or lesser degree of annoyance according to how quickly you slam the apartment door; if you find yourself once more out in the street, your limbs responding with especial agility to the unexpected freedom you have given them; if by this one decision you feel all your capacity for decisive action concentrated within you, if you realize with greater

insight than usual that you do after all have more strength than you
need to bring about the quickest change with ease, that you have the
capacity to weather it; and if you run off down the long streets in the
way you are doing—then for this evening, you have broken utterly
from your family, who fade away into insubstantiality, while you yourself, absolutely solid, black and clear-cut, slapping your thighs, rise and
assume your true form. All this is further reinforced if at this late hour
you go and look up a friend to see how he is doing.

DECISIONS

To pull oneself out of a state of misery must be easy, even if the
energy is forced. I force myself up from my armchair, circle the table,
loosen my head and neck, give a sparkle to my eyes, tense the
muscles around them. Work to counteract every feeling I have: rush
impetuously to greet A. when he arrives, tolerate B. in my room
kindly; in C.'s company* take in all the talk, despite the pain and
trouble, in deep draughts.

But even if it works, with every false move—which is bound to
occur—the whole thing, the easy and the difficult, will come to a halt
and I will be forced to go round in a circle and retreat.

That is why the best counsel is still to put up with everything,
behave like a heavy block, and even if you yourself feel blown away,
refuse to be lured into taking a single unnecessary step; look at the
others with a brutish gaze; feel no remorse; in short, with your own
hand suppress what ghostly remnants of life still remain, that is,
increase the final tomb-like stillness even more, and allow nothing
outside it to exist any further.

A gesture characteristic of such a condition is to run the little
finger across the eyebrows.

THE TRIP TO THE MOUNTAINS

'I don't know,' I cried soundlessly, 'I really don't know. If no one
comes, well then, no one comes. I've done no one any harm; no one
has done me any harm, but no one wants to help me. No one at all.
But it's not really like that. Only that no one is helping me—otherwise
No-one-at-all would be rather nice. I would really quite like—after
all, why not?—to go on a trip with a party of No-one-at-alls. To the

mountains, of course—where else? How these No-one-at-alls are crowding close to one another, with their many arms stretched across or linked, their many feet, only tiny steps apart! Naturally, everyone is wearing a tail-coat. We're walking at our ease; the wind is blowing through the gaps we and our limbs leave open. How free the neck becomes in the mountains! It's a miracle that we're not singing.'

THE BACHELOR'S DISTRESS

It seems so hard to remain a bachelor; as an old man, keeping your dignity with difficulty, to plead for an invitation if you want to spend an evening with people; to be ill and look for weeks at the empty room from the corner of your bed; always to say goodbye in front of the house door, never dash up the stairs at your wife's side; to have nothing but side doors in your room, leading to other people's apartments; to carry your evening meal home in your hand; to gaze in wonder at other people's children and not always have to repeat: 'I have none'; to model your appearance and behaviour on one or two bachelors remembered from your youth.

That is how it will be, only that in reality it will be you yourself standing there, today and later, with a body and a real head, and so with a brow too, to strike with your hand.

THE SMALL BUSINESSMAN

It is possible that some people are sorry for me, but I don't see any sign of it. My small business fills me with worries which give me pain deep inside my forehead and temples, but without offering me any prospect of contentment, for it's a small business.

For hours in advance I have to make arrangements, keep the caretaker's memory alert, warn him of any mistakes I'm afraid he'll make, and in one season calculate the fashions* of the next, not as they will hold sway among the people of my own circle, but among the inaccessible inhabitants out in the countryside.

My money is in the hands of strangers; I am unable to see into their affairs; I have no idea what misfortune might strike them; how would I be able to prevent it! Perhaps they've grown extravagant and are giving a great party in some tavern garden, while others drop in on it for a time en route as they run off to America.

Now that the shop is closed of a weekday evening, and I suddenly see hours stretching before me when I won't be able to do anything about the never-ending needs of my business, I am overwhelmed inside by the tension I put off from the morning, like a returning tide, but I cannot contain it, and it carries me along with it, directionless.

And yet I am unable to turn this mood to use; I can only go home, for my face and hands are dirty and damp with sweat; my jacket is stained and dusty; I'm wearing my tradesman's cap, and my boots are scratched from the nails in the crates. So I walk as if waves were carrying me, snapping the fingers of both hands, and stroking the children's hair as they come towards me.

But my way is short. I am in my block of flats immediately, opening the door to the lift and entering.

I see that I am now, suddenly, alone. Others, who have to climb the stairs, must get rather tired as they go; they have to wait with their lungs gasping until someone comes to open the door to their flat, and that gives them a reason to be irritated and impatient; they enter the hall, where they hang up their hat, and it is not before they have gone down the corridor past several glass doors and into their own room that they are alone.

But I am alone at once in the lift, and, kneeling, gaze into the narrow mirror. As the lift begins to rise, I say:

'Be quiet, go away, all of you, do you want to make for the shade of the trees, or behind the curtains at the window, or down to the arcades?'

I mouth the words as the banisters of the stairs slide, like water flowing, past the opaque glass panes.

'Fly away then; let your wings, which I've never seen, carry you to the valley in the country, or to Paris, if that is where you want to go.

'Still, enjoy the view from the window as the processions come from all three streets, not giving way, but weaving through one another and allowing the open square to emerge again between the ranks at the rear. Wave with your handkerchief, be outraged, be touched, acclaim the pretty lady driving past.

'Cross the brook by the wooden bridge, nod to the children bathing, and listen in amazement to the cheers of the thousand sailors on the distant battleship.

'Go in pursuit of that inconspicuous man, and when you have pushed him into a doorway, rob him,* and then watch him, each of you with your hands in your pockets, as he makes his way sadly into the alley on the left.

'The mounted police galloping here and there bring their horses under control and force you back. Let them. The empty streets will lower their spirits, I know. Already—you see!—they are riding away, two by two, slowly round the street corners, like the wind across the squares.'

Then I have to get out of the lift and send it down; I ring the doorbell and the maid opens the door as I bid her 'Good-evening'.

GAZING OUT IDLY

What will we do in these spring days that are arriving so fast? Early this morning the sky was grey, but now if you go to the window you are surprised, and you rest your cheek against the window-catch.

Down below, you see the light of the sun—though it's sinking already—on the face of a little girl who is just walking along. She looks round, and at the same time you see, falling upon her, the shadow of a man who is walking more quickly behind her.

Then the man has passed her, and the child's face is quite bright.

THE WAY HOME

Just see how persuasive the air is after the thunderstorm! My merits reveal themselves; they overwhelm me—though admittedly I'm not resisting.

I march along, and my tempo is the tempo of this side of the street, of this street, of this quarter of town. I am responsible, and rightly so, for all the knocking on doors, the thumping on tables, the toasts drunk, for all the loving couples in their beds, or in the skeletons of new buildings, pressed close against house walls in dark alleys, or on brothel divans.

I weigh my past against my future and discover that both are excellent; I cannot give precedence to either, and the only fault I can find is in the injustice of Fate, which has favoured me so greatly.

Only when I enter my room, I'm a little thoughtful, but without having found anything worth being thoughtful about as I came upstairs. It doesn't help me much to open the window wide, nor that music is still playing in a garden.

THE RUNNERS

When one is going for a stroll along a lane at night, and a man, already visible from some way off, comes running towards us—the lane ahead of us is on a rise and there is a full moon—we won't attack him, even if he is frail and ragged, even if someone is running after him and shouting, but we will let him go running on.

For it is night, and we can't help it if the lane is rising ahead of us in the full moon, and besides, perhaps these two have put on this chase for fun; perhaps the two are being pursued by a third; perhaps the second has murder in mind, and we would become implicated in the murder; perhaps the two are unaware of each other and are only running home to their beds, each on his own account; perhaps they are sleepwalkers; perhaps the first has a weapon.

And finally, mightn't we be tired? Haven't we drunk all that wine? We are glad that we can no longer see the second man either.

THE PASSENGER

I am standing on the platform of the tram, utterly uncertain of my status in this world, in this city, in my family. I couldn't even say offhand what claims I could justifiably make in any direction. I have no defence at all for standing on this platform, holding on to this strap, allowing myself to travel in this vehicle, nor that people should get out of its way, or walk silently, or pause in front of the shop-windows. After all, nobody is requiring me to do so, but that doesn't matter.

The tram is approaching a stop; a girl stations herself near the steps, ready to get out. She appears as distinct to me as if I had run my hands over her. She is dressed in black; the folds of her skirt hardly stir; her blouse is cut close, with a collar of fine-meshed lace. She is holding her left hand flat against the side; the umbrella in her right hand is resting on the step below the top. Her face is brown; her nose, slightly narrow at the sides, finishes broad and rounded at the tip. She has thick brown hair, with little wisps at her right temple. Her ear lies small and close to her head, but, standing so near her, I can still see all the back of her right ear and the shadow where it joins her head.

I asked myself at the time: how is it that she does not marvel at herself, that she keeps her lips closed and doesn't say anything like this?

DRESSES

When I see dresses with a great many pleats and gathers, hung with ornaments, and sitting beautifully on beautiful bodies, I often think that they won't stay like that for long, but will crease and become past ironing; that they will get dust lying so thick in their decorations that it is past removing, and that nobody would want to make themselves so sad and so ridiculous as to put on the same precious gown every morning and take it off again at night.

And yet I see girls who are undoubtedly beautiful and have lots of charming little muscles and bones, and smooth skin and masses of fine hair, who still appear day after day wearing this one natural fancy dress, always cupping the same face in the same hands, and having it reflected in their mirror.

Only sometimes, at evening, when they come home late from a party, it appears to them in the mirror worn out, puffy, covered in dust, seen by everybody before and scarcely fit to wear any longer.

THE REBUFF

If I encounter a pretty girl and invite her: 'Be nice, come along with me,' and she walks past without speaking, what she means is:

'You're no great lord with your name on the tip of everyone's tongue, nor a broad-shouldered American with the build of a Red Indian, your eyes scanning the horizon and your skin massaged by the wind of the prairies and the rivers pouring through them; you haven't travelled to the great oceans heaven knows where, nor sailed upon them. So I ask you, why should I, a pretty girl like me, go along with you?'

'You forget: you are not riding in an automobile, plunging and jolting down the street; I don't see any gentlemen squeezed into their suits dancing attendance on you, murmuring their benedictions and walking behind you in an exact half-circle; your breasts are laced tidily in your bodice, but your thighs and hips make up for that restraint; you are wearing a taffeta dress with gathered pleats in the style that certainly gave us all pleasure last autumn, and yet—wearing this danger to life and limb—you still smile from time to time.'

'Yes, we are both right, and, so that we do not become undeniably conscious of it, let us rather, shall we? each of us go home alone.'

FOR GENTLEMAN-RIDERS TO THINK ABOUT

Nothing, if you think it over, can tempt you to want to win a race.

The celebrity that comes from being acknowledged as the best rider in the country gives us too much pleasure as the band strikes up, so that we can't help regretting it the morning after.

The envy of our enemies—cunning, quite influential people—is bound to hurt us as we ride in the narrow enclosure towards that flat racecourse which just now lay empty before us, apart from a few horsemen left behind from the last race, small figures charging towards the edge of the horizon.

Many of our friends are in a hurry to claim their winnings, only shouting their cheers casually over their shoulders from the distant booth; but our best friends didn't put any money on our horse, because they were afraid that if they lost they were bound to be angry with us, but now, when our horse came in first and they have won nothing, they turn away when we come past and prefer to look along the grandstands.

Your rivals behind you, firm in the saddle, try to overlook the bad luck that has struck them and the injustice somehow done them; they begin to perk up, as if a new race must be starting, a serious one too, after such child's play.

To many of the ladies the winner seems ridiculous, for there he is, preening himself, but still unable to deal with the endless hand-shaking, greeting, bowing, waving-into-space, while the losers keep their mouths shut and airily clap the necks of their neighing horses.

And finally, out of the lowering sky, it begins to rain.

THE WINDOW ON TO THE STREET

Anyone whose life is lonely, but who would nevertheless wish to make some contact somewhere now and then, or who, depending on changes in the time of day, the weather, conditions at work, and the like, all at once wants to see some arm, any arm he can hold on to—he will not carry on for long without a window on to the street. And if his state of mind is such that he is not especially looking out for anything, and is just going over to stand at his windowsill, a weary man with eyes darting up and down between passers-by and sky, and does not want to look out, leaning his head back a little, then even so the horses will still sweep him down with them into their convoy of carts and din and so at last in the direction of human concord.

WISH TO BECOME A RED INDIAN

Oh to be a Red Indian, ready in an instant, riding a swift horse, aslant in the air, thundering again and again over the thundering earth, until you let the spurs go, for there weren't any spurs, until you cast off the reins, for there weren't any reins, and you scarcely saw the land ahead of you as close-cropped scrub, being already without horse's neck and horse's head!

TREES

For we are like tree-trunks in the snow. Seemingly they are laid on flat, and with a little nudge you could push them away. No, that can't be done, for they are connected firmly to the ground. But look, even that is only seeming.

UNHAPPINESS

When it had already become unbearable—once towards evening in November—and I was pacing the narrow carpet in my room as if it were a racecourse, frightened at the sight of the lighted street, I turned once again and far in the room once again I found a new goal in the depths of the mirror, and I screamed aloud, just so as to hear my scream, the kind of scream that has nothing to answer it and nothing to take away its force, so that it rises without anything to counteract it and cannot stop, even when it falls silent. Just then the door in the wall opened—so hastily because haste was needed any-way, and even the carthorses on the pavement below were rearing like horses driven wild in battle, their throats defenceless.

Like a little ghost, a child wafted out of the utter dark of the cor-ridor where the lamp was still unlit, and stood quite still on tiptoe, on a floorboard that rocked imperceptibly. At first dazzled by the dim light in the room, the child quickly tried to cover its face with its hands, but calmed down unexpectedly as she looked towards the window, for outside its crossbars the haze thrown up by the street lighting finally settled below the darkness. With her right elbow she supported herself against the wall in front of the open door, and let the draught from outside play about her ankles and her neck and her temples.

I looked towards her briefly, then said 'Good evening' and took my coat from the fire-screen, for I didn't want to stand there half-naked. For a while I remained open-mouthed, for my agitation to leave me by that route. My mouth had a sour taste; I could feel my eyelids trembling on my face, in short, this particular visit—which I had been expecting anyhow—was the last thing I needed.

The child was still standing in the same place; she had pressed her right hand against the wall, and, red in the cheeks, was fascinated by the rough texture of the whitewash, scraping her fingertips against it. I said: 'Am I really the person you want? Isn't there some mistake? There's nothing easier than making a mistake in this big building. My name is So-and-so. I live on the third floor. So am I the person you want to visit?'

'Gently, gently,' said the child over her shoulder, 'it's all right.'

'Come further into the room, then. I'd like to shut the door.'

'I've just shut the door. Don't trouble. Just calm down.'

'It's no trouble. But there are a lot of people living on this corridor, and of course they are all acquaintances of mine. Most of them are coming back from work now. If they hear you talking in a room, they simply think they have the right to open the door and look in to see what's going on. That's the way it is. These people have got their day's work behind them and won't be pushed around on their brief evenings of freedom! Besides, you know that as well as I do. Let me shut the door.'

'What is it? What's the matter with you? As far as I'm concerned, the whole block of flats can come in. And I repeat: I've already closed the door. Do you think you're the only one who can shut the doors? I've even locked it with the key.'

'That's all right, then. That's all I wanted. You really didn't have to lock it with the key, though. But now that you're here, make yourself comfortable. You're my guest. You can trust me completely. Relax and don't be afraid. I shan't force you either to remain here or to go away. Do I have to say this? Don't you know me better than that?'

'No, you really don't have to say it. Indeed, you shouldn't have said it at all. I'm a child. Why go to such lengths over me?'

'It's not that bad. A child, of course. But you're not as small as all
that. You're quite grown up. If you were a big girl you wouldn't be
allowed to lock yourself in a room with me so simply.'

'We don't have to worry about that. I only meant: it's not much
protection for me that I know you so well; it only relieves you of the
effort of pretending to me. But you're still paying me compliments in
spite of that. But just leave off, please, just leave off. Besides, I don't
know you everywhere and all the time, especially not in this darkness.
It would be much better if you lit the lamp. No, rather not. In any
case, I shall bear in mind that you've already been threatening me.'

'What? I'm supposed to have threatened you? Come off it.
Anyway, I'm so glad that you are here at last. I say "at last" because
it's so late. I can't understand why you've come so late. It's possible
that in my delight I was speaking so incoherently, and that's how you
understood me. I'll admit ten times over that I did say as much, even
that I made every kind of threat—whatever you like. Only, don't
let's quarrel, for heaven's sake.—But how could you think it? How
could you hurt me so? Why do you want to spoil the little time you're
here like this? A stranger would be more approachable than you.'

'I should think so. That's not much of an insight. By nature I'm
already as close to you as any stranger could come. You know that as
well as I do—so why the melancholy? If you just want to play at
being like that, I'll go right this moment.'

'You will? You're bold enough to say even that to me? You're a bit
too daring. You are in my room, after all. You're scraping your fingers
against my wall like mad! My room! My wall! And besides, what you
say is ridiculous, not just cheeky. You say your nature forces you to
speak to me in this way. That's very nice of your nature. Your nature
is mine. And if I'm acting kindly towards you by nature, then you
shouldn't act otherwise either.'

'Is that kind?'

'I'm talking about earlier.'

'Do you know what I'll be like later?'

'I know nothing.'

And I went over to the table by my bed, where I lit a candle. At that
time I had neither gas nor electric light in my room. I sat down at the
table for a while, until I grew tired of that too. I put on my overcoat,
took my hat from the sofa, and blew out the candle. As I was leaving,
I stumbled over the leg of an armchair.

On the stairs I met a tenant from the same floor.

'You're going out again, you rogue?' he asked, pausing to rest on legs that straddled two steps.

'What am I to do?' I said. 'I've just had a ghost in my room.'

'You say that with the same dissatisfaction as you would if you'd found a hair in your soup.'

'You're joking. But just remember: a ghost is a ghost.'

'Very true. But what if one doesn't believe in ghosts at all?'

'Do you think I believe in ghosts, then? But what good is this not believing to me?'

'Very simple. Just don't be afraid any more if a ghost really turns up.'

'Yes, but that's the lesser fear, after all. The real fear is fear of the cause of the apparition. And that fear sticks. I have it in me on a truly grand scale.' Out of sheer nervousness I started to search in all my pockets.

'But as you weren't afraid of the apparition itself, you could easily have asked it what its cause was.'

'Obviously you've never talked to a ghost; you can never get any clear information out of them. They dither to and fro. These ghosts seem to have more doubts about their existence than we do—no wonder, given how fragile they are.'

'But I've heard that you can feed them up.'

'You're very well informed. You can. But who would do it?'

'Why not? If it's a female ghost, for instance,' he said, jumping onto the upper step.

'I see,' I said, 'but even then it's not worth it.'

I thought hard. My acquaintance was already so high up that he had to bend forward beneath the roof of the stairwell to see me.

'But in spite of that,' I called, 'if you take my ghost away from me up there, then it's over between us, for ever.'

'I was only joking, honestly,' he said, pulling back.

'That's all right then,' I said, and now I could actually have gone for a stroll comfortably. But because I felt so forlorn, I preferred to go upstairs, and went to bed.

The Judgement

It was on a Sunday morning, when spring was at its best. Georg Bendemann,* a young businessman, was sitting in his own room on the first floor of one of the low, flimsily-built houses extending in a long row down the riverside, their height and colour almost the only difference between them. He had just finished a letter to an old friend now in foreign parts, closed it, lingering lightly over the performance, and then, his elbows resting on his desk, he gazed out of the window at the river, the bridge, and the hills on the further bank with their pallid green.

He thought about how this friend, dissatisfied with his progress at home, had years ago literally fled to Russia. He was now running a business in St Petersburg* which had started off very well at first, but for a long time now seemed to be going nowhere, as the friend would complain on visits which were becoming more and more infrequent. So, remote as he was, he was wearing himself out, working to no avail; the beard of foreign cut was an ineffective cover for the face Georg had known since they were children, while the yellow of that face seemed to point to some incipient illness. As he had told Georg, he had no proper connections with the colony* of his own people there, but on the other hand he had almost no social contact with the local families either, so he was finally settling for life as a bachelor for good.

What could you write to a man like that, who had obviously taken the wrong turning, someone you could pity, but not help? Should you perhaps advise him to come back home, transfer his existence back here, resume all his old friendships—there was certainly nothing to stand in the way—and in other respects put his trust in the help of his friends? But that could only mean that you were at the same time telling him—and the more considerately, the more hurtfully—that his efforts so far had come to nothing, that he should finally give them up, that he should return and put up with everyone's wondering stares at somebody who had returned for good, that only his friends knew what was what, that he was an old baby who should simply follow the advice of his friends who had stayed at home? And even then, was it certain that there was any point to all the torment you would have to put him through? Perhaps you mightn't even succeed in persuading him to come back—after all, he said himself that he no longer understood conditions in his home country, and so then, in spite of everything, he would remain in that remote place of his, embittered by all the advice he had been given, and even further estranged from his friends. But if he really did follow this advice and—not intentionally of course, but by the facts—was brought low here, if he couldn't get on with his friends, but couldn't get on without them either, if he suffered from shame, and now no longer had either home, country, or friends, wouldn't it be much better for him to stay there, remote and a stranger, just as he was? In such circumstances, could you really think he could actually do well here?

For these reasons it was impossible, if you wanted to keep any correspondence going with him at all, for you to share any proper information with him, such as you might readily give to even the most distant acquaintance. Georg's friend had not been home now for more than three years, explaining this very feebly by the uncertainty of the political situation in Russia,* which did not permit a small businessman even the briefest of absences, though a hundred thousand Russians were free to go travelling round the world. In the course of these three years, however, a great deal had changed, especially for Georg. About two years ago Georg's mother had died, and since then Georg and his old father had set up house together; the friend had certainly learned of the mother's death, expressing his condolences in a letter of such dryness that its only cause could be that mourning over an event like that was quite unimaginable in such remote parts. But now, since that time, Georg had set about dealing with his business, as he had so much besides, with greater determination. Perhaps while his mother was still alive Georg's father, who insisted on having his view as the only one that counted in the business, had hindered Georg from really acting independently; perhaps since Georg's mother's death, his father, although he still worked in the firm, had become more withdrawn; perhaps happy chance—which was in fact very likely—played a far more important role, but in any case in these two years the business had taken off quite unexpectedly; they had had to double the number of staff, the turnover had increased fivefold, and further progress undoubtedly lay ahead.

But the friend had no inkling of this change. Previously, for the last time perhaps in that letter of condolence, he had tried to persuade

Georg to emigrate to Russia, and enlarged on the prospects that existed in St Petersburg for Georg's branch of business especially. The figures were minute in comparison with the size that Georg's business had now taken on. But Georg had had no desire to write to the friend about his business successes, and if he did so now in retrospect, it would really have looked very odd.

So Georg confined himself to telling his friend only about insignificant incidents, as they pile up at random in the memory on a quiet Sunday. All he wanted was to keep intact the image of his home town that the friend had no doubt created for himself and learned to live with in the long meantime. So it happened that Georg wrote to his friend announcing the engagement of some quite inconsequential person to some equally inconsequential girl three times in three letters with long intervals between, until finally the friend, quite counter to Georg's intention, even started to be interested in this remarkable event.

Georg would much rather write to him about such things than admit that a month ago he had himself become engaged to a Fräulein Frieda Brandenfeld,* a girl from a well-to-do family.* He often spoke to his intended about this friend and about the curious corresponding relationship he had with him. 'So he certainly won't come to our wedding, then,' she said, 'but I do have the right to get to know all your friends, haven't I?' 'I don't want to upset him,' answered Georg. 'I mean, he would probably come, at least I believe he would, but he'd feel forced to come, and hurt; perhaps he would envy me, and certainly feel dissatisfied, and, unable ever to get rid of this dissatisfaction, he would return alone. Alone—do you know what that is?' 'Yes, but mightn't he also find out about our marriage some other way?' 'I can't prevent that, but with his way of life it's not likely.' 'If you have friends like that, Georg, you shouldn't have become engaged at all.' 'Yes, we're both of us to blame for that,* but I wouldn't have it any different now.' And when, panting beneath his kisses, she still managed to bring out: 'It's still hurtful, you know,' he thought it was really quite innocuous to write and tell the friend everything. 'This is how I am, and this is how he has to accept me,' he said to himself. 'I can't trim myself into the sort of human being who might be better fitted to his friendship than I am.'

And in fact, in the long letter he wrote this Sunday afternoon he did indeed report the news that his engagement had taken place, in the following words: 'I have kept the best news till last. I have become engaged to a Fräulein Frieda Brandenfeld, a girl from a well-to-do family who settled here long after you left, so you would scarcely know them. There will be opportunity later to tell you more about my fiancée; for today, let it be enough for you that I am very happy, and that our relationship to each other has changed only to the extent that, instead of having a perfectly ordinary friend in me, you will have a friend who is happy. As well as that, you will have in my fiancée, who sends her warm regards and will write to you herself very soon, a true friend—something not entirely without significance for a bachelor. I know, all sorts of things are holding you back from paying us a visit. But mightn't my wedding be just the right occasion to cast all those impediments aside for once? But, be that as it may, act without considering others, and only as you think fit.'

Holding this letter in his hand, Georg had sat at his desk for a long time, his face turned towards the window. An acquaintance passing by and greeting him from the street, he had barely answered with an absent smile.

Finally, he put the letter in his pocket and went from his own room across a little passage into his father's room, where he had not been for months. Nor was there any need to, for he was in constant contact with his father in the business, and they took lunch in a restaurant at the same time; true, in the evenings each of them looked after himself as he pleased, but then they would mostly sit for a while—unless Georg, which happened most often, joined his friends, or these days visited his fiancée—each with his newspaper, in the living-room they shared.

Georg was amazed at how dark his father's room was, even on this sunny morning. So the high wall that rose on the far side of the narrow yard cast such a long shadow... His father was sitting by the window in a corner decked with various remembrances of his late mother, reading the newspaper and holding it sideways to his eyes, trying to compensate for some weakness in them. On the table were the remains of breakfast, not a great deal of which seemed to have been eaten.

'Ah, Georg!' said his father, going towards him at once. His heavy dressing-gown opened as he walked, the skirts flapping round him—'My father is still a giant,'* Georg said to himself.

'It's unbearably dark in here,' he said then.

'Yes, so it is—dark,' his father replied.

'You've closed the window too?'

'I prefer it that way.'

'It's so warm outside,' said Georg, as if adding to his last remark, and sat down.

His father cleared the breakfast things and put them on a chest.

'Actually, I only wanted to tell you', Georg went on, quite lost as he followed the old man's movements, 'that I have announced my engagement to St Petersburg after all.' He drew the letter a little way out of his pocket, and let it drop back again.

'To St Petersburg?' his father asked.

'Yes, to my friend there,' said Georg, and tried to catch his father's eye. 'In the business he's quite different', he thought, 'from the way he sits here sprawling, with his arms folded on his chest.'

'Yes, to your friend,' said his father with emphasis.

'You know, father, don't you, that at first I wanted to keep my engagement from him? Out of consideration. Not for any other reason. You know yourself he is a difficult person. I told myself that he can easily find out about my engagement from someone else, even though he leads such a solitary life that it's scarcely likely—I can't prevent that—but as it is he shan't hear about it from me.'

'And now you've had second thoughts about it?' asked his father, putting the huge newspaper on the windowsill, and his spectacles on the newspaper, covering them with his hand.

'Yes, I have had second thoughts about it. If he is my good friend, I told myself, then my happy engagement is a happiness for him too. And so I have hesitated no longer in announcing it to him. But I wanted to tell you before I posted the letter.'

'Georg,' said his father, stretching his toothless mouth wide, 'listen to me! You've come to me in this matter to consult me about it. That honours you, certainly. But that's nothing, it is worse than nothing, if you don't tell me the whole truth now. I don't want to stir up things that don't belong here. Since the death of our dear mother,* certain ugly things have been going on. Perhaps the time will come for them too, and perhaps it will come sooner than we think. A great deal escapes me in the business; perhaps it's not being concealed from me—I certainly don't want to make the assumption now that it is being concealed—I'm no longer strong enough, my memory is failing, I no longer have an eye for so many things. In the first place, it's the course of nature, and in the second, the death of our dear mother has stricken me far more than you.—But because we are discussing this matter in particular, this letter, I beg you, Georg, do not deceive me. It's a little thing, it's not worth the breath it takes to say it, so don't deceive me. Do you really have this friend in St Petersburg?'

Georg stood up, at a loss. 'Let's leave my friend be. A thousand friends wouldn't replace my father. Do you know what I believe? You're not looking after yourself enough. But age demands its due. I can't do without you in the business, you know that perfectly well, but if the business was to threaten your health, I'd shut up shop tomorrow for ever. This won't do. We must start a new way of life for you. From top to bottom. Here you are, sitting in the dark, and in the living-room you'd have lovely light. You pick at your breakfast instead of getting your strength up properly. You're sitting with your window closed, and the air would do you so much good. No, father! I'll fetch the doctor, and we'll follow his orders. We'll exchange rooms, you shall move into the front room and I'll move in here. It won't be a great change for you. We'll have all your things carried over with you. But there's time for all that. For now, lie down in bed for a little, you need rest, absolutely. Come, I'll help you to undress, you'll see, I can. Or if you want to go into the front room right away, you can lie down on my bed for the time being. That would be very sensible in any case.'

Georg was standing right next to his father, whose head, with its unkempt white hair, had drooped onto his chest.

'Georg,' said his father softly, without stirring.

Georg knelt down by his father at once. He saw the huge pupils in the tired face focused upon him from the corners of his father's eyes.

'You have no friend in St Petersburg. You've always been a joker, and you've always gone too far, even with me. How could you have a friend there of all places! I can't believe that at all.'

'Just think back a moment, father,' said Georg, and lifted him from the armchair, taking off his dressing-gown for him as he stood there feebly, 'soon it will have been three years ago now that my friend visited us here. I can still remember you didn't particularly take to him. I had to deny him to you at least twice* that he was here, even though he was sitting in my room at that very moment. Of course, I could understand your dislike of him very well, my friend has his oddities. But then you got on with him again perfectly well. I was so proud that time you listened to him, nodded and asked questions. If you think back, you must remember. He was telling incredible stories about the Russian revolution,* for instance when he'd been on a business trip in Kiev and in the middle of a riot he had seen a priest on a balcony who cut a broad cross in blood on the palm of his hand, lifted the hand, and appealed to the mob. You've retold this story yourself now and again.'

While he was speaking, Georg managed to sit his father down again and carefully take off his woollen pants, which he was wearing over his linen underpants, and then his socks. At the sight of the not particularly clean underclothes, he reproached himself for having neglected his father. It should surely have been his duty to look after his father's change of underclothes too. He had not yet expressly discussed with his fiancée how they would arrange his father's future, for they had silently assumed that he would remain in the old home by himself. But now he made up his mind with absolute certainty to take his father with him into his future household. Indeed, on closer inspection, it almost appeared that the care his father would receive there would come too late.

He carried his father to bed in his arms. He had a terrible feeling as he noticed, in the course of the few steps towards the bed, that his father was playing with the watch-chain on his chest. He wasn't able to put him into bed straight away, he clung so tightly to the watch-chain.

But no sooner was he in bed than everything seemed fine. He covered himself up and then drew the bedspread particularly high over his shoulders. He looked up, not unkindly.

'You remember him now, don't you?' asked Georg, nodding to him in encouragement.

'Am I well covered over now?' the father asked, as if he couldn't see whether his feet were covered enough.

'You like it in bed, then?' said Georg, arranging the blankets more tidily around him.

'Am I well covered over?' his father asked once again, and appeared to pay particular attention to Georg's reply.

'Quietly, now. You are well covered over.'

'No!' shouted the father, so sharply that the reply jolted against the question; he threw the bedspread back with such strength that for a moment it opened out completely in its flight, and stood upright in his bed. With only one hand he held lightly onto the ceiling. 'You wanted to cover me over, I know, my little sprig, but I'm not covered over yet. And even if this is the last of my strength, it's enough for you, too much for you. Of course I know your friend. He would have been a son after my own heart.* That is why all these years you have been deceiving him too. Why else? Do you think I haven't wept for him? That is why you lock yourself up in your office; do not disturb; the boss is busy—just so that you can write your bogus little letters to Russia. But fortunately no one has to teach this father to see through his son. Now you believed that you'd got him down, down so low that you can sit with your backside on him and he doesn't stir, that's when his Lordship the son decided to get married!'

Georg looked up at the nightmare image of his father. The friend in St Petersburg, whom the father now suddenly knew so well, moved him as never before. He saw him lost in far-off Russia. He saw him at the door of an empty, plundered shop.* Among the wrecked shelves, the shattered stock, the broken gas brackets, he was just about still standing. Why did he have to go away so far!

'Look at me!' shouted his father, and Georg ran, almost distracted, to the bed, to get a hold on everything, but he stopped short midway.

'Because she lifted her skirts,' his father began to warble, 'because she lifted her skirts like this, the disgusting cow,' and acting the part, he lifted his shirt so high that you could see the scar from his war-wound on his thigh, 'because she lifted her skirts like this and like this and like this, you went for her, and so that you can have it off with her undisturbed you have dishonoured our mother's memory, betrayed your friend, and buried your father in bed so that he can't stir. But can he stir or can't he?' And he stood perfectly free and kicked up his legs. He radiated insight.

Georg stood in a corner, as far from his father as possible. A long while ago he had firmly decided to observe everything with perfect precision so that there was no way he could be taken by surprise, roundabout, from behind, from above. Now he reminded himself of this long-forgotten resolution and forgot it again, in the way one draws a short thread through the eye of a needle.

'But your friend is not betrayed! On the contrary!' his father cried, and his finger wagging to and fro confirmed it. 'I was his representative here on the spot.'

'You were acting!' Georg could not help crying out, recognizing at once the harm this could do, and with his eyes fixed in a stare he bit his tongue—too late—so hard that his knees gave way.

'Yes, of course it was an act! Acting! A good word for it! What other consolation was there left to an old father and a widower? Tell me—and for the moment of your answer, be my living son still—what was left to me, in my back room, persecuted by disloyal staff, with old age deep in my bones? And my son walked the world rejoicing, cutting the deals that I had prepared, wallowing head over heels in his pleasures, and going from them into his father's presence with the grave face of a man of honour! Do you believe I didn't love you, I, whose issue you are!'

'Now he's going to bend forward,' thought Georg, 'what if he were to fall* and smash into pieces!' These words went hissing through his head.

The father did bend forward, but he did not fall. Since Georg didn't draw any closer, as he had expected, he rose again.

'Stay where you are! I don't need you! You think you still have the strength to come over here and you are only restraining yourself because you are in control. What a mistake! I'm still the one who's much more powerful. On my own I might have had to give way, but as it is our mother passed on her strength to me, and I've formed a splendid bond with your friend. As for your customers, I've got them here in my pocket!'

'He's even got pockets in his shirt,' Georg said to himself, believing that with this remark he could make him look ridiculous in the eyes of the whole world. But he only thought this for a moment, for he kept on forgetting everything.

'Just come to meet me arm in arm with your girl! I'll sweep her from your side—you've no idea how!'

Georg made a face as if he didn't believe it. The father merely nodded at Georg's corner, affirming the truth of what he said.

'How you amused me today when you came and asked whether you should write to your friend about your engagement. He knows all about it already, you young fool! He knows all about it already! I wrote to him because you forgot to take my writing things away from me. That's why he hasn't come for years. He knows everything a hundred times better than you do yourself. He crumples up your letters in his left hand, while in his right he holds up my letters to read!'

He waved his arm above his head in his fervour. 'He knows everything a thousand times better!' he cried.

'Ten thousand times!' said Georg, attempting to laugh at his father, but in his mouth the word took on a sound that was deadly serious.

'For years I've been watching out for you to come with this question! Do you believe I'm concerned about anything else? Do you believe I read the newspapers? Here!' And he threw a paper at Georg which had somehow got carried into the bed, an old newspaper with a name that was quite unfamiliar to Georg.

'How slow you were to grow up! Your mother had to die. She didn't live to see the happy day. Your friend is going to ruin in his Russia—as long as three years ago he was yellow enough to throw away, and as for me—well, you can see how things are going with me. You've certainly got eyes for that!'

'So you've been lying in wait for me!' Georg cried.

With compassion his father added: 'You probably wanted to say that earlier. Now it just doesn't apply any longer.'

And louder: 'So now you know all there is to know about everything besides yourself. Until now all you knew was only about yourself! After all, you were an innocent child really—but more really* you were a diabolical human being! And therefore know: I condemn you now to death by drowning!'*

Georg felt driven out of the room; he could still hear the thud as his father fell onto the bed behind him as he fled. On the stairway, where he dashed down the stairs as if they were a slide, he startled his cleaning-woman as she was about to go up to clear up the apartment after the night. 'Jesus!' she cried, covering her face with her apron, but he had already taken off. He bounded through the gateway; something was compelling him to cross the highway and head for the water. He was already clinging on tight to the railings, like a starving man to his food. He swung himself over them, like the excellent athlete he had been, to his parents' pride, as a boy. He still held on* as his hands grew weaker; between the railings he caught sight of an omnibus which would easily cover the sound of his fall; calling softly: 'Dear parents, I did always love you,' he let himself drop.

At this moment there flowed over the bridge an absolutely unending stream of traffic.

The Metamorphosis

I

As Gregor Samsa woke one morning from uneasy dreams, he found himself transformed into some kind of monstrous vermin.* He lay on his hard, armour-like back, and if he lifted his head a little, he could see his curved brown abdomen, divided by arch-shaped ridges, and domed so high that the bedspread, on the brink of slipping off, could hardly stay put. His many legs, miserably thin in comparison with his size otherwise, flickered helplessly before his eyes.

'What has happened to me?' he thought. It was not a dream. His room, a proper, human being's room, rather too small, lay peacefully between its four familiar walls. Above the table, on which his collection of textile samples was spread—Samsa was a commercial traveller—there hung the picture he had recently cut out from an illustrated magazine and mounted in a pretty gilded frame. It showed a lady* posed sitting erect, attired in a fur hat and fur boa, and raising a heavy fur muff, which swallowed her arm right up to the elbow, towards the viewer.

Gregor's gaze then turned towards the window, and the murky weather—one could hear the raindrops striking the window-sill—made him quite melancholy. 'What if I went on sleeping for a while and forgot all these idiocies,' he thought, but that was quite impossible, as he was used to sleeping on his right side and in his present state he was unable to get himself into this position. However energetically he flung himself onto his right side, whenever he did so he would rock onto his back again. He must have tried a hundred times, shutting his eyes so that he didn't have to see his jittery legs, and he only gave over when he began to feel a slight ache in his side, something he had never felt before.

'Oh Lord!' he thought. 'What a strenuous calling I've chosen! Day in, day out on the move. The stresses of making deals are far greater than they are in the actual business at home. And on top of that, I'm burdened with the misery of travelling; there's the worry about train connections, the poor, irregular meals, human contact that is always changing, never lasting, never approaching warmth.

To hell with it all!' He felt a slight itching high on his abdomen. He pushed himself slowly on his back towards the bedpost so that he could lift his head more easily; he found the itching spot, which was covered with lots of little white dots* he had no idea how to interpret. He tried to probe the spot with one of his legs, but drew back at once, for the moment he touched it he was swept by cold shivers.

He slid back into his previous position. 'Getting up so early', he thought, makes you quite dull-witted. A man must have his sleep. Other travellers live like ladies of the harem. For instance, when I go back to the boarding-house to send off the orders I've booked, these gents are only just having their breakfast. I should try that on with my boss—I'd be sacked on the spot. In any case, who knows if that wouldn't be good for me. If it wasn't that I've held back on account of my parents, I'd have given in my notice long ago. I'd have gone to the boss and told him what I thought outright, with real feeling. It would make him fall off his desk.* He's got a peculiar way of perching on his desk and talking down to an employee from on high—who then, what's more, has to come right up close to him on account of his deafness. Well, I haven't entirely given up that hope; once I've got the money together to pay off my parents' debt to him—that ought to take five or six years—I will do so, no two ways about it. Then the great break will be made. But for the present I have to get up, for my train leaves at five.'

And he looked across at his alarm-clock, which was ticking on the chest. 'Father in heaven!' he thought. It was half-past six, and the hands were moving steadily forwards. It was even later than half-past six; it was already approaching a quarter to seven. Was it that the alarm-clock hadn't rung? From the bed it was clear to see that it had been properly set for four o'clock, so it had certainly rung. Yes, but was it possible to sleep peacefully on through this furniture-shattering alarm? Well, he hadn't slept peacefully, though all the more deeply for that, it seemed. But what was he to do now? The next train went at seven; to catch that, he would have to hurry at a frantic speed, and his collection of samples wasn't packed yet, and he certainly didn't feel particularly fresh and lively himself. And even if he managed to catch the train, he couldn't escape a dressing-down from the boss, for the attendant from work had been waiting at the five-o'clock train, and had long ago informed the boss that Gregor had missed it.

He was the boss's creature, stupid and spineless.* What if Gregor were to tell them he was sick? But that would be extremely embarrassing and suspicious, for in all the five years he had been in employment Gregor hadn't once been ill until now. His boss would certainly arrive with the doctor from the Health Insurance, remonstrate with Gregor's parents for having a lazy son, and cut all their objections short by referring to the Insurance doctor, for whom, of course, there was only one kind of human being: healthy, but workshy. And anyway, in the present situation, would he be all that wrong? In fact, apart from feeling quite unnecessarily sleepy after such a long lie-in, Gregor felt perfectly well, and was even particularly hungry.

As he was thinking all this over very quickly without being able to decide to get up—the alarm was just ringing a quarter to seven—there was a cautious knock on the door at the head of his bed, and a call: 'Gregor!'—it was his mother—'it's a quarter to seven. Aren't you going to leave?' That gentle voice! Gregor was startled when he heard his own voice in reply; no doubt, it was unmistakably his previous voice, but merging into it as though from low down came an uncontrollable, painful squealing which allowed his words to remain articulate literally for only a moment, then stifled them so much as they died away that you couldn't tell if you'd heard them properly. Gregor had intended to answer fully and explain everything, but in his present circumstances he confined himself to saying, 'Yes, yes, thank you mother, I'm just getting up.' Because of the heavy wooden door, no doubt the change in Gregor's voice was not noticeable outside, for his mother was content with this explanation, and she shuffled away. However, this little conversation had made the other members of the family aware that Gregor, against expectation, was still at home, and his father was already knocking at one side door, faintly, but with his fist.* 'Gregor, Gregor!' he called, 'what's up?' And after a little while, he admonished him again in a deeper voice: 'Gregor! Gregor!' From the door on the other side, though, his sister was wailing quietly: 'Gregor, are you feeling unwell? Do you need anything?' Gregor answered towards both sides: 'I'm finished.' And by taking the greatest care with his articulation and putting in long pauses between the separate words, he tried hard to rid his voice of anything that might strike them as out of the ordinary. His father even returned to his breakfast, but his sister whispered: 'Gregor, open the door, I beg you.' But Gregor certainly had no intention of opening it; instead, he applauded the habit of caution he had adopted from his travels in locking all the doors at home overnight as well.

He wanted first to get up quietly without any disturbance, get dressed, and above all have his breakfast, and only then put his mind to what next, for, as he understood perfectly well, he wouldn't come to any sensible conclusion if he stayed in bed. He recalled that, perhaps through lying awkwardly, he had often felt some slight pain in bed, which, once he got up, turned out to be pure imagination. And he was curious to see how his present impressions would gradually fade away. He hadn't the slightest doubt that the change in his voice was nothing but the herald of a really bad cold, an occupational disease for travellers.

Throwing off the bedspread was quite simple; he needed only to puff himself up a little and it fell down of its own accord. But after that it got difficult, particularly because he was so uncommonly wide. He would have needed arms and hands to raise himself; but instead of those, he had only these many little legs, which were continually fluttering about, and which he could not control anyhow. If he tried to bend one of them, it was the first to stretch; and if he finally managed to get this leg to do what he wanted, all the others were flapping about meanwhile in the most intense and painful excitement, as if they had been let loose. 'Just don't stay uselessly in bed,' Gregor said to himself.

At first he tried to get out of bed with the lower part of his body, but this lower part, which in any case he hadn't yet seen, nor could have any proper idea of, proved to be too sluggish; it was such slow going; and when finally, driven nearly crazy, he heaved himself forward regardless with all his might, he found he had chosen the wrong direction and bumped violently against the bottom bedpost; and the burning pain he felt told him that it was the lower part of his body that was perhaps the most sensitive.

So he attempted to get his upper body out of the bed first, cautiously turning his head towards the edge. This worked easily enough, and in the end, despite its width and weight, the mass of his body slowly followed the way his head was turning. But when at last he held his head in the air outside the bed, he became afraid of moving any further forward in this way, for if he did finally let himself drop, it would need a sheer miracle for his head to remain unharmed. And right now was no time to lose consciousness, not at any price; he would sooner stay in bed.

But, as he lay there as before, once again sighing heavily after repeating the effort and once again watching his little legs struggling among themselves, if anything worse than ever, and saw no possibility of bringing calm and order to this unruliness, once again he told himself he couldn't possibly stay in bed, and the most sensible thing was to sacrifice everything if there was just the slightest hope that this would release him from his bed. But at the same time he did not forget to remind himself between whiles that calm, the calmest, reflection was far better than desperate decisions. At such moments he turned his eyes as keenly as he could towards the window, but unfortunately the sight of the morning fog, which even shrouded the other side of the narrow street, had little confidence or cheer to offer. 'Seven o'clock already,' he said to himself as the alarm-clock began to ring again, 'seven o'clock already, and still so foggy.' And for a little while he lay quietly, his breathing shallow, as if he were expecting that perhaps the utter stillness would bring a return of the real, true, ordinary state of affairs.

But then he said to himself: 'Before it rings a quarter-past seven, I absolutely must have got out of bed, all of me. Besides, by that time somebody will have come from the business to ask after me, for it opens before seven o'clock.' And he set about rocking the entire length of his body out of bed all in one piece. If he fell out of bed in this way, his head, which he meant to lift sharply as he was falling, would as far as he could see remain unscathed. His back seemed hard; it would probably come to no harm as he fell on to the carpet. His greatest misgivings came from his concern over the loud crash which was bound to follow and would probably rouse if not terror then certainly apprehension on the far side of all the doors. Still, that would have to be risked.

As Gregor was already rearing halfway out of bed—the new method was more play than effort, for he only needed to rock backwards—it occurred to him how simple it would all be if someone came to help him. Two strong people—he thought of his father and the maid—would have been entirely up to it; all they would have to do was put their arms under the dome of his back, unpeel him out of his bed in this way, stoop down with their load, and then merely wait patiently with him until he had managed to swing over on the floor, when, he hoped, his legs would do what they were intended to do. Well now, quite apart from the fact that the doors were locked, should he really have called for help? In spite of his distress, he couldn't suppress a smile at the thought.

In rocking so strongly, he had already reached the point where he could scarcely keep his balance, and very soon he had to make up his mind once and for all, for in five minutes it would be a quarter-past seven—when there came a ring at the door of the apartment. 'That's somebody from the office,' he said to himself, and almost froze, while his little legs only danced all the faster. For a moment, everything was silent. 'They're not going to open it,' said Gregor to himself, seized by some sort of absurd hope. But then of course, as always, the maid walked with a firm tread to the door, and opened it. Gregor only needed to hear the first words of greeting from the visitor and he knew who it was—the chief clerk himself. Why was Gregor the only one condemned to serve in a firm where the slightest lapse pro-voked the greatest suspicion? Were all their staff rogues, the lot of them? Wasn't there one loyal, devoted person among them who, if he had merely neglected to make use of a few morning hours for busi-ness, went crazy with remorse and was literally incapable of leaving his bed?* Wouldn't it really be enough to send an apprentice to enquire—if all this questioning was necessary in the first place? Did the chief clerk himself have to come, and did he have to show the entire, innocent family that the investigation of this suspicious mat-ter could only be entrusted to the intelligence of the chief clerk? And more as a consequence of the agitation these reflections roused in Gregor than as the consequence of a proper decision, he swung him-self with all his might out of the bed. There was a loud thump, but it was not a real crash. The fall was broken slightly by the carpet, and his back was more yielding than Gregor had thought. Hence the not-so-very-noticeable dull thud. Only he had not held his head in position carefully enough and had hit it; he turned it and rubbed it on the carpet in anger and pain.

'Something fell in there,' said the chief clerk in the room on the left. Gregor tried to imagine whether one day something akin to what had befallen him now could also happen to the chief clerk; after all, the possibility shouldn't actually be discounted But as if in brusque answer to this question, the chief clerk took a few decisive steps in the next room, making his patent-leather boots squeak. From the room on the right, his sister whispered to Gregor in explanation: 'Gregor, the chief clerk is here.' 'I know,' said Gregor to himself; but he did not risk raising his voice high enough for his sister to hear.

'Gregor,' his father said in turn from the room on the left, 'the chief clerk has come to find out why you didn't leave on the early train. We don't know what to tell him. Besides, he also wants to talk to you personally. So please open the door. He will be kind enough to excuse the disorder in your room.' 'Good morning, Herr Samsa,' the chief clerk broke in with a friendly tone. 'He isn't well,' Gregor's mother was saying to the chief clerk while his father was still speaking at the door. 'He's not well, believe me, sir. What other reason could there be for Gregor to miss a train! Indeed, the boy thinks of nothing but the business. I get almost angry that he never goes out of an evening; just lately he was in town for a week, but he was home every evening. There he sits at the table with us, reading the newspaper or studying the railway timetables. It's diversion enough for him to do his fretwork. For instance, he cut out a little picture-frame in the course of two or three evenings; you'll be amazed at how pretty it is; it's hanging in there in his room; you'll see it at once when Gregor opens the door. However, I'm very glad you are here, sir; we wouldn't have been able to persuade Gregor to open the door on our own; he's so stubborn; and he is definitely not well, although he denied it this morning.' 'I'll be right with you,' said Gregor slowly and deliberately, not moving so as not to lose a word of the conversation. 'I can't think of any other explanation, dear lady,' said the chief clerk, 'I hope it is nothing serious. Though on the other hand I have to say that often we businessmen—unfortunately or fortunately, as you will—simply have to overcome any slight indisposition, for the sake of doing business.' 'So can the chief clerk come into your room?' asked Gregor's father impatiently, knocking on the door again. 'No,' said Gregor. A painful silence fell in the room on the left. His sister began to sob in the room on the right.

Why didn't his sister join the others? She had probably only just got out of bed and hadn't dressed yet. And why was she crying? Because he wasn't getting up and wasn't letting the chief clerk in, because he was in danger of losing his job, and because then the boss would pursue their parents with his old demands again? Surely for the time being these were unnecessary worries. Gregor was still here and didn't have the slightest thought of deserting his family. True, for the moment he was lying there on the carpet, and no one who knew the state he was in would seriously have expected him to let the chief clerk enter. Surely Gregor could not be dismissed on account of this small discourtesy, for which a suitable excuse could easily be found later. And it seemed to him that it would be much more sensible for them to leave him in peace instead of upsetting him with all these tears and appeals. But it was this very uncertainty that distressed the others and excused their behaviour.

'Herr Samsa,' the chief clerk now called with his voice raised. 'What's going on? You're barricading yourself in your room, answering merely with "yes" and "no", causing your parents severe, unnecessary worries and neglecting—this just by the by—your business obligations in a quite unheard-of way. I am speaking here in the name of your parents and your employer, and I beg you in all seriousness for a straight explanation right now. I'm amazed, amazed. I thought I knew you to be a quiet, sensible person, and now all of a sudden you seem to want to start showing off with these strange whims of yours. Indeed, the boss hinted this morning at a possible explanation for your absence—it concerned the job of cash-collecting recently entrusted to you—but truly, I almost pledged my word of honour that this explanation couldn't be the right one. But now that I see your incomprehensible obstinacy, I lose all wish to put in the least word for you, utterly. And your position is by no means the most secure. I had originally intended to tell you this between ourselves, but as you have me waste my time to no purpose, I do not see why your parents should not hear it as well. For your performance recently has been very unsatisfactory; true, it is not the season for doing particularly good business, we acknowledge that; but a season for doing no business at all, Herr Samsa, there is no such thing, and there cannot be.'

'But sir,' Gregor cried, beside himself, and forgetting everything else in his distress. 'I'll open the door at once, this very moment. A slight indisposition, an attack of giddiness, prevented me from getting up. I'm still lying in bed. But I'm quite fresh again now. I'm just getting out of bed! Just a little moment's patience! It's not yet going as well as I thought. But I'm fine now. Oh, the things that can come over a person! Yesterday evening I felt fine, my parents can tell you, or rather, yesterday evening I already had a little premonition.

They must have noticed it. Why didn't I let you know in the firm! But one always thinks one can get over the illness without staying at home. Sir, sir, spare my parents! There is no cause for all the accusations you are making; no one has said a word about it to me. Perhaps you haven't yet read the last orders I sent in. In any case, I can still take the eight o'clock train and be off. The few hours' rest have given me strength. Don't let me hold you up, sir. I'll be at the office myself in no time, and please be so kind as to say that, and give my regards to our esteemed employer.'

And while Gregor was hurriedly pouring all this out, scarcely knowing what he was saying, he had drawn near the wardrobe with ease, probably as a result of the practice he had already had in bed, and he now tried to haul himself upright against it. He really did want to open the door, really did want to show himself and speak with the chief clerk; he was eager to learn what the others, who were asking for him now so much, would say at the sight of him. If they were terrified, then Gregor no longer bore the responsibility and could be at peace. But if they took it all calmly, then he too had no cause to get upset, and could, if he hurried, really be at the station at eight o'clock. At first he slid down a few times from the smooth wardrobe, but finally he gave himself one last swing and stood there upright; he no longer paid any attention to the pain in his lower abdomen, however sore it was. Now he let himself drop against the back of a chair close by and clung fast to the edges with his little legs. But in doing so he had also regained control of himself, and fell silent, for now he was able to hear the chief clerk.

'Could you understand a single word?' the chief clerk was asking his parents. 'He's not making a fool of us, is he?' 'For heaven's sake,' his mother cried, already in tears, 'perhaps he's seriously ill, and here we are, harassing him. Grete! Grete!' she screamed. 'Yes, Mother?' called his sister from the other side. They were communicating across Gregor's room. 'You must go to the doctor's this instant. Gregor is ill. Did you hear Gregor speaking just now?' 'That was an animal's voice,' said the chief clerk, noticeably quiet compared with the mother's screaming. 'Anna! Anna!' called his father through the hall into the kitchen, and clapped his hands. 'Fetch a locksmith at once!' And already the two girls were running through the front hall, their skirts rustling—how had his sister dressed so quickly?—and flinging open the apartment door. There was no sound of the doors slamming; they had probably left them open, which tends to happen in dwellings where some great misfortune has occurred.

But Gregor had become much calmer. So it was true they could no longer understand his words, even though they had seemed clear enough to him, clearer than before, perhaps because his ear was adapting. But now at any rate they did believe there was something not quite right about him, and were ready to help him. The confidence and certainty with which the first arrangements had been made did him good. He felt drawn back into the sphere of humanity, and had high hopes of impressive and surprising achievements from both, from the doctor and from the locksmith, without really distinguishing very clearly between them. For his voice to be as intelligible as possible for the coming consultations, he cleared his throat a little, though he took care to muffle the noise, as it was possible that this too sounded different from human coughing, something he no longer trusted himself to decide. In the next room meanwhile, everything had fallen silent. Perhaps his parents were sitting at the table with the chief clerk, talking about him behind his back; perhaps they were all leaning against the door, listening.

Gregor pushed himself with the armchair slowly towards the door, let go of it there, flung himself at the door, clung to it upright—the pads on his little legs were slightly sticky—and for a moment rested there from the effort. Then he set about using his mouth to turn the key in the lock. Unfortunately, it seemed that he didn't have any proper teeth—what was he to grip the key with?—but to make up for that, his jaws were very strong, certainly, and with their aid he really did get the key moving, not caring that he was undoubtedly doing himself some sort of harm, for a brown liquid ran from his mouth, trickled over the key, and dripped on to the ground. 'Listen,' said the chief clerk in the next room, 'he's turning the key.' This encouraged Gregor greatly; but they should all of them have been calling to him, including his father and mother. 'Go on, Gregor,' they should have been calling, 'Keep at it! Go for the lock!' And, imagining that they were all following his labours with excitement, using all the strength he could muster and nearly fainting, he bit blindly into the key. As the key turned further round in the lock, he danced wildly round it too. He kept himself upright only by his mouth now, dangling from the key as necessary or pressing it down again with the entire weight of his body. The sharper sound of the lock as it finally clicked back literally brought him to his senses. Heaving a sigh of relief, he said to himself: 'So I didn't need the locksmith after all,' and laid his head on the handle to open the door all the way.

As he'd had to unlock the door in this way, it was actually quite wide open by now, and he himself was still not to be seen. First he had to manoeuvre himself round the one half of the double-door, and very cautiously too, if he didn't want to fall plump onto his back just before he entered the room. He was still engaged in that difficult movement and hadn't time to attend to anything else, when he heard the chief clerk utter a loud 'Oh!'—it sounded like the wind whistling—and now he could see him as well, the nearest to the door, as he pressed his hand against his open mouth and retreated step by step, as if some invisible power were steadily at work, driving him away. Gregor's mother—her hair, despite the chief clerk's presence, still dishevelled from the night and right now standing on end—looked first with hands clasped together at his father, then took two steps towards Gregor and collapsed, surrounded by her outspread skirts, her face sunk and quite hidden in her breast. His father clenched his fist with a hostile expression, as if meaning to drive Gregor back into his room, but then he looked uncertainly round the living-room, covered his eyes with his hands, and wept so that his mighty breast shook.

Gregor made no attempt to enter the room now, but leaned against the other, firmly bolted, wing of the door on the inside, so that all there was to be seen of him was half his body and his head leaning towards one side as he peered across to the others. Meanwhile it had become much brighter; on the other side of the road a section of the endless grey-black building opposite—it was a hospital—was clearly to be seen, with its regular windows sharply interrupting the frontage; the rain was still falling, but only in large drops, each single one visible and each single one literally hurled onto the ground. The table was still laid with the china from breakfast, far too much of it, for Gregor's father regarded breakfast as the most important meal of the day, dragging it out for hours as he read various newspapers. Directly opposite, a photograph of Gregor from his time in the reserve* hung on the wall, showing him as a lieutenant, with his hand on his sword, smiling light-heartedly, demanding respect for his stance and uniform. The door to the front hall was open, and, as the door to the living-room was also open, it was possible to see out on to the apartment landing and the top of the downward stairs.

'Well now,' said Gregor, fully aware that he was the only one who had remained calm, 'I shall get dressed straight away, pack my samples, and leave. Will you, will you let me leave? And you sir, well, you see I am not obstinate and I do my work willingly; the travelling is arduous, but without travelling I couldn't live. Where are you going, sir? To the firm? You are? Will you report everything faithfully? A person may be momentarily incapable of working, but that is just the right time to recall his earlier achievements and consider that later, once the impediment has been removed, he will certainly work with all the more vigour and concentration. After all, I am so very much indebted to our esteemed employer, as you very well know. On the other hand, I have the care of my parents and sister. I'm in a cleft stick, but I will work my way out of it. But don't make it more difficult for me than it is already. Speak on my behalf in the firm! Not much love is lost on the traveller there, I know. They think he earns a fortune and leads a great life at the same time. They just have no particular reason to think this preconception through. But you, sir, you have a better view of the situation than the other personnel—confidentially, a better view than our esteemed boss himself, who, in his capacity as entrepreneur, can easily be swayed in his judgement, to the disadvantage of his staff. And you know very well too how the traveller, who is away from the firm for almost the whole year, can so easily become the victim of gossip, chance events, and unfounded complaints, which are quite impossible for him to fend off, as he mostly doesn't get to hear of them and it's only by the time he has ended a trip exhausted, once he is at home, that he comes to feel in his flesh the serious consequences they entail, with causes that can no longer be clearly understood. Don't go away, sir, without having said a word to me to show me that you think I am at least just a little bit right.'

But the chief clerk had already turned away at Gregor's first words, and it was only over his twitching shoulder that he looked back at Gregor, his lips drawn back in a grimace. And while Gregor was speaking he did not stand still for a moment, but instead retreated towards the door without letting Gregor out of his sight—but very gradually, as if there were some mysterious prohibition against leaving the room. He was already in the outside hall, and from the sudden movement he made as he drew his leg out of the living-room for the last time, one might have thought he had just burnt the sole of his foot. However, once in the hall he stretched his right hand as far out as he could towards the stairs, as if nothing less than deliverance* from heaven awaited him there.

Gregor perceived that there was no way he could let the chief clerk leave in this mood, if his position in the firm was not to be in the utmost danger. His parents didn't really understand it all. In the course of the long years they had convinced themselves that Gregor was provided for in this business for life, and on top of that, they were now so caught up in their present worries that they had lost any view into the future. But Gregor had this view. The chief clerk must be detained, pacified, convinced, and finally won over; after all, Gregor's future, and his family's, depended on it! If only his sister were here! She was clever; she had been crying while Gregor was still lying peacefully on his back. And certainly the chief clerk, that lady's man, would have let her talk him round; she would have closed the living-room door and talked him out of his terror in the front hall. But his sister was just not there. Gregor himself had to act. And without thinking that as yet he was not in the least familiar with the movements he was capable of performing in his present state; without thinking too of the possibility, indeed probability, that once again his speech had not been understood, he abandoned the wing of the door; pushed himself through the opening, and made to approach the chief clerk, who was already clinging ludicrously with both hands to the banisters on the landing. But as he was looking for support, Gregor promptly fell down onto his many legs, giving a little cry. No sooner had this happened than he felt at ease with his body for the first time this morning; his little legs had firm ground beneath them; they obeyed perfectly, as he observed with pleasure; they even did their best to carry him where he wanted to go; he already believed that his final recovery from suffering was about to take place there and then. But the moment he lay on the ground not far from his mother, right opposite her, rocking with suppressed emotion, all at once, even though she had seemed so utterly lost within herself, she leapt up with arms outstretched and fingers outspread, and cried: 'Help! For God's sake, help!' She put her head to one side as if she wanted to see Gregor better, but then, contrariwise, ran back point-lessly, forgetting that the table was behind her, still laid. When she reached it she sat down on it in haste, as though distraught, and did not seem to notice at all that the coffee was spilling in floods onto the carpet from the huge pot she had just upset.

'Mother, mother,' Gregor said softly, looking up at her. For a moment he had entirely forgotten the chief clerk; on the other hand, at the sight of the coffee pouring out he could not stop himself snapping his jaws several times into the empty air. At that his mother screamed once more, fled from the table, and fell into the arms of Gregor's father as he came hurrying towards her. But Gregor had no time now for his parents; the chief clerk was already on the stairs, his chin on the banister, looking back for the last time. Gregor took a run-up, to be as sure as he could to catch up with him; the chief clerk must have sensed something, for he took a leap down several stairs and disappeared. But he was still crying 'Aah!', which echoed right up the entire stairwell. Unfortunately Gregor's father, who until now had been relatively composed, appeared to be thrown into complete confusion by this flight of the chief clerk, for instead of running after the chief clerk himself, or at least not hindering Gregor in his pursuit, with his right hand he seized the chief clerk's walking-stick, left behind by their visitor on an armchair as well as his hat and overcoat, and with his left he fetched a large newspaper from the table, and stamping his feet, set about driving Gregor back into his room by waving the stick and the paper. None of Gregor's pleas helped, none of his pleas was understood; however submissively he turned his head, his father stamped all the more vigorously with his feet. Over on the other side of the room his mother had flung open a window despite the cold weather, and, leaning far outside, she pressed her face into her hands. A strong draught rose between street and stairwell, the curtains flew up at the windows, the newspapers rustled on the table, single sheets sailed over the floor. Implacably his father forced him back, hissing like a savage. As yet Gregor had had no practice at all in moving backwards, it was really very slow going. If he had only been allowed to turn around, he would have been in his room in no time, but he was afraid of making his father impatient if he tried this time-consuming manoeuvre, and every moment the stick in his father's hand threatened him with a fatal blow on his back or his head. However, in the end Gregor had no alternative, for he noticed with horror that in going backwards he didn't know how to keep in the right direction; and so, constantly looking sideways in fear at his father, he began to turn around as quickly as possible, but still in reality only very slowly. Perhaps his father noticed his good-will, for he didn't interrupt him in his efforts, but even guided his turning movements from a distance now and then with the tip of his stick. If only there weren't this intolerable hissing from his father! It made Gregor lose his head entirely. He had made an almost complete turn when he lost track, still heedful of the hissing, and briefly went into reverse. But when at last his head had managed to reach the doorway, it turned out that his body was too wide to get through the opening without more ado. Of course, in his father's present state of mind it didn't even remotely occur to him to do something like open-ing the other wing of the door, for instance, so as to create sufficient passage for Gregor. His fixed idea was merely that Gregor had to get into his room as quickly as possible. And he would never have per-mitted the elaborate preparations Gregor needed to pull himself upright and perhaps get through the door in that way. Rather, he drove Gregor on, as if there were no obstacles, making a particular commotion as he did so. Behind Gregor it no longer sounded like the voice of one single father merely; it was really no longer a joke by now, and Gregor forced himself—come what may—into the door-way. The one side of his body rose; he lay tilted in the opening; his one flank had been scraped raw, and there were nasty spots left on the white door. Soon he was stuck fast and would not have been able to move of his own accord; his legs on one side hung quivering up in the air, those on the other side were pressed painfully down on the floor—then his father gave him a vigorous kick from behind, which this time was truly a deliverance, and he flew, bleeding heavily, into the depths of his room. More, the door was slammed shut with the stick; and then at last all was still.

II

It was not until dusk that Gregor woke from a sleep as heavy as if he had fainted. He wouldn't have woken much later, certainly, even if he hadn't been disturbed, for he felt he'd had a good night's rest and sleep; but even so, it seemed to him that he had been wakened by a fleeting footstep, and by the sound of the door to the front hall being opened cautiously. Here and there the light from the electric street-lamps lay pale upon the ceiling and the upper parts of the furniture, but down below where Gregor lay all was in gloom. Slowly he pushed himself towards the door, still groping clumsily with his antennae, whose value he was only now learning to appreciate, in order to check what had happened there. His left side seemed to be one long scar, uncomfortably taut, and he literally had to limp on his two rows of legs. In any case, one little leg had been badly hurt in the course of the morning's events—it was almost a miracle that only one had been damaged—and it dragged lifelessly after him.

It was only when he reached the door that he noticed what had actually attracted him there: it was the smell of something to eat. For there stood a bowl of sweet milk, with little pieces of white bread floating in it. He might almost have laughed for joy, for he was even more hungry than he had been in the morning, and straight away he plunged his head into the milk almost over his eyes. But he soon drew it back again in disappointment; not only because eating caused him difficulties on account of his tender left side—and he was able to eat only if his entire body joined in, puffing and panting—but even more because he had no taste at all for the milk, which used to be his favourite drink and surely the reason why his sister had put it down for him; indeed, he turned away from the bowl almost in revulsion and crawled back to the middle of the room.

In the living-room the gas was lit, as Gregor could see through the crack in the door, but where it had once been his father's habit at this time of day to read in a loud voice to Gregor's mother and sometimes to his sister from his afternoon newspaper, now there was not a sound to be heard. Well, perhaps this custom of reading aloud, which his sister had always told him of and written to him about, had recently been abandoned. But round about too it was all so still, although the apartment was certainly not empty. 'What a quiet life the family leads anyway,' said Gregor to himself, and as he stared ahead into the dark he felt very proud that he had been able to provide his parents and his sister with such a life in such a fine apartment. But what if now all peace, all prosperity, all content, were to end in terror? So as not to lose himself in such thoughts, Gregor chose rather to get moving and began crawling up and down in his room.

Once only during the long evening one side door was opened, and once only the other was opened by a small crack and quickly closed again; someone probably felt the need to come in, but again had too many misgivings. Gregor now came to a stop right by the living-room door, resolved all the same to bring the hesitant visitor in somehow, or at least find out who it was; but now the door was no longer being opened, and Gregor waited in vain. Early this morning, when the doors were locked, they all wanted to come in to him, but now, when he had opened the one door and the others had obviously been opened during the day, no one came any longer, and in addition the keys were now in the locks on the outside.

It was not until late at night that the light in the living-room was put out, so it was easy to conclude that parents and sister had been awake all the time, for, as he could clearly hear, they now departed, all three on tiptoe. It was certain now that no one would come in to Gregor until the morning, so he had a long time to reflect undisturbed on how he was to order his life anew. But the room, with its height and freedom, where he was forced to lie flat on the floor frightened him, though he could not think why, for after all, this was the room he had dwelt in for five years—so, making a half-unconscious turn and not without a slight feeling of embarrassment, he scuttled under the sofa, where, although his back was squashed slightly and he couldn't lift his head, he immediately felt comfortable and was only sorry that his body was too wide to be accommodated all the way underneath.

He remained there all night, which he passed partly dozing, starting up from hunger again and again, but partly with anxieties and vague hopes which all still led to the conclusion that for the time being he should keep calm, and by his patience and consideration make these inconveniences, which in his present state he was bound to cause his family, at least tolerable for them.

In the early hours of the morning—it was still almost night—Gregor soon had an opportunity to test the strength of the resolutions he had just made, for his sister, almost fully dressed, opened the door from the hall and looked nervously inside. She didn't find him at once, but when she noticed him under the sofa—Heavens, he must be somewhere, he couldn't have flown away!—she was so startled that, losing control of herself, she slammed the door shut again from the outside. However, as if she were sorry for her behaviour, she promptly opened the door again and entered on tiptoe, as if she were in the room of a serious invalid or even a stranger. Gregor had pushed his head out as far as the edge of the sofa, and was watching her, wondering whether she would notice that he had left the milk, though certainly not because he wasn't hungry, and whether she might bring in some different food that suited him better. If she didn't do it of her own accord, he would rather starve than draw her attention to it, although actually he had a tremendous urge to dive out from under the sofa, throw himself at his sister's feet, and beg her for something good to eat. But his sister noticed at once with surprise that the bowl was still full, with just a little milk spilt around it; she picked it up straight away, not, indeed, with her bare hands, but using a rag, and carried it out. Gregor was extremely curious to see what she would bring instead, and he imagined all sorts of things. But he would never have guessed what his sister in her kindness really did. To try out his taste she brought him a large selection, all spread out on an old newspaper. There were some old, half-rotten vegetables, bones from yesterday's supper covered in a white sauce that had gone solid, a few raisins and almonds, some cheese which two days ago Gregor had declared was uneatable, one piece of dry bread, one piece of bread spread with butter, and one piece spread with butter and salt. As well as these she also put down the bowl, now probably intended once and for all for Gregor, which she had filled with water. And out of tact,* for she knew Gregor would not eat in front of her, she left hastily and even turned the key, just so that Gregor might see that he could make himself as easy as he wanted. His little legs went whirring away as they bore him to his meal. His wounds too must be fully healed already; he no longer felt handicapped; he was astonished, and reflected how over a month ago he had cut his finger with a knife and only the day before yesterday this injury had still hurt him badly enough. 'Might I have become less sensitive?' he thought, already greedily sucking at the cheese, which had immediately, and insistently, attracted him ahead of all the other food on offer. With eyes weeping in gratification, he speedily devoured the cheese, the vegetables, and the sauce one after the other; on the other hand, he had no palate for the items of fresh food; he could not even stand the smell of them, and went as far as to drag the things he wanted to eat a bit further away. He had long been finished with them all, and was still lying lazily in the same place when his sister turned the key, slowly, as a sign that he should withdraw. That made him start up in fright immediately, although he had almost nodded off, and he hurried under the sofa once more. But it cost him a great deal of will-power to stay under the sofa, if only for the short time his sister was in the room, for his abdomen had swollen slightly from so much to eat, and he could scarcely breathe there in the narrow space. Amid short spells of suffocation, his eyes protruding slightly, he watched how his unsuspecting sister used a broom to sweep up not only his leftovers, but even the food he had not touched at all, as if this too were no longer any use, and how she hastily shook it all into a bucket, which she closed with a wooden lid, afterwards carrying it all out. She had hardly turned her back before Gregor crawled out from under the sofa and puffed himself up.

This was how Gregor was given his food every day, once in the morning when parents and maid were still asleep, the second time after everyone's midday meal, for then the parents would also take a little nap, and his sister would send the maid away on some errand. Certainly, they didn't want Gregor to starve either, but perhaps they wouldn't have been able to bear finding out more about his food than they were told, or perhaps his sister wanted to spare them even what was possibly only a small grief, for they had really suffered enough. What excuses they had invented on that first morning to get the doctor and the locksmith out of the apartment was something Gregor could never find out, for, as he couldn't be understood, no one, not even his sister, even dreamt that he was able to understand others, and so, when his sister came into his room, he had to be content simply with hearing her sighs and cries to the saints* now and then. Not until later, when she had grown used to everything just a little—of course, getting used to it entirely was out of the question—Gregor sometimes caught a remark that was kindly meant, or could be interpreted as such. 'He's enjoyed his meal today,' she would say, if Gregor had tucked into his food heartily, while in the opposite case, which gradually became all too frequent, she would say, almost sadly: 'Now he's left everything again.'

But while Gregor was not able to learn any news directly, he gathered quite a lot from listening at the rooms adjoining his, and whenever he heard voices he would run at once to the appropriate door and press the whole length of his body against it. In the early days especially, there was not a conversation that didn't refer to him in some way, if only obscurely. For two whole days, at every mealtime he heard nothing but discussions about what attitude they should take towards it all; but the same topic filled their conversation between meals too, for there were always at least two members of the family at home, as it seemed nobody wanted to stay at home on their own, and there was no way they could leave the apartment all at the same time. Also, on the very first day the maid—it was not entirely clear what or how much she knew of what had happened—begged her mistress on her knees to allow her to leave at once, and when she made her farewells a quarter of an hour later, she thanked them with tears in her eyes for dismissing her, as if they had shown her the greatest of favours, and she swore a terrible oath, without even being asked, that she would never betray the least thing to anyone.

Gregor's sister, together with their mother, now had to do the cooking as well, though that did not make a great deal of work, for they ate almost nothing. Again and again Gregor would hear one of them encouraging the other in vain to eat, and always receiving the same reply: 'Thank you, I've had enough,' or something like it. Perhaps they drank nothing, either. Sister would often ask father whether he would like some beer, and lovingly offer to go and fetch it herself; then, when her father was silent, to allay his misgivings, she would say she could also send the caretaker out for it, but then at the last he would utter an emphatic 'No,' and nothing more was said about it.

In the course of the first day, the father explained their present financial situation and prospects to mother as well as daughter. Now and again he got up from the table and fetched some document or account-book from the small strongbox he had salvaged from the collapse of his business five years ago. Gregor could hear how he would unfasten the complicated lock and, after he had taken out what he had been looking for, lock it again. These explanations of his father's were in a way the first welcome news Gregor had heard since his imprisonment. He had supposed that his father had had nothing at all left from the business, at least his father had never told him anything to the contrary, and anyway Gregor hadn't asked him about it. Gregor's concern at the time had been only to do his utmost to have his family forget as quickly as possible the financial misfortune that had brought them to a state of utter hopelessness. And so he had begun to work with an especial passion, turning almost overnight from a little clerk into a commercial traveller, who naturally enjoyed very different opportunities to earn money, and any successful deal he made could promptly be transformed as a commission into hard cash, which could be laid on the table at home to the astonishment and joy of the family. They had been good times, which never occurred again, at least not in such glory, even though later Gregor made so much money that he was in a position to take on the expenditure of the whole family—and did so. They just got used to it, the family as much as Gregor; they accepted the money gratefully, he provided it gladly, but there was no longer any particular warmth about it. Only his sister had remained close to him, and because, unlike Gregor, she was very fond of music and could play the violin most affectingly, it was his secret plan to send her to the conservatoire next year, regardless of the inevitable expense, which he would surely clear in some other way. During the short periods when he was able to stay in town, the conservatoire would often come up in conversation with her, but always as a beautiful dream impossible to realize, and their parents didn't even like hearing these innocent allusions to it. But Gregor had definite thoughts on the subject, and intended to make a solemn announcement about it on Christmas Eve.*

Such were the thoughts, quite useless now in his present state, which would go through his head as he clung there erect, stuck to the door as he eavesdropped. Sometimes he was so tired all over that he was no longer able to listen in, and would vacantly let his head bump against the door, but then he would promptly hold it firm again, for even the little noise he caused had been heard in the next room and made them all fall silent. 'What's he up to now, I wonder,' said his father after a while, evidently turning towards the door, and only then their interrupted conversation would gradually be resumed.

Gregor now learned only too well—for his father was in the habit of repeating himself frequently as he explained, partly because for a long time he himself had not been engaged in these things, partly too because his mother didn't understand it all straight away at first hearing—that in spite of their misfortune, some financial assets, though not large, were still left from the old days, and had meanwhile been increased a little by the untouched interest. But apart from that, the money Gregor had brought home every month—he had kept only a small amount for himself—had not all been spent and had built up into a modest capital sum. Gregor, behind his door, nodded eagerly, pleased at this unexpected foresight and thrift. Actually, he would have been able to pay off more of his father's debts to the boss, and the day when he might have been free of this position would have arrived far sooner, but now it was undoubtedly better the way his father had arranged things.

But this money was not at all sufficient for the family to live on the interest; it was sufficient perhaps to keep the family going for a year, or two years at most, but there wasn't more than that. So it was merely a sum that they shouldn't actually draw on and should put aside for emergencies; living expenses, however, they would have to earn. Now the father was an elderly man; true, he was fit, but he hadn't worked for five years and didn't think he might be capable of very much; during these five years, which were the first holiday he had had in his hard though unsuccessful life, he had put on a lot of weight, which had made him very slow and heavy. And as for Gregor's old mother, was she to go out perhaps and earn money, although she suffered from asthma, which made merely walking through the apartment effort enough for her, having to spend every other day on the sofa with the window open, breathing with difficulty? And was his sister supposed to earn money, and she just a child of seventeen, with a way of life up till then that he had been delighted for her to enjoy: dressing nicely, sleeping late, helping about the house, taking part in a few modest entertainments, and above all playing the violin? Whenever they began to discuss this need to earn money, Gregor would always first let go of the door and then hurl himself onto the cool sofa next to the door, for he burned with shame and sorrow.

He often lay there the whole night through, not sleeping for a moment, only scrabbling for hours on the leather. Or he would go to great lengths to push an armchair up to the window, then crawl up to the windowsill, and, jammed into the chair, he would lean against the window, evidently with some memory of the sense of deliverance he had once had from gazing out of the window. For in fact, things that were even quite near he saw more and more indistinctly from day to day. The hospital opposite, which he used to curse for the all-too-intrusive sight it offered, no longer came into view at all, and if he had not known specifically that the street he lived in was the quiet but completely urban Charlottenstrasse,* he might have believed he was gazing from his window out into a desolation in which the grey sky and the grey earth were indistinguishably merged. His watchful sister only needed to see the armchair by the window twice, before, once she had finished clearing up the room, she would always push the chair right back to the window again—indeed, from now on she even left the inside window casement open.

If only Gregor could talk with his sister and thank her for everything she had to do for him, he would have endured her help more easily; but as things were, he suffered under it. True, his sister tried as far as possible to dull the distress of it all, and the more time went by, naturally, the more she succeeded, but in time Gregor also came to understand everything much more clearly. Her mere entrance was dreadful for him. She would scarcely come in before she dashed straight to the window, without pausing to shut the doors, however careful she usually was to spare everyone the sight of Gregor's room, and she would fling it open in haste as if she were almost suffocating; she would also remain by the window for a while even on the coldest of days, taking in deep breaths of air. Twice a day she terrified him with all these alarums and excursions; he trembled all the while under the sofa, knowing full well that she would no doubt have been glad to spare him the commotion if it had only been possible for her to stay in the same room as Gregor with the window shut.

Once—perhaps a month had gone by after Gregor's transformation and his sister surely had no further cause in particular to be surprised at his appearance—she arrived a little earlier than usual, and came upon Gregor as he was gazing out of the window motionless, propped upright, enough to terrify her. Gregor wouldn't have been surprised if she hadn't come in, for his position prevented her from opening the window straight away, but she not only didn't enter, she even shrank back and closed the door; a stranger might really have thought that Gregor had been lying in wait for her and wanted to bite her. Of course, Gregor hid under the sofa at once, but he had to wait until midday before his sister returned, and she seemed much more uneasy than usual. He understood from this that the sight of him was still intolerable to her and was bound to remain intolerable for the future, and that she probably had to force herself not to run away from the sight of just the small part of his body that stuck out from under the sofa. To spare her even this sight, one day he carried the sheet onto the sofa on his back—he needed four hours to do it—and arranged it in such a way that he was now completely covered, and his sister, even if she bent down, couldn't see him. If she considered this sheet was unnecessary, then of course she could have removed it, for it was clear enough that there was no pleasure for Gregor in cutting himself off so completely; but she left the sheet as it was, and Gregor even believed he caught a grateful glance when on one occasion he cautiously lifted the sheet with his head to see how his sister was taking the new arrangement.

For the first two weeks the parents could not bring themselves to come in to him, and he often heard how greatly they appreciated the work his sister was now doing, whereas up to now they had frequently been annoyed at her, because she had appeared to them to be a rather useless girl. But now both of them, father and mother, would often wait outside Gregor's room while his sister cleared up inside, and she would scarcely have emerged before she had to tell them exactly what it was looking like in the room, what Gregor had eaten, how he had behaved this time, and whether perhaps some small improvement could be observed. Besides, his mother wanted to visit Gregor relatively soon, but father and sister restrained her at first with rational arguments, which Gregor listened to very attentively and approved of entirely. But later they had to hold her back by force, and when she cried out: 'Let me go to Gregor! He is my unhappy son, after all! Don't you understand, I must go to him?' Gregor then thought it would be a good thing if his mother did come in to him, not every day of course, but perhaps once a week; after all, she understood everything much better than his sister, who despite all her courage was only a child and had perhaps taken on such a heavy task only out of childish silliness.

Gregor's wish to see his mother was soon fulfilled. He didn't want to show himself at the window during the daytime, if only out of consideration for his parents; and he wasn't able to crawl all that much on the few square metres of the floor; during the night he found lying quietly hard to bear; soon eating no longer gave him the least pleasure, and so for diversion he developed the habit of crawling all over the walls and ceiling. He was particularly fond of hanging high up under the ceiling. This was something different from lying on the floor; one breathed more freely; an easy swinging motion passed through the body; and in this almost happy state of distraction up there, it could happen that to his own surprise he would let go and fall smack! to the ground. But now of course he had his body under control, quite unlike before, and didn't hurt himself even after such a great fall. His sister noticed at once the new amusement that

Gregor had found for himself—for when he was crawling he also left sticky traces here and there—so she got it into her head to make it easier for Gregor to crawl to a much greater extent by getting rid of the furniture that prevented it, which meant chiefly the wardrobe and the writing-desk. But she wasn't able to do this alone; she didn't dare ask her father for help; the housemaid would certainly not have helped her, for though this girl of about sixteen years old held out bravely with them since the first cook had been allowed to leave, she had begged the privilege of keeping the kitchen permanently locked and only having to open it when specially summoned. So his sister had no choice but, on an occasion when her father was not in the house, to fetch her mother. She arrived with cries of joy and agitation, but fell silent at the door outside Gregor's room. At first of course his sister looked in to see if everything in the room was in order; only then she let her mother enter. In the greatest of haste Gregor had pulled the linen sheet still lower, with more folds in it; it all really looked just like a sheet that happened to have been thrown over the sofa by chance. This time too Gregor refrained from spying from under the sheet; he gave up his claim to see his mother for now, and was only glad that she had come anyway. 'Do come; we can't see him,' said his sister, evidently leading her mother by the hand. Gregor could hear how the two frail women shifted the old wardrobe, pretty heavy for anyone, from its place, and how his sister took on the greatest part of the work without listening to the words of warning from her mother, who was afraid she would overstrain herself. It took a very long time. After a quarter of an hour's work, the mother said it would be better to leave the wardrobe where it was, for in the first place it was too heavy and they wouldn't have finished before the father arrived, and with the wardrobe in the middle of the room it would bar every path Gregor might take; and in the second place it wasn't at all certain anyway that it was doing Gregor a favour to remove the furniture. It seemed to her that the opposite was the case; it really weighed upon her heart to see the empty wall; and why shouldn't Gregor also have the same feeling, when he had been used to this furniture for so long and would feel abandoned in the empty room. 'And wouldn't it look,' she ended very quietly, almost in a whisper, not knowing Gregor's exact whereabouts—as if she wanted to spare him hearing even the sound of her voice, for she was convinced he didn't understand her words—'and wouldn't it look as though by removing the furniture we had given up any hope of recovery and callously abandoned him to himself? I believe it would be best if we tried to keep the room as it was before, so that when Gregor comes back to us, he will find everything unchanged and be able to forget the interim more easily.'

As he listened to these words of his mother's, Gregor came to see that in the course of these two months, lack of any direct human attention, combined with the monotonous life within the family, must have confused his mind, for there was no other way he could explain how he could seriously have desired his room to be emptied. Had he really wanted them to transform his cosy room, comfortably fitted with old family furniture, into a lair where he would indeed be able to crawl undisturbed in all directions, but at the same time he would be rapidly consigning his human past to utter oblivion? Wasn't he even now already close to forgetting, and only his mother's voice, unheard for so long, had shaken him out of it. Nothing was to be removed. Everything should stay. He could not do without the positive effects the furniture had on his condition. And if the furniture prevented him from carrying on this senseless crawling round, then that did no harm, it was rather a great benefit.

But unfortunately his sister took a different view. When discussing anything that concerned Gregor she had become accustomed, and not unjustifiably, to taking on the role of special expert towards her parents, and so on this occasion too her mother's advice was sufficient reason for her to insist not just on removing the wardrobe and the writing-desk, which were the only things she had thought to move at first, but also on removing all the furniture entirely, excepting the indispensable sofa. Naturally it was not only childish defiance that set her on this course, nor the unexpected and hard-won self-confidence she had achieved of late; she had, after all, actually observed that Gregor needed a great deal of space to crawl in, while on the other hand, as far as one could see, he hadn't the slightest use for the furniture. But perhaps some part was also played by the wayward fancy of girls of her age, which looks for any opportunity to indulge itself and now tempted Grete to exaggerate Gregor's terrifying situation still further, in order to do even more for him than she had up until now. For a room where Gregor ruled the empty walls alone was surely a space which no one except Grete would ever dare to enter.

And so she refused to let her mother dissuade her from her decision; from sheer agitation her mother seemed insecure in this room; she soon fell silent and helped Gregor's sister, as far as she was able, to move the wardrobe outside. Now, Gregor could if necessary manage without the wardrobe, but the writing-desk at least had to stay. And the women had hardly left the room with the wardrobe, groaning as they clung to it, when Gregor thrust his head out from under the sofa to see how he might intervene, cautiously and as considerately as possible. But unfortunately it had to be his mother who came back first, while in the next room Grete had her arms round the wardrobe, rocking it to and fro by herself, without of course being able to budge it. But his mother was not used to the sight of Gregor; it might make her ill, so Gregor rushed backwards in terror to the other end of the sofa, but he couldn't prevent the linen sheet from stirring a little at the front. That was enough to attract his mother's attention. She stopped, stood still for a moment, and then went back to Grete.

Although Gregor had to tell himself over and over again that nothing extraordinary was happening, only a few pieces of furniture being rearranged, still, this toing and froing of the women, their little calls to each other, the furniture scraping on the floor, affected him like some vast tumult fed from all sides, and however tightly he tucked in his head and legs and pressed his body close to the ground, he was forced to tell himself that he wouldn't be able to stand it all for long, no argument about it. They were clearing out his room; they were depriving him of everything that was dear to him, they had already carried out the wardrobe, which held his fretsaw and his other tools; they were now tugging at the writing-desk, fast embedded in the floor, where he had written his homework as a student at business school, as a secondary schoolboy, indeed, even as a pupil at elementary school—enough! He really had no more time to examine the good intentions of the two women, whose existence, incidentally, he had almost forgotten, for they were now working in silence, exhausted, and only their heavy, lumbering steps were to be heard.

And so he broke out—the women were just leaning against the bureau in the next room to catch their breath. He changed direction four times as he ran; he really had no idea what to rescue first, when, hanging on the wall, which was otherwise bare, he was struck by the picture of the lady dressed in nothing but fur. He crawled up to it hurriedly and pressed himself against the glass, which held him fast and did his burning stomach good. This picture at least, which Gregor now covered completely, no one would take away from him—that was certain. He turned his head towards the door of the living-room to watch the women as they came back.

They hadn't given themselves much of a rest and were already returning. Grete had put her arm round her mother, almost carrying her. 'Well, what shall we take now?' said Grete, looking round. Then her eye caught Gregor's, on the wall. No doubt it was only because of her mother's presence that she kept her composure, bent her face to her mother to prevent her from looking round, and said, though trembling and without thinking: 'Come, let's go back into the living-room for a moment, shall we?' Grete's intention was clear to Gregor: she wanted to bring her mother to safety and then drive him down from the wall. Well, she could always give it a try! He was sitting on his picture and he wasn't giving it up. He would rather make a leap for Grete's face.

But Grete's words really did perturb their mother; she moved aside, caught sight of the monstrous brown patch on the flowered wallpaper, and before it actually dawned on her that what she was looking at was Gregor, she gave a hoarse scream and cried: 'Oh, my God! Oh, my God!' and fell across the sofa with arms outspread as though she were just giving up, motionless. 'Gregor!' his sister called, raising her fist with a compelling look. These were the first words she had spoken to him directly since his transformation. She ran into the next room to fetch some smelling-salts to rouse her mother from her faint. Gregor wanted to help too—there was still time to rescue the picture—but he was sticking fast to the glass and had to use force to tear himself off; then he too ran into the next room, as if he could give his sister some kind of advice, as he used to do in the past; but he could only stand behind her, doing nothing; while she was hunting among various little flasks, she was startled the moment she turned round; one bottle fell to the ground and broke in pieces; a splinter hurt Gregor in the face; some sort of medicine spilled around him, smarting; without waiting any longer, Grete took as many little flasks as she could hold, and ran with them to her mother; she slammed the door shut with her foot. Gregor was now cut off from his mother; perhaps through his fault she was close to death; he oughtn't to open the door, not unless he wanted to drive his sister away, and she had to stay with their mother; all he could do was wait, and, weighed down by self-reproach and anxiety, he started to crawl. He crawled over everything, walls, furniture, ceiling, and finally, as the entire room began to whirl around him, in his desperation he fell down onto the big table, right in the middle.

A little while passed; Gregor lay there limp; round about all was quiet; perhaps that was a good sign. Then came a ring. The maid was of course locked in her kitchen, so Grete had to go and open the front door. Father had arrived. 'What's happened?' were his first words; no doubt Grete's appearance had revealed all. Grete replied in a stifled voice; evidently she was pressing her face to her father's breast: 'Mother fainted, but she's better now. Gregor has broken out.' 'I always expected he would,' her father said, 'I've always said so, but you women didn't want to listen.' It was clear to Gregor that his father had wrongly interpreted Grete's all-too-brief report, and assumed that he was guilty of some violent act. So Gregor now had to try to pacify his father, for he had neither the time nor the ability to explain to him. And so he fled to the door of his room and pressed himself against it, so that when his father came in from the front hall he could see straight away that Gregor had every intention of going back into his room at once, and that it wasn't necessary to drive him back, rather, that they only needed to open the door and he would promptly vanish.

But his father was in no mood to notice such delicacy. 'Aha!' he cried as soon as he came in, in a tone that suggested he was full of rage and elation at the same time. Gregor pulled his head back from the door and raised it towards his father. He had really never imagined his father as he was standing there now, though recently, absorbed in this new skill of crawling around, he had no longer been concerned about what was going on in the rest of the apartment, as he once had been, and he should really have been prepared to encounter changed conditions. Nevertheless, nevertheless, was this still his father? The same man who lay buried deep in his bed when Gregor had set off on a business trip in earlier times; who had greeted him from his armchair, still wearing his dressing-gown, on the evenings when he returned; who wasn't really capable of getting to his feet, but had only raised his arms to signal he was glad to see him; the same man, when they had taken a rare stroll together on a few Sundays in the year and on high holidays, father between Gregor and mother, already slow enough themselves, who always walked a bit more slowly still, wrapped in his old overcoat, working his way forward, all the time cautiously planting his crutch, and who, when he wanted to say something, almost always stopped still and gathered his entourage around him? But now he stood firm and erect; dressed in a tight blue uniform* with gold buttons, of the sort worn by the servants of a bank; his powerful double chin unrolled above the stiff high collar of his coat; his black eyes looked out clear and sharp from beneath his bushy eyebrows; his white hair, once dishevelled, was combed down in a shining, meticulously straight parting. He threw his cap with its gold monogram, probably a bank's, in a curve right across the whole room onto the sofa, and walked, the tails of his long uniform coat pushed back, his hands in his pockets, his face grim, towards Gregor. He probably didn't know what he had in mind himself; in any case, he lifted his feet unusually high, and Gregor was amazed at the gigantic size of his boot-soles. But he didn't linger in his amazement; he knew from the very first day of his new life that in his father's eyes only the greatest severity was the right way to deal with him. And so he ran ahead of his father, stopped when his father came to a halt, and hurried forward again if his father only stirred. They went round the room several times like this without anything decisive happening, indeed, without appearing to be a pursuit, it was so slow. That is also why Gregor stayed on the floor for the present, especially as he was afraid his father might take his flight on to the walls or ceiling as an act of particular wickedness. In any case, Gregor had to tell himself that he wouldn't be able to keep up even this way of running, for where his father took one step, he had to perform countless movements. Breathlessness was already becoming noticeable, just as in the past he had possessed lungs that were also not entirely reliable. As he staggered along in this way, trying to gather all his strength together for the race, he scarcely kept his eyes open; with his mind so dulled he didn't think of any other deliverance at all than by running, and he had almost forgotten that the walls were open to him, though here they were obstructed by carefully fretted furniture, carved jagged and sharp—when something tossed lightly flew down and landed right next to him, and then rolled in front of him. It was an apple; at once a second flew after it; Gregor stood still in terror—running any further was useless, for his father had decided to bombard him. He had filled his pockets from the fruit-bowl on the sideboard and, without aiming very exactly for the moment, threw apple after apple. These little red apples rolled about on the ground as if they were electrified, bouncing off one another. One badly thrown apple skimmed Gregor's back, but slid off without harming him. On the other hand, the one that flew straight after it literally penetrated Gregor's back; Gregor tried to drag himself on further, as if the surprising, unbelievable pain would pass with a change of place; but he felt as if he were nailed fast,* and collapsed in a total confusion of all his senses. Only with his last glance he was still able to see how the door to his room was flung open and his mother rushed forward, his sister ahead of her screaming, his mother in her shift, for his sister had undressed her so that she could breathe more easily during her faint; he could see how his mother ran to their father, how on the way her layered skirts slipped to the ground one after another, and how she stumbled over the skirts to urge herself upon their father, embracing him, in total union with him—Gregor's sight was already failing—and with her hands circling the back of his father's head she begged him to spare Gregor's life.

III

Gregor's wound was serious and gave him pain for over a month—the apple remained, since no one dared remove it, as a visible memorial in his flesh*—but it seemed to have reminded even his father that, despite his present sad and repulsive form, Gregor was a member of the family who was not to be treated as an enemy; instead, family duty towards him commanded that they should swallow their disgust, and put up with him in patience, just put up with him.

And even though it seemed his wound had made Gregor lose his mobility for ever, and though for the present, like some disabled veteran, he needed long, long minutes to cross his room—crawling aloft on the ceiling was out of the question—he drew some recompense for this deterioration in his condition, one he considered was entirely adequate: towards evening the door to the living-room, which he grew used to watching keenly for as much as two hours beforehand, was always opened, so that, lying in the darkness of his room, invisible from the living-room, he might see the whole family at the lamp-lit table and hear what they had to say, with their general permission as it were, a very different arrangement from before.

Certainly, there were no longer the lively conversations of the past, which Gregor had always thought about with some longing in his tiny hotel rooms when he was obliged to throw himself wearily into damp bedclothes. Now things were very quiet in the main. Soon after supper the father would fall asleep in his armchair; mother and sister would remind each other to be quiet; bending far forward over the lamp, the mother would sew fine lingerie for a fashion shop; the sister, who had taken a job as a sales assistant, was learning shorthand and French in the evening so that she could perhaps get a better position later on. Sometimes the father would wake up and say to the mother, as if he wasn't aware he had been sleeping: 'What a long time you've been sewing again!' and would go back to sleep at once, while mother and sister would smile at each other wearily.

With a kind of obstinacy, the father refused to take off his uniform, even at home; and while his dressing-gown hung uselessly on its hook, he would slumber fully dressed in his proper place, as if he were always ready for duty and waiting here too for the voice of his superior. Consequently his uniform, which hadn't been new in the first place, began to look less clean and tidy, despite the care mother and daughter gave it, and Gregor would often gaze for entire evenings at this coat with its many, many stains and its gold buttons radiant from constant polishing, which the old man wore as he slept—in discomfort but at peace.

As soon as the clock struck ten, the mother would try to wake the father, talking to him gently, and then try to persuade him to go to bed, for this wasn't sleeping properly, was it?—and he needed his sleep, for he had to start work at six. But, with the obstinacy that had come over him when he became a bank attendant, he always insisted on staying at the table longer, even though he regularly fell asleep and it was only with the greatest of trouble that he could be induced to exchange his armchair for his bed. Then, however much mother and sister would urge him, cajoling gently, he would shake his head slowly for a quarter of an hour at a time, keep his eyes closed, and stay where he was. The mother would tug at his sleeve, whisper sweet words into his ear, the sister would leave her homework to help her mother, but her father wasn't to be caught out by that. He would just sink lower in his armchair. Only when the women seized him under the arms, he would open his eyes, look from mother to sister in turn, and habitually say: 'What a life! So this is the peace of my old age.' And supported by the two women, he would heave himself up, making heavy weather of it, as if he were the greatest of burdens to himself, allow himself to be led by the women as far as the door, dismiss them there with a gesture, and continue on his own, while the mother would hastily fling down her sewing things and the sister her pen to run after him and help him some more.

Who, in this worn-out and overtired family, had time to care for Gregor more than was necessary? The household had to economize more and more. The maid was dismissed in the end; a huge, bony charwoman with a head of flying white hair came morning and evening to do the heaviest work; the mother took care of everything else, as well as all her sewing. Things even went so far that various pieces of family jewellery, which mother and sister used to wear with great delight for entertainments and celebrations, were sold, as Gregor gathered in the evening from the general discussion of the prices they had fetched. But the biggest complaint was constantly that they were unable to give up the apartment, which was far too big for their present situation, as they could not work out how they were to move Gregor. But Gregor could see that it wasn't just consideration for him that prevented them from moving house, for they could easily have transported him in a suitable box with a few holes in it for air; what chiefly held the family back from changing address was far more their utter hopelessness, and the thought that they were stricken with a misfortune like no one else in their entire circle of friends and relations. What the world requires of the poor they fulfilled to their limits; the father fetched breakfast for minor bank clerks, the mother sacrificed herself for the lingerie of strangers, the sister ran to and fro behind the counter at the customers' behest, but further than that the family's powers did not stretch. And the wound in Gregor's back began to hurt again as if it were fresh, when the mother and sister, after taking the father to bed, would return and, putting their work aside, would sit cheek to cheek; and when his mother, pointing to Gregor's room, would say: 'Do close the door, Grete'; and when Gregor was once more in darkness, while in the next room the women would weep together or stare dry-eyed at the table.

The nights and the days Gregor spent almost entirely without sleep. Sometimes he dwelt on the thought that when the door was next opened he might take the family's affairs fully in hand again, as he had before; figures reappeared in his thoughts after long absence: the boss, the chief clerk, the lesser clerks and the apprentices; the porter who was so stupid; two or three friends from other firms; a chambermaid in a hotel in the provinces, a sweet, fleeting memory; a girl, cashier in a millinery shop, he had been seriously courting, but too slowly—they all appeared mixed in with strangers or people already forgotten, and he was glad when they vanished. But afterwards he was not at all in the mood to worry about his family; he was simply full of rage at how badly they looked after him. And though he couldn't imagine anything he might enjoy eating, he still made plans about getting into the larder, even if he wasn't hungry, to take what was his rightful due anyway. Now, no longer giving any thought to what she might do for Gregor that would give him particular pleasure, morning and noon before she dashed off to the shop, his sister would hurriedly push any old food into Gregor's room with her foot, and then in the evening sweep it up with a whisk of her broom, indifferent to whether he had merely tasted it or—which was mostly the case—left it untouched. Clearing out his room, which she always did in the evening now, couldn't be done quickly enough. The walls were stained with trails of grime, and tangles of dust and filth lay here and there. In the early days, when his sister arrived Gregor would station himself in corners where such dirt was particularly noticeable, taking this position to some extent as a reproach to her. But he could well have stayed there for weeks without her mending her ways; she saw the dirt every bit as clearly as he did, but she had just decided to leave it. On the other hand, she watched with a touchiness that was quite new in her, and which, indeed, had seized the whole family, to make sure that the task of clearing up Gregor's room remained in her hands. His mother had once given his room a thorough clean-out, and only managed it after several buckets of water—in any case, all that damp hurt Gregor's feelings too, as he lay wide, embittered, and immobile on the sofa. But his mother did not escape punishment, for that evening his sister had barely noticed the change in Gregor's room before she rushed into the living-room, highly affronted, and despite her mother's hands uplifted in entreaty, broke into convulsive sobbing, while her parents—the father of course was startled out of his armchair—gazed at her, amazed and helpless at first, until they too began to stir; to his right the father scolded the mother for not leaving it to the sister to clean Gregor's room; to his left on the other hand he yelled at the sister that she would never be allowed to clean Gregor's room again; while the mother tried to drag the father, who was beside himself with rage, into the bedroom, the sister, shaking with sobs, hammered on the table with her little fists; and Gregor hissed aloud with fury that it didn't occur to anyone to shut the door and spare him this sight and this commotion.

But even if his sister, exhausted from her job, had had enough of looking after Gregor as she had once done, his mother certainly would not have to take her place, and Gregor still wouldn't need to be neglected. For now the cleaning-woman was there. This old widow, whose powerful frame must have helped her to survive the worst in her long life, had no real feelings of revulsion towards Gregor. Without being in any way curious, she had once chanced to open the door to his room and immediately stopped short in amazement, her hands folded on her stomach, at the sight of Gregor, who was taken by complete surprise and, although no one was chasing him, began to run to and fro.* Since then she never failed to open the door a little for just a moment every morning and evening to look in on Gregor. To begin with she even called him up to her with words that she evidently regarded as friendly, such as: 'Come on, you old dung-beetle!' or 'Well, look at the old dung-beetle then!' Gregor didn't answer to such modes of address, but stayed where he was, as if the door hadn't opened at all. Instead of letting this charwoman disturb him pointlessly as the fancy took her, if only they had told her to clean his room every day! Once, early in the morning—heavy rain, already perhaps a sign of the coming Spring, was beating against the window-panes—Gregor was so incensed when the charwoman started using her pet names again that he turned on her, however slowly and feebly, as if to attack her. But instead of being afraid, the charwoman merely lifted a chair that happened to be near the door, and as she stood there, with mouth gaping, her intention was clear: she would only close her mouth when the chair in her hand crashed down on Gregor's back. 'Well, aren't you going to have another go, then?' she asked, when Gregor turned around again, and calmly put the chair back into the corner.

Gregor was now eating almost nothing. Only when he happened to pass by the food put ready for him, he would play at taking a bite of it into his mouth, keep it there for hours, and then mostly spit it out again. At first he thought it was mourning over the condition of his room that kept him from eating, but he very soon became reconciled to the changes in his room. The family had become used to putting things they couldn't accommodate anywhere else into this room, and there were now a great many such things, as they had let one room in the apartment to three gentleman-lodgers. These grave gentlemen—all three wore full beards, as Gregor discovered once as he peered through a crack in the door—were scrupulously concerned about order, not only in their own room, but, now that they had moved in as lodgers, in the entire household, which meant particularly in the kitchen. They wouldn't put up with useless, let alone dirty, junk. Besides, they had mainly brought their own furniture with them. For this reason many things that were admittedly not saleable, but which the family still didn't want to throw away, had become superfluous. All these made their way into Gregor's room. Likewise too the ash-can and the rubbish-bin from the kitchen. Whatever she had no use for at the moment the charwoman, who was always in a hurry, simply slung into Gregor's room; fortunately Gregor mostly saw only the object in question and the hand that was holding it. Perhaps the charwoman intended to take the things back when time and opportunity offered, or throw them out together all at one go, but in fact they just stayed where they had landed when she first threw them, unless Gregor wriggled through the lumber and shifted it around, at first forced to do so, because otherwise there was no room for him to crawl, but later with increasing pleasure, although after such excursions he would once again remain motionless for hours, sad and tired to death.

As the lodgers sometimes also took their evening meal in the shared living-room, there were many evenings when the living-room door remained closed, but Gregor found it quite easy to get by without having it opened; after all, he hadn't taken advantage of a number of evenings when it had been opened, but instead, unnoticed by the family, he had lain in the darkest corner of his room. However, the charwoman had once left the door to the living-room ajar, and it remained like that, even when the gentleman-lodgers came in that evening and the lamp was lit. They sat on high at the table where in the past father, mother, and Gregor used to sit, unfolding their serviettes and taking their knives and forks in their hands. Immediately, Gregor's mother appeared in the doorway with a dish of meat, and close behind her came the sister holding a dish piled high with potatoes.

Dense steam rose from the food. The gentleman-lodgers bent over the dishes placed before them as if they wanted to test them before eating, and in fact the one sitting in the middle, seemingly regarded by the others as the authority, cut up one piece of meat while it was still in the dish, evidently to ascertain whether it was tender enough or whether it shouldn't possibly be sent back to the kitchen. He was satisfied, and mother and sister, who had been watching nervously, sighed with relief and began to smile.

The family itself ate in the kitchen. Nevertheless, before the father went into the kitchen, he would enter the living-room and, making a single bow, his cap in his hand, do a round of the table. The gentlemen all rose together, murmuring something into their beards. Then, when they were alone, they ate in almost total silence. It seemed strange to Gregor that out of all the various sounds of eating they made, over and over again he could make out the champing of their teeth, as if he had to be shown that one needs teeth to eat, and that even with the finest jaws, if they were toothless, nothing could be achieved. 'I do have an appetite,' said Gregor sorrowfully to himself, 'but not for these things. How these gentlemen feed themselves, and I perish.'

On the very same evening—Gregor couldn't remember having heard it all this time—the violin sounded from the kitchen. The gentlemen had already finished their supper; the one in the middle had taken out a newspaper, given a page to each of the other two, and now they leaned back, reading and smoking. When the violin started to play, they began to take notice, rose, and tiptoed to the hall door, where they remained, standing crammed together. The family must have heard them from the kitchen, for the father called: 'Perhaps the gentlemen are displeased by the playing? It can be stopped at once.' 'On the contrary,' said the middle gentleman, 'wouldn't the young lady like to come in to us and play here in the living-room where it is much more comfortable and friendly?' 'By all means,' called the father, as if it was he who was playing. The gentlemen went back into the room and waited. Soon, in came father with the music-stand, mother with the music, and sister with the violin. Calmly the sister put everything ready for playing: the parents, who had never rented out rooms before and so overdid the politeness towards the lodgers, did not venture to sit in their own armchairs; the father leaned against the door, his right hand hidden between two buttons on the tightly fastened coat of his livery; the mother, on the other hand, accepted the armchair offered by one of the gentlemen and, letting it stay on the spot where he had happened to leave it, sat in a corner, out of the way.

Gregor's sister began to play; father and mother followed the movements of her hands attentively from either side. Attracted by the playing, Gregor had ventured a little further out until his head was already in the living-room. He was hardly surprised that he had shown so little consideration for the others of late; in the past this consideration had been his pride. And besides, right now he would have had even greater reason to hide, for, because of the dust on everything in his room, which rose at the slightest movement, he too was quite covered in it; he dragged threads, hairs, bits of left-over food about on his back; his indifference towards it all was far too great for him to do what he had previously done several times a day, lie on his back and scrub it against the carpet. And in spite of this condition, he did not hesitate to advance some way forward on the spotless floor of the living-room.

In any case, no one took any notice of him. The family was wholly taken up by the playing; the gentlemen on the other hand had at first positioned themselves, hands in pockets, much too close behind the sister's music-stand, which was surely bound to disturb her; they soon withdrew, conversing in low voices with heads lowered, back to the window, where, under the father's anxious eye, they remained. It really seemed more than obvious that they were disappointed in their assumption that they were to hear some beautiful or entertaining violin-playing, had had enough of the entire performance, and were only consenting to this interruption to their quiet out of politeness. The way they all blew out their cigar-smoke from nose and mouth in particular suggested great irritability. And yet his sister was playing so beautifully. Her face was inclined to one side; her eyes followed the lines of the music closely and sadly. Gregor crawled forward a little more, keeping his head close to the floor so that he could, if possible, meet her glance. Was he a beast, that music should move him like this? He felt as if the way to the unknown nourishment he longed for was being revealed. He resolved to advance right up to his sister, pluck her by the skirt to intimate that he was asking her to come with her violin into his room, for no one here was rewarding her playing as he would reward it. He wouldn't let her out of his room ever again, at least not while he was alive; his terrifying figure should be useful to him for the first time; he would post himself by all the doors of his room at once and go hissing to meet his attackers; but his sister should stay with him, not under duress, but of her own free will; she should sit next to him on the sofa, incline her ear down to him, and he would confide to her his firm intention of sending her to the conservatoire, and, if this misfortune hadn't got in the way, he would have told everybody last Christmas—Christmas was over, wasn't it?—without caring about any kind of objection to it. After this explanation his sister would burst into tears of emotion and Gregor would rear up as far as her shoulders and kiss her throat, which, ever since she had been working at the shop, was free of ribbon or collar.

'Herr Samsa!' called the middle gentleman, and without wasting another word pointed with his forefinger at Gregor, who was moving slowly forward. The violin fell silent. Shaking his head, the gentleman-lodger in the middle smiled just once at his friends and then looked in Gregor's direction once more. Instead of driving Gregor off, the father seemed to think it was more necessary to calm the gentlemen down first, although they were not in the least agitated, and Gregor seemed to amuse them more than the violin. He rushed up to them, and with outstretched arms tried to urge them back into their room, his body at the same time depriving them of their view of Gregor. They now became actually quite angry; it was unclear whether this was on account of the father's behaviour or because it now dawned on them that, without knowing it, they had possessed a neighbour like Gregor. They demanded explanations from the father, raised their own arms, plucked restively at their beards, and only slowly retreated towards their room. Meanwhile Gregor's sister had got over the bemused state she had fallen into after the sudden interruption of her playing, and, after she had held violin and bow in her drooping hands for a while and then gone on looking at her music as if she were still playing, she suddenly pulled herself together, put the instrument into her mother's lap (who was still sitting in her chair gasping, her lungs heaving violently), and dashed into the next room, which the gentlemen, driven on by her father, were already approaching even faster. Gregor saw how her practised hands made blankets and pillows on the beds fly into the air and settle themselves tidily. Before the gentlemen had reached their room she had finished making the beds and slipped out. The father seemed to be carried away by his stubbornness again, so that he forgot the respect which, after all, he owed his tenants. He drove them and drove them until, already in the doorway, the middle gentleman stamped thunderously with his foot, bringing the father to a standstill. 'I hereby declare', he said, looking round to include mother and sister too, 'that in view of the revolting conditions prevailing in this apartment and this family'—so saying, he spat briefly and decisively onto the floor—'I am giving my notice this instant. Naturally I shall not pay a penny, and that goes for the days I have been living here too; and then again I shall also consider whether I shan't make any claims—believe me, easy to justify—against you.' He fell silent, looking straight in front of him, as if he were expecting something. His two friends did in fact promptly break in with the words: 'We are giving notice this instant too.' At that he seized the latch and slammed the door shut with a crash.

The father staggered, groping his way to his armchair and falling into it. It looked as if he were stretching out for his usual evening nap, but the severe bobbing of his head, as if it had lost its support, showed that he certainly wasn't sleeping. All along, Gregor had lain still on the spot where the gentleman-lodgers had first caught him listening. Disappointment at the way his plan had miscarried, but also perhaps his infirmity after starving for so long, made it impossible for him to move. He feared with some certainty that a general cataclysm was about to be visited on him, and waited. He didn't even start when the violin, slipping from his mother's trembling fingers, fell from her lap and gave out a resounding note.

'Parents dear,' said his sister, striking the table with her hand by way of introduction, 'it can't go on like this. I will not utter my brother's name in front of this monster, so I will simply say: we must try to get rid of it. We have tried everything humanly possible, looking after it and putting up with it; I don't think anyone can reproach us in the slightest for that.'

'She's right a thousand times over,' said her father to himself. Her mother, who still could not catch her breath, with a wild look in her eyes, began a stifled coughing into the cover of her hand.

Gregor's sister rushed to her mother and held her forehead. The father seemed to have been jolted into thinking more sharply by the sister's words; he sat down, straight-backed, played with his uniform cap amongst the plates, which were still lying on the table after the gentlemen's meal, and now and then looked across at Gregor as he lay motionless.

'We must try to get rid of it,' his sister now said solely to their father, since their mother couldn't hear anything for coughing, 'it will be the death of you both, I can see it coming. If we all have to work already as hard as we do, we can't put up with this endless agony as well. I certainly can't go on any more.' And she broke into crying so vehemently that her tears fell on to her mother's face, which she wiped dry with mechanical movements of her hand.

'But my child,' said her father compassionately and with remarkable understanding, 'what are we to do?'

Gregor's sister only shrugged her shoulders, indicating the helplessness that had overcome her while she cried, quite unlike her earlier assurance.

'If he understood us,' said the father, half questioningly, but the sister waved her hand vehemently in the midst of her tears, indicating that this was inconceivable.

'If he understood us,' the father repeated, and by closing his eyes, took in the sister's conviction that it was out of the question, 'then perhaps some accommodation with him might be possible. But as it is—'

'It has to go,' cried the sister, 'that is the only way, father. You must just try to get rid of the thought that it is Gregor. Our real misfortune is that we have believed it for so long. But how can it be Gregor? If it were Gregor, he would have understood long ago that it's not possible for human beings to live with a beast like that, and he would have left of his own free will. We wouldn't have a brother then, but we would be able to go on living, and honour his memory. But as it is, this beast is pursuing us and driving away our lodgers; it obviously wants to take over the entire apartment and put us out to sleep on the street. Just look, father,' she suddenly shrieked, 'he's at it again!' And in a fit of terror, which was utterly beyond Gregor's understanding, the sister even abandoned their mother, literally pushing her out of her armchair, as if she would sooner sacrifice her mother than remain so near to Gregor; she rushed behind her father, who also got to his feet, agitated simply by her behaviour and half-raising his arms as though to protect her.

But it hadn't occurred to Gregor for a moment to want to scare anyone, least of all his sister. He had simply begun to turn round to make his way back into his room, though the effect of his attempts was alarming, for, owing to the sorry state he was in, he had to use his head to help him perform the difficult manoeuvre of turning, raising it several times as he did so, and hitting it on the floor. He paused and looked round. His good intentions seemed to have been recognized; it had only been a momentary fright. Now they all looked at him silently and sadly. His mother was lying in her armchair, her legs pressed together and stretched out straight; her eyes were almost closing from exhaustion; father and sister sat next to each other, the sister had laid her hand round her father's neck.

'Well, now perhaps they'll let me turn round,' thought Gregor, and began his labour once more. He wasn't able to suppress the puffing and panting the effort entailed, and now and again he was also obliged to rest. But no one was forcing him either; it was all left to him. Once he had completed the turn, he began to head straight back. He was astonished at the great distance separating him from his room, and couldn't understand at all how a short time ago, weak as he was, he had covered the same stretch almost without noticing. With his mind all the time on crawling fast, he was scarcely aware that not a word, not a cry, came from his family to disturb him. Only when he was in the doorway he turned his head, not fully, because he could feel his neck stiffening, but even so he could still see that behind him nothing had changed; only his sister was standing up. His last glance fell on his mother, who by now had fallen fast asleep.

He was hardly inside his room before the door was hastily shut, bolted fast, and locked. Gregor was so startled at the sudden noise that his little legs collapsed. It was his sister who had moved so fast. She had already been standing there waiting, and then, light-footed, she had leapt forward. Gregor hadn't heard her coming at all, and then: 'At last!' she cried to her parents, as she turned the key in the lock.

'And now?' Gregor asked himself, and looked around in the darkness. He soon discovered he was no longer able to move at all. He wasn't at all surprised; rather, it seemed to him to be unnatural that up till now he had actually been able to move about on these thin little legs. Otherwise he felt relatively comfortable. True, he had aches and pains all over his body, but it seemed to him that they were gradually getting weaker and weaker and in the end would vanish entirely. He could scarcely feel the apple in his back, rotten by now, nor the inflammation around it, covered all over in a thin film of dust. He thought back on his family with affection and love. His own opinion that he should vanish was, if possible, even more determined than his sister's. He remained in this state of vacant and peaceful reflection until the tower clock struck three in the morning. He still lived to see the dark begin to grow generally lighter outside the window. Then his head sank down without his willing it, and from his nostrils his last breath faintly flowed.

When the charwoman came early in the morning—from sheer hustle and bustle she would slam all the doors so hard, however often they had asked her not to, that once she had arrived it was impossible to sleep peacefully anywhere in the apartment—when she paid her usual brief visit to Gregor, at first she found nothing peculiar. She thought he was lying there without moving on purpose, sulking: she gave him credit for all sorts of intelligence. She happened to be holding the long broom in her hand, so she tried to tickle Gregor with it from the doorway. When this didn't work, she became annoyed and gave Gregor a prod, but it was only when she had shoved him unresisting from the spot that she began to pay some attention. It did not take her long to recognize the true state of affairs; she opened her eyes wide, whistled to herself, wasted no more of her time, but threw open the bedroom door and shouted into the darkness in a loud voice: 'Come and see; it's snuffed it; it's lying in there, snuffed it. Completely!'

The marital couple sat up straight in the marital bed; they had enough to do to get over the fright the charwoman had given them before they took in her announcement. But once they had, Herr and Frau Samsa got out of bed at speed, one from each side; Herr Samsa threw the bedspread over his shoulders, Frau Samsa emerged wearing only her nightdress; so clad, they entered Gregor's room. Meanwhile the door opened from the living-room, where Grete had been sleeping since the gentleman-lodgers had moved in; she was fully dressed, as if she hadn't slept at all; and her pale face seemed to show it. 'Dead?' said Frau Samsa, looking up at the charwoman questioningly, although she could check it all for herself and recognize it even without checking. 'I'll say he is,' said the charwoman, and to prove it pushed Gregor's corpse a fair way to one side with her broom. Frau Samsa made a move as if she wanted to restrain the broom, but did not do so. 'Well,' said Herr Samsa, 'now we can thank God.' He crossed himself, and the three women followed his example. Grete, whose eyes had been fixed on the corpse, said: 'Just see how thin he was. He hasn't eaten now for so long. Just the way his food went in, that's how it came out.' And indeed, Gregor's body was completely flat and dry; it was only now they actually perceived it, when he was no longer supported by his little legs and there was nothing else besides to distract their gaze.

'Come in to us for a little while, Grete,' said Frau Samsa with a melancholy smile, and Grete followed her parents, not without looking back at the corpse, into their bedroom. The charwoman closed the door and opened the window wide. Although it was early morning, there was already a touch of mildness in the fresh air. It was just the end of March.

The three gentleman-lodgers emerged from their room and looked around for their breakfast in astonishment; the family had forgotten them. 'Where's our breakfast?' the one in the middle asked the charwoman gruffly. She put her finger to her lips and beckoned the gentlemen hastily and silently to come into Gregor's room. And come in they did, and with their hands in the pockets of their rather shabby jackets, they stood in the room, by now fully bright, around Gregor's corpse.

Then the bedroom door opened and Herr Samsa appeared in his uniform, his wife on one arm, his daughter on the other. They all showed signs of weeping; from time to time Grete pressed her face against her father's arm.

'Leave my home at once!' said Herr Samsa, and pointed towards the door without letting go of the women. 'What do you mean?' said the middle gentleman, rather taken aback, with a sickly smile. The other two put their hands behind their backs, all the time rubbing them together, as though in joyful expectation of a huge row which was bound to end in their favour. 'I mean exactly what I say,' replied Herr Samsa, and, lined up with his two companions, he made for the gentleman-lodger, who first of all stood still, looking at the floor, as if the things in his head were rearranging themselves in a new order. 'Then we'll go,' he said, looking up at Herr Samsa as if, overcome by sudden humility, he required further permission even for this decision. Herr Samsa merely nodded shortly to him several times, with a glare. At that the gentleman actually strode into the front hall; his two friends had already been listening for a while with their hands quite still, and they practically hopped after him now, as if they were afraid Herr Samsa might enter the front hall ahead of them and break the connection with their leader. Once in the hall, the three took their hats from the hat-rack and their sticks from the umbrella-stand, bowed in silence, and left the apartment. In—as it turned out—utterly unfounded mistrust, Herr Samsa, still with the two women, went out on to the landing. Leaning on the banisters, they watched as the three gentlemen went slowly but steadily down the long staircase, disappearing at a bend in the stairs at each floor and reappearing after a few moments; the lower they went, the more the Samsa family lost interest in them, and when a butcher's boy came climbing proudly towards them and then higher up above them, tray on head, Herr Samsa soon left the landing with the women and they all returned, as if relieved, into their apartment.

They decided to use the present day to rest and take a stroll; they had not only earned this interruption to their work, they absolutely needed it. And so they sat down at the table and wrote three notes of excuse, Herr Samsa to his head manager, Frau Samsa to her client, and Grete to the proprietor of her shop. While they were writing, the charwoman came in to tell them that she was about to go, as her morning's work was done. Busy with their writing, at first the three merely nodded without looking up. It was only when the charwoman still made no attempt to leave that they looked up in annoyance. 'Well?' asked Herr Samsa. The charwoman stood smiling in the doorway, as if she had some great good fortune to tell the family, but would only do so if questioned closely. The little ostrich feather, sticking almost upright in her hat, which had annoyed Herr Samsa all the time she had worked for them, waved lightly in all directions. 'So what is it you want?' asked Frau Samsa, the one the charwoman respected most. 'Well,' answered the charwoman, who was unable to continue speaking at first for sheer good-natured laughter, 'about how to get rid of that stuff in the next room, you don't have to worry about it. I've seen to it.' Frau Samsa and Grete bent over their letters, as if they wanted to go on writing; Herr Samsa, who observed that the charwoman was about to describe everything in detail, dismissed this firmly with outstretched hand. But as she was not allowed to tell her tale, she remembered the great hurry she was in and called out, obviously offended: 'Bye, all,' turned wildly, and left the apartment with a terrible slamming of doors.

'She'll get her notice this evening,' said Herr Samsa, but received no answer, neither from his wife nor from his daughter, for the charwoman seemed to have upset their barely gained composure again. They rose, went to the window, and remained there, arms round each other. Herr Samsa turned towards them in his armchair and watched them quietly for a while. Then he called: 'Come over here. Let go of the old things at last. And show a little consideration for me too.' At once the women did as they were told, hastened to him, caressed him, and quickly finished their letters.

Then all three left the apartment together, something they had not done for months, and took the tram out into the open country outside the town. The sun shone warm right through the carriage where they were sitting. Leaning back comfortably in their seats, they discussed their prospects for the future, and it emerged on closer inspection that these were not at all bad, for the jobs all three of them held, which they had never actually asked one another about, were extremely good, and, looking ahead, particularly promising. For the moment of course the greatest improvement in their situation was bound to come simply from a change of dwelling; they proposed to take an apartment that was smaller and cheaper, but in a better location and generally more practical than their present one, which was still the one that Gregor had chosen. While they were talking like this together, it occurred to Herr and Frau Samsa at almost the same time, as they looked at their daughter becoming more and more full of life, how, in spite of all the distress that had made her cheeks so pale, she had blossomed of late into a handsome, full-figured girl. Growing quieter and coming almost unconsciously to an understanding as they exchanged glances, they reflected that it was also getting to be time to look for a good husband for her. And they felt it was like a confirmation of their new dreams and good intentions when, as they came to the end of their journey, their daughter was the first to rise from her seat, and she stretched her young body.

In the Penal Colony

'It is a remarkable apparatus,' said the officer to the enquiring travel-ler,* surveying the apparatus with some admiration in his eyes, though it must have been long familiar to him. It seemed that it was only out of courtesy that the traveller had accepted the command-ant's invitation to attend the execution of a soldier who had been condemned for disobedience and insulting behaviour towards his superior. In the penal colony, too, interest in this execution was probably not very great. At least, here in the deep, sandy little valley, cut off by the bare hillsides all round, the only figures present, apart from the officer and the traveller, were the condemned man, a dull-witted, wide-mouthed being with unkempt hair and a wild expres-sion, and one soldier, who was holding the heavy chain attached to the small chains which fettered the condemned man by his ankles and wrists as well as by his neck, and which were also linked to one another by connecting chains. However, the condemned man looked so submissive and dog-like that it seemed as if one could let him run free on the hillsides, and would only have to whistle at the start of the execution for him to come.

The traveller had little interest in the apparatus, and paced to and fro behind the condemned man with almost visible detachment, while the officer attended to the final preparations, at one moment crawling beneath the apparatus, which had been built deep in the earth, at another climbing a ladder to examine the upper parts. These were tasks that really could have been left to a mechanic, but the officer carried them out with great zeal, whether it was because he was a devotee of the apparatus, or whether it was for other reasons that the work could not be entrusted to anyone else. 'Now everything is ready!' he called at last, and climbed down from the ladder. He was utterly exhausted, breathed with his mouth wide open, and he had pushed two delicate ladies' handkerchiefs into his uniform collar. 'Surely these uniforms are too heavy for the tropics,' said the travel-ler, instead of enquiring after the apparatus as the officer had expected. 'Indeed,' said the officer, washing hands dirty from oil and grease in a waiting bucket of water, 'but they mean home; we don't want to lose contact with our home country. But just look at this apparatus,' he promptly added, drying his hands on a towel, at the same time pointing to the apparatus. 'Up to this point it needs to be adjusted by hand, but from now on it will work quite of its own accord.' The traveller nodded and followed the officer. The officer, attempting to cover himself against all possible accidents, then said: 'Of course, malfunctions do occur; I certainly hope that won't happen today; all the same, we have to reckon with them. The apparatus should actually run for twenty-four hours without interruption. But even if malfunctions do occur, they are very slight after all, and they will be put right straight away.'

'Won't you sit down?' he asked finally, pulling a wicker chair from a pile of them and offering it to the traveller, who could hardly refuse. He sat at the edge of a ditch, and cast a fleeting glance into it. It was not very deep. To one side the excavated earth had been heaped up into a rampart; on the other side stood the apparatus. 'I don't know', said the officer, 'whether the commandant has explained the apparatus to you already.' The traveller made a vague gesture with his hand. The officer desired nothing better, for now he could explain it himself. 'This apparatus', he said, taking hold of a crank-shaft, 'is an invention of our old commandant. I was involved from the start in the very first trials, and took part in all the work until it was completed. However, the credit for the invention belongs solely to him. Have you heard of our old commandant? No? Well, I am not putting it too strongly when I say that the organization of the entire penal colony is his work. As his friends, we already knew by the time he died that the organization of the colony was so highly integrated that his successor, however many thousands of new plans he has in his head, will not be able to change anything the old one set up, at least not for many years. And what we predicted has come true; the new commandant has had to acknowledge it. A shame that you didn't know our old commandant!—But,' the officer interrupted himself, 'I'm chattering, and here is his apparatus before us. It is made up, as you see, of three parts. In the course of time what you might call popular names have developed for each of them. The lower part is called the Bed; the upper part is called the Marker, and this pulsating part between them is called the Harrow.' 'The Harrow?' queried the traveller. He had not been listening with full attention—the sun was too strong, trapped in the shadeless valley; it was hard to collect one's thoughts. The officer seemed to him all the more admirable as he explained his purpose so eagerly in his tight uniform, weighed down with epaulettes and hung with cords, fit for parade, and in addition, even while he was speaking, he was also still busy with his screw-driver on a screw here or there. The soldier seemed to be in a condition similar to the traveller's. He had wrapped the condemned man's chain round both his wrists, supporting himself with one hand on his rifle and letting his head hang back, paying no attention. The travel-ler was not surprised, for the officer spoke French,* and certainly neither the soldier nor the condemned man understood French. Indeed, it was all the more striking that nevertheless the condemned man made every effort to follow the officer's explanations. With a kind of somnolent persistence he kept turning his gaze wherever the officer happened to be pointing, and now, as the officer was inter-rupted by a question from the traveller, like him, he too looked at the traveller.

'Yes, the Harrow,' said the officer. 'The name fits. The needles are arranged as spikes are in a harrow, and the entire part moves like a harrow, though merely on the same place and far more efficiently. Anyway, you will soon understand it. The condemned man is placed on the Bed. I will describe the apparatus first and then have the pro-cedure itself carried out. You will be able to follow it better like that. Also, one cog-wheel in the Marker is very badly worn; it grates so much when it's in operation, it's hard to make oneself understood; unfortunately, it is difficult to get hold of replacement parts here.—So, here is the Bed, as I said. It is entirely covered with a layer of padding; you will find out the purpose of that later. The condemned man is laid on this padding face-down, naked, of course; straps for his hands are here, for his feet here, for his neck here, to bind him fast. Here at the head of the Bed, where the man, as I said, is at first lying face-down, you have this small stump of felt which can easily be adjusted so that it is forced straight into the man's mouth. Its purpose is to prevent him from screaming and biting his tongue. Of course the man has to take the felt in his mouth, other-wise his neck would be broken by the strap.' 'That's padding?' quer-ied the traveller, leaning forward. 'Yes, certainly,' said the officer, smiling, 'feel it for yourself.' He took the traveller's hand and passed it over the Bed. 'It is a specially treated padding—that's why it looks so strange. I shall say something about its purpose later.' The travel-ler's interest in the apparatus was already won over a little; sheltering his eyes against the sun with his hand, he looked up at the apparatus above him. It was a huge structure. The Bed and the Marker were the same size, and they looked like two dark chests. The Marker was mounted about two metres above the Bed. Both were connected at the corners by four brass rods which were almost radiating light in the sun. Between the chests, suspended on a strip of steel, was the Harrow.

The officer had hardly noticed the traveller's previous indifference, but he certainly sensed his dawning interest; so he broke off his explanations to give the traveller time to observe without interruption. The condemned man copied the traveller; unable to cover his eyes with his hand, he squinted upwards with open eyes.

'So now the man is lying there,' said the traveller, leaning back in his chair and crossing his legs.

'Yes,' said the officer, pushing back his cap a little and passing his hand across his hot face, 'now, listen! Both the Bed and the Marker have their own electric battery; the Bed requires it for its own use, the Marker for the Harrow. As soon as the man is bound fast, the Bed is set in motion. It vibrates with minute, very rapid tremors, from side to side and at the same time up and down. You will have seen similar apparatus in private clinics; only with our Bed all the movements are exactly calculated; they have to be exactly coordinated with the movements of the Harrow. It is the Harrow that has the actual task of executing the sentence.'

'How does the sentence run?' asked the traveller. 'You don't know that either?' said the officer in amazement, biting his lip. 'Forgive me if my explanations have been rather incoherent; please excuse me. It's just that previously it was the custom for the commandant to give them; but the new commandant has avoided this great duty; even so, with the attendance of such an esteemed visitor'—the traveller attempted to dismiss the honour, gesturing with both hands, but the officer insisted on the term—'of such an esteemed visitor, not even to have let him know the form our sentence takes is another of his innovations that—' He had a curse on the tip of his tongue, but he pulled himself together and said only: 'I was not informed of this; it is not my fault. Besides, I am after all the best person to explain the kind of sentence we pass, for I have here'—he struck his breast-pocket—'the relevant designs in the hand of our old commandant.'

'Designs in the hand of the commandant himself?' queried the traveller. 'Did he unite everything in himself, then? Was he soldier, judge, engineer, chemist, draughtsman all in one?'

'Indeed,' said the officer, nodding his head with fixed and brooding gaze. Then he examined his hands; they didn't seem to him clean enough to be handling the designs; so he went over to the bucket and washed them once again. Then he drew out a small leather case and said: 'Our sentence doesn't sound harsh. The commandment that the condemned man has broken is inscribed upon his body with the Harrow. This man for example'—the officer pointed to him—'will have inscribed upon his body: "Honour thy superior!"'

The traveller glanced briefly towards the man; he kept his head down as the officer pointed to him, and seemed to be straining his ears to gather something from what was being said. But the movements of his thick, tight-shut lips plainly showed that he could understand nothing. The traveller had a number of different questions he wanted to ask, but under the man's gaze he asked only: 'Does he know what his sentence is?' 'No,' said the officer, and was about to carry on explaining straight away, but the traveller interrupted him: 'He doesn't know his own sentence?' 'No,' said the officer again, stopping short for a moment as if he expected the traveller to explain his question further; then he said: 'It would be pointless to tell him. He will feel it in his own flesh.' The traveller was about to fall silent, but he sensed the condemned man turning his eyes in his direction. He seemed to be asking if the traveller was able to give his approval to the procedure. This made the traveller, who had already leaned back, bend forward once more and ask again: 'But he does know that he has actually been condemned?' 'Not that either,' said the officer, and smiled at the traveller as if he were expecting further strange admissions from him. 'No,' said the traveller, 'so even now the man doesn't know how his defence was received?' 'He had no opportunity to defend himself,' said the officer, looking to one side as if he were talking to himself and didn't want to embarrass the traveller by telling him these—to him quite normal—things. 'But he must have had an opportunity to defend himself,' said the traveller, getting up from his chair.

The officer realized that he ran the risk of getting held up for a long time in his explanation of the apparatus; so he went over to the traveller, put his arm in his, and pointed with his hand at the condemned man, who, now that attention was so evidently being turned towards him, stood up straight—the soldier also gave a tug at the chain. 'The situation is as follows,' said the officer. 'I have been appointed judge here in the penal colony. Despite my youth. For I also assisted our old commandant in all criminal affairs, and I am also the person most familiar with the apparatus. The fundamental principle of my decisions is: "Guilt is always beyond question." Other courts are unable to follow this principle, for they are made up of many persons and are also subject to courts higher than themselves. That is not the case here, or at least it was not the case under the old commandant. It is true, the new one has already shown a desire to interfere in my court, but so far I have managed to hold him off, and shall continue to do so.—You wanted to have the present case explained; it is as simple as the rest. This morning a captain filed a report that this man, who has been assigned to him as his servant and sleeps outside his door, had been asleep on duty. For it is his task to get up every hour and salute outside the captain's door. Certainly not a hard task, but a necessary one, for he is supposed to stay fresh both as a sentry and as a servant. Last night the captain wanted to make sure that his servant was doing his duty. On the stroke of two he opened his door and found him curled up asleep. He fetched his riding-whip and struck him across the face. Instead of getting up and begging forgiveness, the man seized his master round the legs, shook him, and shouted: "Throw your whip away, or I'll eat you up." Those are the facts of the case. The captain came to me an hour ago. I wrote up his statement, and the sentence directly afterwards. Then I had the man put in chains. That was all very simple. Only confusion would arise if I had summoned the man and interrogated him first. He would have lied, and if I had succeeded in refuting his lies, he would have replaced them with fresh lies, and so on. But now I've got him, and I shan't let him go.—Does that explain everything? But time is passing; the execution should have started by now and I still haven't finished explaining the apparatus.' He pressed the traveller on to his seat, went up to the apparatus once more, and began: 'As you see, the Harrow corresponds to the shape of a human being; this is the harrow for the upper torso; these are the harrows for the legs; only this small spike is intended for the head. Is that clear?' He bowed amiably to the traveller, ready for the most comprehensive explanations.

The traveller looked at the Harrow, frowning. What he had just heard about the judicial procedure had not left him pleased. All the same, he had to tell himself that this was a penal colony; that special measures were necessary here, and that they had to act along military lines to the last. Anyway, he placed some hopes on the new commandant, who obviously intended to introduce new procedures, however slowly, which this officer's narrow mind couldn't take in. Pursuing this train of thought, the traveller asked: 'Will the commandant be attending the execution?' 'It's not certain,' said the officer, embarrassed by the direct question. His affable expression contorted: 'That's just why we must make haste. Sorry as I am to do so, I shall even have to cut my explanations short. But of course I could catch up on the more detailed explanations tomorrow, when the apparatus has been cleaned once again—its only drawback is that it gets so fouled. Now for the moment, only what is most essential.—When the man is lying on the Bed, and it is set vibrating, the Harrow is lowered onto the body. It adjusts itself automatically so that it only touches his body very lightly with its needles; once the adjustment is completed, this steel rope stiffens at once into a rod. And now the performance begins. From outside, the uninitiated do not notice any outward difference in the punishments. The Harrow appears to work uniformly. As it vibrates it stabs its needles into the condemned man's body, which is also vibrating from the Bed. Now to make it possible for everyone to observe the sentence as it is being carried out, the Harrow is made of glass. This caused some technical difficulties in fixing the needles into it, but after a number of attempts it worked. There were no lengths we didn't go to. And now everybody can watch through the glass how the inscription is carried out on the body. Won't you come closer and look at the needles?'

The traveller rose slowly, went across, and bent over the Harrow. 'You can see', said the officer, 'two kinds of needle in various arrangements. Each long needle has a short one next to it. The long one is for writing, and the short one sprays water to wash away the blood and keep the inscription clear at all times. The mingled blood and water is then piped into these little channels here and finally into this main channel, and its drainage-pipe leads into the ditch.' With his finger the officer pointed out precisely the path the blood and water had to take. And when, to make the picture as vivid as possible, he practically caught it in cupped hands at the outlet of the drainpipe, the traveller raised his head and, groping backwards with his hand, tried to return to his seat. Then to his horror he saw that like him the condemned man too had followed the officer's invitation to look at the arrangement of the Harrow from close quarters. He had tugged the sleepy soldier by his chain, and was likewise bending over the glass. One could see that he was also looking uncertainly for what the two gentlemen had just been observing, but that without the explanation, it was not possible for him to do so. He bent this way and that. Again and again his eyes scanned the glass. The traveller tried to drive him back, for what he was doing was probably a punishable offence. But with one hand the officer held the traveller fast, and with the other took a clod of earth from the rampart and threw it at the soldier. With a start the soldier raised his eyes and saw what the condemned man had dared to do, dropped his rifle, braced his heels against the ground, pulled the condemned man back so sharply that he fell down at once, and looked down on him writhing and rattling his chain. 'Get him to his feet!' shouted the officer, for he noticed that the traveller was being distracted far too much by the condemned man. The traveller even leaned right over the Harrow, without bothering with it, wanting only to find out what was happening to the condemned man. 'Handle him carefully!' the officer shouted again. He ran round the apparatus, himself caught hold of the condemned man under the arms, and, with the soldier's help stood him on his feet, though they kept on sliding beneath him.

'Now I know everything about it,' said the traveller when the officer returned. 'Except the most important thing,' came the reply, as the officer took the traveller by the arm and pointed upwards: 'Up there in the Marker you have the mechanism that controls the movement of the Harrow, and this mechanism is arranged according to the design that the sentence requires. I still use the old commandant's designs. Here they are'—he drew some pages from the leather folder—'but unfortunately I can't put them into your hands; they are the most precious things I have. Do sit down; I will show them to you from this distance. Then you'll be able to see them all quite easily.' He showed the first page. The traveller would gladly have said something appreciative, but all he could see was something like a maze of criss-crossing lines covering the paper so closely that it was only with difficulty that one could make out the white spaces in between. 'Read it,' said the officer. 'I can't,' said the traveller.

'But it's perfectly clear,' said the officer. 'It's very elaborate,' said the traveller evasively, 'but I can't decipher it.' 'Yes,' said the officer with a laugh, putting the case back into his pocket, 'it's not a script* for schoolchildren's copy-books. One has to read it over a long period. You would certainly be able to make it out for yourself in the end. Of course it shouldn't be a simple script; after all, it's not supposed to kill immediately, but only within a space of twelve hours on average; the turning-point has been calculated to come at the sixth hour. So the actual script has to be surrounded by many, many flourishes; the real script encircles the body only in a narrow girdle; the rest of the body is intended for decoration. Now can you appreciate the work of the Harrow and the whole apparatus?—Just watch!' He leapt onto the ladder, turned a wheel, and called down: 'Look out! Move aside!' and it all began to function. If the wheel had not grated, it would have been magnificent. As if the officer were surprised at the noise of the wheel, he shook his fist at it, but then, in excuse, spread out his arms towards the traveller and clambered down quickly to observe the operation of the apparatus from below. Something that only he had noticed was still not in order; he clambered up again, plunged both hands into the interior of the Marker, and then, to get down faster, instead of using the ladder slid down one of the poles. Making a great effort to be heard above the noise, he shouted into the traveller's ear: 'Do you understand what is going on? The Harrow is beginning to write; once it has finished the preliminary layout of the script on the man's back, the layer of padding rolls over, and slowly turns the body onto its side to give the Harrow fresh space. Meanwhile the places that have been written raw are lying on the pad. Because of its special treatment this will stop the bleeding at once and prepare for engraving the script more deeply. Then, once the body is turned again, these teeth at the edge of the Harrow will tear the padding away from the wounds and eject it into the ditch—and there is fresh work for the Harrow. In this way it writes deeper and deeper the entire twelve hours long. For the first six hours the condemned man is alive almost as before, except that he suffers pain. After two hours the felt is removed, for the man no longer has any strength left to scream. Into this electrically heated bowl here at the head of the Bed, there is placed warm rice porridge, and if he wants, the man may take what he can manage to lick up with his tongue. Not one misses the opportunity. I don't know anyone who has, and my experience is great. Only at the sixth hour will he lose his pleasure in eating. Then I usually kneel here and observe this phenomenon. The man rarely swallows his last mouthful; he just turns it round in his mouth and spits it into the ditch. Then I have to duck, for otherwise it will land in my face. But how still the man becomes at the sixth hour! Understanding dawns upon even the most stupid. It begins with the eyes. From there it spreads further. A sight that might tempt you to join him lying beneath the Harrow. Indeed, nothing further happens; the man simply begins to decipher the script; he purses his lips as if he were listening. You have seen it is not easy to decipher the script with one's eyes; but our man deciphers them with his wounds. Admittedly, it is hard work. He needs six hours to accomplish it. But then the Harrow spears him right through and throws him into the ditch, where he splashes down onto the blood and water and padding. Then the process of judgement is at an end, and we—myself and the soldier—cover him over.'

The traveller had inclined his ear to the officer and, hands in pockets, watched the machine as it worked. The condemned man watched too, but without understanding. He was bending over slightly, following the quivering needles, when, at a signal from the officer, the soldier took a knife and cut through the man's shirt and trousers so that they fell away from him; he tried to grab at them as they fell to cover his nakedness, but the soldier lifted him up and shook the last tatters from him. The officer turned off the machine, and as the silence now fell, the condemned man was laid beneath the Harrow. His chains were removed and the straps fastened in their place. For the condemned man it seemed for a moment, at first, to come almost as a relief. And now the Harrow sank a little lower, for he was thin. As the points touched him, a shudder ran through him; while the soldier was busied with his right hand, he stretched out his left, without knowing in what direction; in fact, it was towards where the traveller was standing. All the time the officer was watching the traveller from one side, as if trying to tell from his face what impression the execution, which he had explained to him at least superficially, was making on him.

The strap meant for the wrist snapped; probably the soldier had pulled it too tight. Expecting the officer to help, the soldier showed him the torn bit of strap. And the officer did go across to him, and with his face turned towards the traveller he said: 'The machine is very complex; something is bound to snap or break now and again; but one shouldn't let that mislead one when making an overall judgement. Besides, we can find a substitute for the strap straight away; I shall use a chain; though, it's true, that will interfere with the sensitivity of oscillation for the right arm.' While he was fixing the chain, he added: 'Resources for maintaining the machine are at present very restricted; under the old commandant funds were freely available to me intended solely for this purpose. There was a depot here holding every possible kind of spare part. I admit, I was almost extravagant in using them—I mean previously, not now, as the new commandant asserts, for he uses everything just as an excuse to work against old institutions. Now he has the fund for the machine under his own control, and if I send for a new strap, the torn one will be required as evidence, and the new one won't arrive for another ten days, and then it is of inferior quality and pretty worthless. But in the interim, no one cares in the least how I am supposed to keep the machine functioning.'

The traveller pondered: it is always a dubious business, to intervene decisively in others' affairs. He was a citizen neither of the penal colony, nor of the state it belonged to. If he tried to condemn this execution, or even obstruct it, they could tell him: 'you're a foreigner; hold your tongue.' To that he would have no answer, being able only to add that he himself couldn't understand why he was doing so in this instance, for he was travelling simply as an observer and not with the smallest intention of changing the legal constitution of a foreign country. Though the situation here was a great temptation to do so. There was no doubt about the injustice of the procedure and the inhumanity of the execution. No one could assume any self-interest on the traveller's part, for the condemned man was a stranger to him; he wasn't a fellow-countryman and certainly not a person to arouse one's compassion. The traveller himself had recommendations from high places, had been received here with great civility, and to have been invited to this execution even seemed to indicate that his judgement was desired. This was all the more likely, surely, given that the commandant—as he had heard all too plainly on this occasion—was no devotee of the procedure and almost hostile in his attitude towards the officer.

At that moment the traveller heard a cry of rage from the officer. He had, not without difficulty, just pushed the gag into the condemned man's mouth, when the man closed his eyes in an uncontrollable attack of nausea, and vomited. The officer pulled him away sharply from the gag and tried to turn his head towards the ditch; but it was too late, the vomit was already dripping down the machine. 'It's all the commandant's fault,' the officer shouted, shaking the brass poles at the front in blind rage. 'The machine is being fouled like a sty in front of my eyes.' With shaking hands he showed the traveller what had happened. 'Haven't I spent hours attempting to make the commandant understand that no food is to be given on the day before the execution. But this new soft line takes a different view. Before the man is led away, the commandant's ladies stuff the man's stomach with bon-bons. All his life he has fed on stinking fish and now he has to eat bon-bons! But that might be just acceptable—I wouldn't have anything against it—but why don't they send a fresh gag, as I've been requesting these past three months. How can a man take this gag in his mouth without revulsion, when over a hundred men have been retching and biting on it as they were dying?'

The condemned man had laid down his head, and looked peaceful. The soldier was busy cleaning the machine with the man's shirt. The officer approached the traveller, who took a step back with some misgiving, but the officer seized him by the hand and drew him aside. 'I wish to say a few words to you in confidence,' he said, 'I may, I hope?' 'Certainly,' said the traveller, and listened with lowered eyes.

'This procedure and this execution, which you now have the opportunity to admire, no longer have any open followers in our colony at the present time. I am their sole champion, and at the same time the sole champion of the old commandant's legacy. I can no longer think of developing the procedure further; I spend all my energies just on maintaining what is still there. When the old commandant was alive, the colony was full of his followers; I possess in some part the persuasiveness of the old commandant, but I lack his power; consequently his followers have gone into hiding; there are many of them still, but no one will admit to it. If you visit a teahouse today, on an execution day, that is, and keep your ears open, all you will hear is perhaps a few ambiguous remarks. They are all of them followers, but under the present commandant, and with his present opinions, they are no use at all to me. And now I ask you: is such a life's work'—he pointed at the machine—'to be ruined on account of this commandant and the ladies who influence him? Should one permit it? Even if, as a foreigner, one is visiting our island only for a few days? But there is no time to lose: they are planning something against my judicial authority; discussions, where I have not been consulted, are already taking place in the commandant's headquarters; even your visit today seems to me indicative of the entire situation; they are cowards, and they are sending you ahead as a cover for themselves. How different the execution was in earlier times! A day before the execution the entire valley was already overflowing with people; they all came just to watch; early in the morning the commandant would appear with his ladies; fanfares would rouse the entire encampment; I would deliver the announcement that everything had been made ready; the company—every high official was under orders to attend—took their places around the machine; this heap of wicker chairs is a miserable remnant of that time. The machine was freshly cleaned and shining; I used new spare parts for every execution. Before a hundred eyes—as far as the hills over there all the spectators were standing on tip-toe—the condemned man was laid under the Harrow by the commandant himself. What a common soldier is permitted to do now was my task, as president of the court, and an honour for me. And now the execution would begin! Not a discordant sound disturbed the work of the machine. Many gave up watching entirely, lying instead on the sand with their eyes shut; they all knew: now Justice is being done. In silence one only heard the groaning of the condemned man, muffled by the gag. Today the machine can no longer manage to force a sigh out of the condemned man stronger than the gag can stifle; but in those days, as they wrote, the needles dripped a corrosive fluid which today we are no longer allowed to use. And then came the sixth hour! It was impossible to grant everyone their request to be allowed to watch from near at hand. The commandant in his wisdom ordered that first and foremost the children should be considered; though I myself, by virtue of my office, could always be present; I often crouched on that spot there, a little child in each arm to right and left. How we all took in the look of transfiguration from the suffering face, how we bathed our cheeks in the reflection of a justice finally attained and already passing! What times they were, my comrade!' The officer had obviously forgotten who was standing in front of him; he had embraced the traveller and laid his head upon his shoulder. The traveller was deeply embarrassed; impatiently he looked past the officer and away.

The soldier had finished his cleaning, and was still pouring rice-porridge into the bowl from a can. The condemned man, who seemed to have recovered completely, scarcely laid his eyes on it before he began to lick at the porridge with his tongue. The soldier kept pushing him away, as it was surely meant for later, but in any case it was also offensive that the soldier should be digging into it with his filthy hands and eating some of it for himself in front of the ravenous condemned man.

The officer pulled himself together quickly. 'I didn't mean to stir your feelings,' he said, 'I know it's impossible today to make those times intelligible. Besides, the machine still works, and functions of its own accord. It functions of its own accord even when it is alone in this valley. And the corpse still falls in the end, dropping with incomprehensible softness into the ditch, even though people no longer gather in their hundreds like flies, as once they did, around the ditch. In those days we had to put up a strong fence around the ditch—it was torn down long ago.'

The traveller tried to turn his face away from the officer, and looked around aimlessly. The officer thought he was contemplating the desolation of the valley; so he seized his hands, circled round him to catch his eye, and asked: 'Do you see the disgrace?'

But the traveller was silent. The officer let him be for a moment; with legs apart and hands on hips, he stood still, looking at the ground. Then he smiled at the traveller encouragingly, and said: 'I was near you yesterday, when the commandant invited you. I heard his invitation. I know the commandant. I understood at once what he was driving at with the invitation. Although his power would be great enough to take action against me, he is not risking it yet, but there is no doubt he wants to expose me to the judgement of a respected foreigner. He has worked it out carefully; this is your second day on the island; you didn't know the old commandant, nor the way he thought. Your mind is trapped in European attitudes; perhaps out of principle you oppose the death-penalty in general and this kind of execution by machine in particular. Moreover, you can see how without public interest the execution is a dismal process, on a machine already showing signs of damage—so wouldn't it be possible, all things taken together (this is how the commandant thinks), that you might consider my procedure to be wrong? And if you don't think it right (I am still giving the commandant's point of view), you will not keep silent about it, for you will certainly have the confidence of your tried and tested convictions. On the other hand, though, you have seen many strange customs in many lands, and have learned to respect them, so it is likely you won't speak out against the procedure as vigorously as perhaps you would in your own country. But the commandant doesn't need that. One word in passing, no more than one casual word, is enough for him. It doesn't have to express your convictions at all as long as it just seems to meet his wishes. He will question you craftily, I'm quite sure. And his ladies will sit round him in a circle, pricking up their ears; you will say something like: "where I come from, we have a different criminal procedure", or "where I come from, the defendant is examined in advance of the verdict", or "where I come from, the condemned man is informed of his sentence", or "where I come from, there are other penalties besides death", or "where I come from, torture existed only in the Middle Ages". These are all remarks that seem to you as right as they are natural, innocent remarks that do not impugn my procedure. But how will the commandant take them? I can see him, our good commandant, pushing his chair aside and rushing on to the balcony; I can see his ladies pouring after him; I can hear his voice—the ladies call it a voice of thunder—and he pronounces: "A great Western expert, appointed to examine criminal procedure in many lands, has just said that our procedure, following old custom as it does, is an inhuman one. After this judgement from such a distinguished person, it is of course no longer possible for me to tolerate this procedure, so as of today I give the order—et cetera." You try to interrupt: you didn't say what he is proclaiming; you didn't call my procedure inhuman; on the contrary, in the light of your profound insight, you consider it to be most human, most humane; you also admire this machinery—but it is too late; you cannot get on to the balcony at all—it's already full of ladies; you try to draw attention to yourself; you want to scream; but a lady's hand stops your mouth—and we—myself and the old commandant's work—are lost.'

The traveller had to suppress a smile; so his task was as easy as that—and he had thought it was so difficult. Avoiding the issue, he replied: 'You overestimate my influence; the commandant has read my letter of recommendation; he knows I am not an expert in criminal procedure. If I were to give an opinion, it would be the opinion of a private person, no more significant than the opinion of anyone else, and in any case far more insignificant than the view of the commandant, who has, I understand, very extensive rights in this colony. If his view of this procedure is as certain as you believe it is, then I fear the end of this procedure is at hand without any need of my modest aid.'

Did the officer grasp the point? No, he still didn't grasp it. He shook his head vigorously, looked back briefly at the condemned man and the soldier, who both gave a start and left off eating the rice. He went up quite close to the traveller, not looking him in the face, but somewhere in the region of his jacket, and said, more softly than before: 'You don't know the commandant; your attitude towards him and towards all of us—forgive the expression—is rather naive; your influence, believe me, cannot be estimated highly enough. Indeed, I was more than happy when I heard that you were to attend the execution alone. This order of the commandant's was supposed to get at me, but now I can bend it to my own advantage. Without being distracted by false insinuations and looks of contempt—which would have been unavoidable if there had been greater attendance at the execution—you have listened to my explanations, you have seen the machine, and you are now about to view the execution. Your judgement on it, I am sure, is already quite firm; if a few little uncertainties persist, the sight of the execution will remove them. And now I will make my plea to you: "help me against the commandant!"'

The traveller would not let him go on speaking. 'How could I do that?' he cried. 'It's quite impossible. I can do as little to help you as I can to harm you.'

'You can,' said the officer. With some anxiety, the traveller noticed that the officer was clenching his fists. 'You can,' he repeated more urgently still. 'I have a plan that is bound to succeed. You believe your influence is not sufficient. I know that it is. But even if we grant that you are right, then isn't it necessary, for the preservation of this procedure, to try everything, even what might possibly be inadequate? So listen to my plan. To carry it out, it will be necessary above all for you to be as reticent as possible in the colony about your judgement on the procedure; unless you are asked directly, you shouldn't utter a word about it; but what you say must be brief and imprecise; they ought to notice that you find it difficult to talk about it, that you are aggrieved, and that if you were forced to speak about it, you couldn't help breaking into outright curses. I am not asking you to lie; not at all; you should only answer briefly, along the lines of: "yes, I observed the execution", or "yes, I heard all the explanations". That is all; nothing further. As for the bitterness they are to perceive in you, there is certainly enough cause for it, even though not as the commandant sees it. He of course will misunderstand it completely and interpret it in his own way. That is the basis of my plan. Tomorrow an important conference of all the higher government officials is to take place, chaired by the commandant. The commandant of course knows how to turn these sittings into a show. He has had a gallery built which is always full of spectators. I am forced to take part in these meetings, but they fill me with disgust. You will certainly be invited to the meeting in any case; if you act today according to my plan, the invitation will turn into an urgent request. But if for some mysterious reason you are not asked after all, you should by all means demand an invitation; there can be no doubt that you will receive it. So tomorrow you will be sitting with the ladies in the commandant's box. Looking up frequently, he will make sure that you are there. After various unimportant, ridiculous items for negotiation, mainly intended for the spectators—it's mostly harbour works! always harbour works!—the question of criminal procedure will also come up. If the commandant doesn't raise it, or doesn't raise it soon enough, I will take care that it happens. I will rise to my feet and make the announcement of today's execution. Quite briefly. Only the announcement. Such an announcement is not customary there, it's true, but I shall make it even so. The commandant thanks me with a friendly smile, and—well—he can't restrain himself, but seizes the favourable opportunity. "The announcement," he will say, or something of the sort, "the announcement of the execution has just been delivered. I would only wish to add that this is the actual execution attended by the great scientist whose visit, such an extraordinary honour for our colony, you all know about. The significance of our present session is also greatly enhanced by his presence. Shall we not ask this great scientist to give us his judgement on the execution as carried out according to old custom, and also on the procedure prior to it?" Of course, applause everywhere, and general agreement. I am the loudest. The commandant bows to you and says: "Then in the name of all those present, I put that question to you." And now you approach the balustrade. You place your hands on it for all to see—otherwise the ladies will take hold of them and play with your fingers.—And now at last you speak. I don't know how I'll be able to bear the tension of the hours until then. In your speech, you mustn't put any restrictions on what you say; noise the truth abroad; lean over the balustrade and roar—yes, roar—your opinion, your unshakable opinion, to the commandant. But perhaps you don't want to do that; perhaps it's not in your character; perhaps in your country people behave differently in such situations; that is all right too; that will be perfectly sufficient; don't even stand up; just say a few words; whisper them so that the officials below you can only just hear them; it's enough; you don't have to speak at all yourself about the lack of public interest in the execution, or the grating wheel, the torn strap, the disgusting gag, no, I shall deal with everything else, and believe me, if my speech doesn't drive him out of the hall, then it will force him to his knees, so that he has to confess: "Old commandant, I bow before you."—That is my plan; will you help me to carry it out? But of course you will; more than that, you must.' And the officer seized the traveller by both his arms and looked into his face, panting heavily. He had shouted the last sentences so loudly that even the soldier and the condemned man began to pay attention; although they could understand nothing, they paused in their eating and looked across at the traveller as they chewed.

For the traveller, the answer he had to give was in no doubt from the start; he had experienced too much in his life for him to waver here; he was fundamentally honourable, and he had no fear; all the same, he hesitated now for the space of drawing breath under the eyes of the soldier and the condemned man. Finally, however, he said, as he was bound to say: 'No.' The officer blinked several times, but kept staring at him. 'Do you want me to explain?' asked the traveller. The officer nodded silently. 'I am an opponent of this procedure,' resumed the traveller, 'and even before you took me into your confidence—which of course I will under no circumstances abuse—I was already considering whether I would be justified in taking some action against it, and whether any action from me could have even a small prospect of success. It was clear to me which person I should turn to first: of course, the commandant. You have made it even clearer, but without having made my decision any stronger; on the contrary, I am touched by the integrity of your conviction, even though it cannot shake me.'

The officer remained silent; he turned to the machine, grasped one of the brass poles, and then, leaning back slightly, looked up at the

Marker, as if to make sure that everything was in order; the soldier and the condemned man seemed to have made friends with each other; although it was difficult for him to manage, bound as he was so fast, the condemned man was making signs to the soldier; the soldier bent down to him; the man whispered something to him, and the soldier nodded.

The traveller followed the officer, and said: 'You don't yet know what I intend to do. I shall certainly give the commandant my views on the procedure, not at a full session though, but in private; nor shall I stay here long enough to get drawn into such a session; I shall leave early tomorrow morning, or at the least board ship.'

It didn't look as if the officer had been listening. 'So the procedure did not convince you,' he murmured, and smiled as an old man smiles at a child's prattle, guarding his real thoughts behind the smile.

'So it is time then,' he said at last, and suddenly looked at the traveller with bright eyes that held some kind of challenge, some kind of summons to participate.

'Time for what?' asked the traveller, disturbed, but he received no reply.

'You are free,' said the officer to the condemned man, in the man's own language. At first the man did not believe it. 'Go on, you're free,' said the officer. For the first time the condemned man's face had some real life in it. Was it the truth? Was it only a whim of the officer's that wouldn't last? Had the stranger interceded for him? What was it? That is what the expression on his face seemed to be asking. But not for long. Whatever it might be, if they were letting him, he wanted to be really free, and he began to struggle, as far as the Harrow allowed.

'You'll break the straps,' shouted the officer, 'keep still. We're undoing them now.' He made a sign to the soldier, and with his help he set about it. The condemned man laughed softly to himself without speaking, one moment turning his face to the officer on his left, the next to the soldier on his right, not forgetting to include the traveller.

'Pull him out,' the officer ordered the soldier. Because of the Harrow, it had to be done carefully. The condemned man already had a few small wounds on his back as a consequence of his impatience.

But from now on the officer no longer bothered about him. He went up to the traveller, took out the little leather case once more, leafed through it, and finally found the page he was looking for. He showed it to the traveller: 'Read it,' he said. 'I can't,' said the traveller, 'I told you, I can't read these papers.' 'Look at the page closely,' said the officer, coming to the traveller's side to read it with him. When that didn't help either, he moved his little finger high above the paper, as if the page were under no circumstances to be touched, to make reading it easier for the traveller. The traveller also made an effort, to oblige the officer at least in this, but found it impossible. The officer began to spell out the inscription letter by letter, then connected them up and read them out once more: ' "Be just!" it says. Surely you can read it now.' The traveller bent so closely over the paper that the officer, afraid he would touch it, moved the sheet further away; indeed, the traveller said nothing more, but it was clear he still had not been able to read it. ' "Be just!" it says,' repeated the officer, and he climbed the ladder, still holding the page; he laid it with great care in the Marker and, it seemed, completely rearranged the mechanism; it was very laborious work, and it must also have involved very small wheels, for sometimes the officer's head vanished entirely into the Marker, he had to examine the mechanism so closely.

The traveller continued to follow the work from below; his neck grew stiff, and his eyes ached from the sunlight flooding the sky. The soldier and the condemned man were each concerned only with the other. With the point of his bayonet the soldier fished out the condemned man's shirt and trousers, which were already lying in the ditch. The shirt was horribly filthy, and he washed it in the bucket of water. Afterwards, when he put on his shirt and trousers, both soldier and condemned man couldn't help laughing out loud, for they should have known the clothes had been slit in two at the back. Perhaps the condemned man felt obliged to keep the soldier amused, for he turned round and round, showing the slashes in his clothes in front of the soldier, who squatted on the ground, striking his knee and laughing. Nevertheless they kept their laughter subdued in view of the gentlemen's presence.

When the officer had finally finished up above, with a smile he surveyed the machine and all its parts once more; this time he slammed the lid of the Marker shut, for it had been open until then, climbed down, looked into the ditch and then at the condemned man, and noted with satisfaction that he had recovered his clothes from it. He then walked to the bucket of water to wash his hands, but perceived the disgusting dirt too late, and, sad that now he wasn't able to wash his hands, finally plunged them—this substitute wasn't enough for him, but he had to accept it—into the sand. Then he stood up, and began to undo the buttons of his uniform coat. At first, as he did so, the two ladies' handkerchiefs he had forced under his collar fell into his hands. 'Here, have your handkerchiefs,' he said, and threw them to the condemned man. And to the traveller he said in explanation: 'presents from the ladies'.

Despite the obvious haste with which he took off his uniform coat and then undressed completely, he still treated each article of clothing meticulously; he stroked the silver lacing on the coat with special care, and shook a tassel straight. Though it was hardly consistent with this care that, as soon as he finished seeing to a garment, he should promptly throw it with a reluctant flick into the ditch. The last thing he had left was his short sword with its belt. He drew the sword from the scabbard, broke it in pieces, gathered them all up—the bits of sword, the scabbard, and the belt—and threw them away so violently that they clashed together in the ditch.

Now he stood there naked. The traveller bit his lip and said nothing. True, he knew what would happen, but he had no right to prevent the officer from doing anything. If the criminal procedure that the officer was so attached to really was so close to being suspended—possibly as a consequence of the traveller's intervention, which for his part he felt it was his duty to make—then the officer was acting perfectly correctly; in his place the traveller would not have acted differently himself.

The soldier and the condemned man understood nothing at first; in the beginning they did not even look. The man was delighted to have the handkerchiefs back, but he couldn't enjoy them for long, for the soldier snatched them from him in a quick, unexpected move. Now the condemned man tried to pull the handkerchiefs out of the belt where the soldier had tucked them, but the soldier was alert. So they struggled, half playfully. It was only when the officer was completely naked that they began to pay attention. The condemned man in particular seemed to have been struck by a sense of some great reversal of things. What had happened to him would now happen to the officer. Perhaps it would go on like this to the bitter end. Probably the stranger had given the order for it. So that was vengeance.

Without having suffered to the end himself, he was himself avenged to the end. Silent laughter spread across his face, and did not go away.

The officer himself had turned towards the machine. If it had been clear before that he was expert in the ways of the machine, now it was almost astounding to see how he dealt with it and how it obeyed him. His hand had barely approached the Harrow, and it rose and fell a number of times until it had found the right position to receive him; he took hold merely of the edge of the Bed, and it already started to vibrate; the gag came to meet his mouth; one could see that the officer did not actually want to accept it, but his hesitation lasted only a moment; he submitted straight away and took it to him. Everything was ready. Only the straps hung down at the sides, but they were obviously unnecessary; the officer did not have to be strapped in. That was when the condemned man noticed the loose straps; in his opinion the execution was not complete if the straps were not fastened; he beckoned eagerly to the soldier, and they ran over to strap the officer in. But he had already stretched out one foot to push the crank that was to set the Marker working; then he saw the pair had arrived, so he drew back his foot and allowed himself to be strapped in. Now, though, he could no longer reach the crank; neither the soldier nor the condemned man would be able to find it, and the traveller was determined not to stir. It was not necessary; the straps had hardly been attached before the machine began to operate; the Bed vibrated, the needles danced on his skin; the Harrow swung up and down. The traveller had already been staring at it all for a while before he recalled that one wheel in the Marker should have been grating; but everything was silent; not the slightest humming was to be heard.

By operating so silently, the machine almost escaped his notice. He looked across at the soldier and the condemned man. Of the two, the condemned man was the livelier; everything about the machine interested him; one moment he would bend down, the next he would stretch up; he was constantly stretching out his finger to point something out to the soldier. The traveller found it upsetting. He was determined to stay here to the end, but he couldn't have borne the sight of the two for long. 'Go home,' he said. Perhaps the soldier might have been ready to do so, but the condemned man felt the order as outright punishment. He begged, pleading with hands folded, to be allowed to remain here, and when the traveller, shaking his head, refused to give in, he even knelt before him. The traveller perceived that commands were no use here; he was about to go across and drive the two away when he heard a noise up in the Marker. He looked up. So that cog-wheel was giving trouble after all? The lid of the Marker was lifting slowly, and then opened completely. The teeth of a cog-wheel appeared, rising until soon the entire wheel was visible; it was as if some strong force were compressing the Marker, so that there was no more room left for this wheel; the wheel rolled to the edge of the Marker, fell to the ground, trundled upright for a while in the sand, and then lay still. But already another wheel was rising at the top; it was followed by many more—some large, some small, some almost identical—the same thing befell them all; one kept thinking all the time that by now the Marker should be empty when a fresh, particularly large cluster of wheels would appear, fall to the ground, roll along in the sand, and lie still. This process made the condemned man forget the traveller's command completely; the cog-wheels filled him with delight; he kept trying to catch one, at the same time urging the soldier to help him, but then he would draw back his hand, flinching, for another wheel would follow at once, startling him as it began to roll.

The traveller on the other hand was much disturbed; the machine was obviously collapsing; its smooth operation was an illusion; he had the feeling he should take care of the officer, who was no longer able to look after himself. But all the time the falling cog-wheels were claiming his attention he had failed to keep an eye on the rest of the machine; but now, after the last cog-wheel had left the Marker, as he bent over the Harrow he had a fresh, even more dreadful, surprise. The Harrow was not writing, it only stabbed; and the Bed was not turning the body, but as it vibrated, only lifted it into the needles. The traveller wanted to intervene, possibly stop the whole thing; this wasn't the torture the officer was aiming for, but outright murder. He stretched out his hands, but the Harrow was already rising to one side with the body pierced upon it, which it usually did only at the twelfth hour. The blood flowed in a hundred streams, not mingled with water, for this time the water-jets too had failed. And now the final process failed: the body was not released from the long needles; blood was streaming from it, but it hung over the ditch without falling into it. The Harrow was already trying to return to its old position, but as if it noticed of its own accord that it was not yet free of its burden, it remained hanging over the ditch. 'Come and help, won't you!' the traveller shouted over to the soldier and the condemned man, and took hold of the officer's feet himself. He wanted to push down on the feet from his end, while on the other side the two of them were supposed to take hold of the officer's head; in this way he was to be slowly removed from the needles. But the two couldn't make up their minds to come; indeed, the condemned man actually turned his back; the traveller was obliged to go over to them and urge them forcibly towards the officer's head. As he was doing so, almost against his will, he saw the face of the corpse. It was as it had been in life; not a sign of the promised deliverance was to be discovered; what all the others had found in the machine, the officer had not found; his lips were pressed tight; his eyes were open, and had the appearance of life; his gaze was calm with conviction; the point of a great iron spike pierced his brow.

When the traveller, followed by the soldier and the condemned man, reached the first houses of the colony, the soldier pointed to one of them, saying: 'Here's the teahouse.'*

On the ground floor of one of the houses was a deep, low, cavernous room, its walls and ceiling stained with smoke and open to the street along its entire width. Although there was little to distinguish the teahouse from the other houses of the colony, which, including the palatial buildings of the commandant's headquarters, were all very dilapidated, nevertheless it roused the impression of historical memory in the traveller, and he felt the force of earlier times. He drew nearer, and followed by his companions, walked through, past the empty tables standing in the street in front of the teahouse, and breathed deeply the cool, dank air that came from inside. 'The Old Man is buried here,' said the soldier. 'The priest refused him a place in the graveyard. They were undecided for a time where they should bury him; in the end they buried him here. I'm sure the officer told you nothing about that, for of course that is what he was most ashamed of. He even tried to dig him up at night a few times, but he was always driven away.' 'Where is the grave?' asked the traveller, who couldn't believe the soldier. Straight away both of them, the soldier and the condemned man, ran ahead of him, and with outstretched hands pointed to where the grave was supposed to be.

They led the traveller up to the back wall, where guests were sitting at a few tables. They were apparently dock-workers, strong men with shining, short black beards. None of them wore a jacket; their shirts were torn; they were poor, downtrodden people. As the traveller approached, a few of them got up, pressed themselves against the wall, and watched him as he drew near. 'He's a foreigner,' came the whisper around him: 'he wants to see the grave.' They pushed a table aside, and under it there really was a gravestone to be seen. It was a simple gravestone, low enough to be hidden under a table. It bore an inscription in very small lettering; the traveller had to kneel down to read it. It ran: 'Here rests the old commandant; his followers, who may not be named today, have dug him this grave and raised this stone. There is a prophecy that after a certain number of years the commandant will rise again and lead his followers from this house to reconquer the colony. Believe, and await the day!' After he had read it, the traveller rose and saw the men standing round him, smiling as if they had been reading the inscription with him, and finding it ludicrous were challenging him to join them in their view. The traveller acted as if he hadn't noticed, distributed a few coins among them, waited until the table was pushed over the grave, left the teahouse, and made his way to the harbour.

The soldier and the condemned man had come upon some acquaintances in the teahouse, who held them up. They must have torn themselves away from them quite soon, though, for the traveller was only halfway down the long flight of steps leading to the boats when they were already running behind him. It seemed that at the last minute they wanted to make him take them with him. While he was negotiating with the boatman to ferry him across to the steamer, the two rushed down the steps—in silence, for they dared not shout out. But by the time they reached the bottom, the traveller was already in the boat and the ferryman just casting off from the bank. They might still have been able to leap into the boat, but the traveller raised a heavily knotted rope from the floor and, threatening them with it, prevented them from making the leap.

Letter to his Father

Dearest Father,

You asked me once recently why it is I maintain I am afraid of you. As usual, I wasn't able to give you any answer, partly on account of that very fear, partly because if I am to explain the reasons for it, there are far too many relevant details for me to be able to hold them even halfway together when I speak about them. And if I try to answer you here on paper, it will still be very incomplete, because even in the writing, the fear and its consequences still get in the way when I am confronted with you, and because the sheer extent of the material goes far beyond my memory and my understanding.

To you the issue has always appeared very simple, at least as far as you have spoken about it in front of me, and, indiscriminately, in front of a number of other people. It seemed to you more or less like this: you have worked hard all your life, sacrificed everything for your children, especially for me; consequently I have lived 'like a lord', had complete freedom to study what I wanted, had no occasion to worry about my next meal, and hence no worries at all; you haven't asked for any gratitude in return—you know 'the gratitude of children' all too well—but at least for some give-and-take, some sign of fellow-feeling. Instead, for as long as you can remember, I have crept away from you, to my room, to my books, to crazy friends, to wild ideas; I have never talked frankly with you; I have never approached you in temple;* I never visited you in Franzensbad,* nor had any family feeling at any other time either; I never concerned myself with the shop, nor your other business affairs; I saddled you with the factory* and then left you to it; I supported Ottla in her wilfulness,* and whereas I don't stir a finger for you (I don't even get you a theatre ticket), there is nothing I won't do for strangers. If you sum up your judgement on me, it emerges that you are not, it's true, accusing me of anything outright indecent or wicked (except perhaps for my recent intention to marry),* but of coldness, distance, ingratitude. And you accuse me in such a way as if it were all *my* fault, as if by a turn of the wheel I could have set it all up differently, whereas you are not in the least to blame, unless it is that you have been too good to me.

This, your usual way of representing our relations, is in my view right only to the extent that I too believe you are wholly guiltless of our estrangement. But I am just as wholly guiltless as well. If I could persuade you to acknowledge that, there might be a possibility, not of a new life—we are both of us too old for that*—but still of a kind of peace, not an end to your unceasing accusations, but still some tempering of their excess.

Curiously enough, you have some inkling of what I mean. For instance, you said to me recently: 'I've always been fond of you, even if on the outside I haven't behaved towards you as other fathers usually do; that is because I can't pretend like the others.' Now Father, I have never on the whole doubted your affection for me, but as I see it, this remark is wrong. You cannot pretend, that is so; but to claim for this reason alone that those other fathers do pretend is either mere self-righteousness, not worth discussing further, or—and in my opinion that is what it really is—a veiled way of expressing that something between us is not as it should be, and that you have a part in causing it, but without being to blame. If that is what you really mean, then we are of one mind.

After all, I am not saying that I have become what I am only through your influence. That would be a great exaggeration (and one I am even prone to making). It is very possible that even if I had grown up free of your influence, I still couldn't have become a human being after your own heart. Probably I would still have become a weakly, timorous, hesitant, unquiet person, neither Robert Kafka* nor Karl Hermann,* but even so quite different from what I am in reality, and we could have got on with each other splendidly. I would have been happy to have you as a friend, as an employer, as my uncle, as my grandfather, even (though with more hesitation) as my father-in-law. Only, simply as my father, you were too strong for me, especially as my brothers died when they were small and my sisters didn't come along until much later, and so I had to survive the first onslaught quite alone—and for that I was much too weak.

Compare the two of us: I—to put it very briefly—a Löwy on a certain Kafka foundation, but simply not to be bestirred by the Kafkas' will to life, business, and conquest, but rather by a spur from the Löwy side, which works more secretly, more warily, in a different direction—and often fails to work at all. You, by contrast, a real Kafka, in strength, health, appetite, voice of thunder, self-satisfaction, superiority over the rest, stamina, presence of mind, worldly wisdom, a certain liberality—and of course all the failings and weaknesses that belong to these qualities and to which you are driven by your temperament and sometimes by your quick temper. You are not wholly a Kafka perhaps in your general view of the world, as far as I can compare you with Uncle Philipp or Uncle Ludwig or Uncle Heinrich.* That is curious—and I can't quite work it out. After all, they were all more cheerful, lighter, more relaxed, more easygoing, less severe than you. (In this, by the way, I have inherited a great deal from you, and managed my inheritance far too well, but even then without having in my nature the necessary counterweights, as you have.) But then, on the other hand, in this respect you have also gone through different stages in life; perhaps you were more cheerful before your children, myself in particular, disappointed and depressed you at home (when strangers arrived you were different, of course), and indeed, perhaps you have become more cheerful once again now that your grandson and your son-in-law are giving back to you something of the warmth that your own children, apart from Valli* perhaps, couldn't give you.

In any case, we were so different, and in this difference so dangerous to each other, that if anyone had tried to calculate in advance how I, the child and slow developer, and you, the grown man, would behave towards each other, he could well have assumed that you would simply stamp on me and nothing would be left of me. Well, that hasn't happened. Life does not submit to calculation. But perhaps something worse has happened. In saying that, I am still begging you not to forget that I have not the remotest belief in any guilt on your part, not at all. The influence you had on me was the influence you could not help having—only, you should stop regarding it as some special malice on my part that I have succumbed to that influence.

I was a timorous child, though I was certainly stubborn too, as children are; and mother certainly spoiled me too, but I can't believe that I was particularly unmanageable; I can't believe that a friendly word, or taking me gently by the hand, or a kindly glance, wouldn't have persuaded me to do everything you wanted. Now you are fundamentally a kind and tender person (what follows will not contradict that, for of course I am speaking only of your image as it affected the child). But not every child has the resilience and the courage to go on searching until he comes upon the kindness. You are only able to treat a child according to your own nature, with force, noise, and outbursts of rage; and over and above that, in this case it also seemed to you to be a very suitable approach, because you wanted to bring me up to be a brave, strong boy.

Of course, I can't give a direct description today of your methods of child-rearing in my earliest years, but I can imagine more or less what they were like by inference from my later years and from the way you treat Felix,* which makes one more sharply aware that you were younger then, that is, you were also wilder, earthier, even more ruthless than you are today, and besides, you were completely tied to the shop and it was scarcely possible for me to see you once in the day, so you made all the greater impression upon me, which hardly ever settled into merely getting used to you.

I have a direct memory of only one event from my earliest years. Perhaps you remember it too. One night I kept whining for water, certainly not because I was thirsty, but partly to annoy you, I suppose, and partly to amuse myself. After several powerful threats had not worked, you picked me up from my bed, carried me out on to the *pawlatsche*,* and left me standing there for a little while, outside the locked door, alone in my nightshirt. I don't mean to say that it was wrong; perhaps at the time there was really no other way to get a night's sleep; but I want to use it to characterize your methods of bringing up a child and their effect on me. After that I was pretty docile, no doubt, but it left me damaged inwardly. It is in my nature that I was never able to make the proper connection between my silly crying for water, to me a matter of course, and the extraordinary and terrible experience of being carried outside on to the *pawlatsche*. For years afterwards I suffered agonies imagining that the giant man, my father, the ultimate authority, could come almost without cause and carry me from my bed at night out on to the *pawlatsche*, and that I was such a nothing to him.

That was only a small beginning at the time, but this feeling of nullity that often dominates me (in other respects after all a noble and productive feeling) springs in many ways from your influence. I could have done with a little encouragement, a little kindness, a little keeping-my-path-clear-for-me, but you blocked it—admittedly with the well-meaning intention of having me take another path. But I wasn't cut out for that. You would encourage me if I saluted and marched bravely, for example, but I was no future soldier; or you would encourage me if I could eat up my dinner and even drink beer along with it; or if I joined in songs I couldn't understand, or parroted your favourite sayings. But none of that belonged to my future. And it is telling that even today you really only encourage me in anything when you yourself are also affected, when it is a matter of your own good opinion of yourself that I am injuring (by my intention to marry, for example), or that has been injured in me (for example, when Pepa* rails at me). Then I am given encouragement, I am reminded of my worth, my attention is drawn to this or that good match I would be entitled to make—and Pepa is utterly condemned. But quite apart from the fact that at my age I am almost impervious to encouragement, what good would it be to me anyway if it only appears when I am not the main person concerned?

It was back then, and then in everything, that I could have done with the encouragement. I was already oppressed by your sheer physical presence. I remember, for example, how we would often undress together in the same cabin. There was I—skinny, weak, thin; and you—strong, big, broad. Before we had even left the cabin I seemed pathetic in my own eyes, not just in front of you but in front of the whole world, for to me you were the measure of all things. Then, when we had stepped out of the cabin in front of the other people, I holding your hand, a little skeleton, barefoot and unsteady on the boards, afraid of the water, incapable of copying your swimming movements, which you kept demonstrating to me, meaning well, but in fact filling me with profound shame, then I was in deep despair, and at such moments all my worst experiences in every domain came together in grand accord. I felt easiest when you would sometimes undress first, and I could stay in the cabin and put off the shame of making a public entrance for so long that in the end you would come and see what was the matter, and drive me out of the cabin. I was grateful to you that you didn't seem to notice my distress, and I was proud, too, of my father's body. Something like this difference, by the way, exists between us even today.

It had its further counterpart in your intellectual dominance. You had worked your way up so far solely by your own efforts that consequently you had unbounded confidence in your own opinions. That was not nearly so confusing for me when I was a child as it was later when I was a young person growing up. In your armchair you ruled the world. Your opinion was right; every other one was crazy, eccentric, *meschugge*,* not normal. At the same time, your self-confidence was so great that you didn't have to be consistent at all, and still didn't cease to be right. It could even happen that on some topic you had no opinion whatever, so consequently every opinion that could possibly be relevant to the matter was bound, without exception, to be wrong. For example, you were able to abuse the Czechs, then the Germans, then the Jews, not only selectively but in every respect, until in the end no one was left except you. For me you acquired that mysterious quality that all tyrants have who base their right on their person and not on their arguments. At least, that's how it seemed to me.

Now towards me, it is astonishing how often you were in fact in the right; in conversation that went without saying, though it hardly ever got as far as a conversation, but in reality too. Still, there was nothing especially puzzling about that, either. For in my every thought I was under heavy pressure from you, even in the thoughts that didn't fit in with yours—particularly in those. All the thoughts that appeared to be independent of you were from the start weighted down with your dismissive judgement. To carry that burden and still develop a thought through to the stage where it was fully worked out and permanent was almost impossible. I'm not talking here about any great thoughts, but of every little childhood concern. One only had to be happy about something, only had to be full of it, and come home and pour it out—and the answer would be an ironical sigh, a shake of the head, a finger tapping on the table: 'Oh, I've seen something much better than that', or 'You and your troubles', or 'I've no time for it now', or 'You don't say?' or 'Here's a penny'. Of course, one couldn't ask you to be enthusiastic about every little childish trifle when your own life was full of care and concerns. That wasn't the issue. The issue was rather that you were always and in principle bound to create disappointments for the child because your nature was the opposite of his, and further, that this opposition went on growing stronger and stronger as the occasions for it accumulated, so that in the end it would make its presence felt out of sheer habit, even if for once you had the same opinion as mine, and that ultimately these disappointments imposed on the child were not the disappointments of ordinary life, but rather—since what was at issue was your person as the measure of all things—they struck at the core.

The courage, resolution, confidence, joy in this thing and that, couldn't survive if you were against them, or merely if your opposition could be taken for granted—and it could almost certainly be taken for granted for nearly everything I did.

That applied to thoughts as much as to people. It was enough for me to show a little interest in a person—on account of my nature that didn't happen very often—for you to butt in without any consideration for my feelings or respect for my judgement with abuse, slander, and vilification. Innocent, childlike persons, like the Yiddish actor Löwy,* for example, had to pay the price. Without knowing him, you compared him, terribly, in a way I've now forgotten, to some kind of vermin,* and, as you so often did with people who were dear to me, you were automatically ready with the saying about dogs and fleas. I recall the actor particularly because I made a note of what you said at the time about him: 'My father speaks like that about my friend (whom he doesn't know at all) only because he is my friend. I will always be able to use that against him when he accuses me of lacking filial love and gratitude.' What was always incomprehensible to me was your total insensitivity to the kind of suffering and shame you were able to inflict on me; it was as if you had no inkling of your power. Certainly I too have hurt you with my words, but then I always knew it; it distressed me, but I wasn't self-controlled enough to hold them back; I was already regretting them even as I was uttering them. But you would lay about you with your words without a second thought; you were sorry for no one, not while you were uttering them, not afterwards—one was completely defenceless against you.

But your entire approach to bringing up children was like that. You have, I believe, a talent for it; you could certainly have done some good for a person of your own kind in bringing him up; he would have perceived the good sense in what you told him, would not have troubled himself any further and carried it out as you had said. But for me as a child, everything you shouted at me was a command from heaven; I never forgot it; it stayed with me as the most important means of judging the world, above all of judging you, and there you failed completely. As I was in your company mainly at mealtimes, instruction from you was largely instruction in table-manners. What arrived on the table had to be eaten; there was to be no discussion of the quality of the food—but you frequently found the food uneatable, called it 'cattle-fodder'; 'the cow' (the cook) had spoiled it. Because, since it suited your huge hunger and the way you preferred to eat, you ate everything fast, hot, and in vast mouthfuls, the child had to hurry up; grim silence reigned at table, interrupted by admonitions: 'eat first, then talk,' or 'faster, faster, faster,' or 'look, I finished ages ago'. Bones were not to be crunched. But you could. Vinegar was not to be slurped. But you could. The main thing was to cut one's bread straight. It didn't matter that you did so with a knife dripping with gravy. One should take care that no scraps of food fell on the floor. By the end the most scraps were lying under your chair. At table the only activity allowed was eating. But you would tidy and trim your nails, sharpen pencils, clean your ears with a toothpick. Please, Father, understand me aright: in themselves these would have been totally insignificant details. They became oppressive for me only because you, who were for me so monstrously the measure, did not yourself keep the commandments you imposed upon me. This divided the world for me into three parts: one where I, the slave, lived, under laws that were invented only for me, and which, for reasons unknown, I could never wholly live up to anyway; then a second world which was infinitely distant from mine, in which you lived, engaged in government, in issuing commands, and displeasure when they were not obeyed; and lastly, a third world where other people lived happily, free of commanding and obeying. I was always in disgrace; either I complied with your commands—and that was a disgrace; or I was defiant—and that was a disgrace too, for how could I be defiant towards you? Or I wasn't able to follow them because I didn't have your strength, for instance, or your appetite, or your dexterity, though in spite of that, you always demanded it of me as something to be taken for granted; that, of course, was the greatest disgrace. That was the drift—not of the child's feelings—but of his reflections.

My situation at that time will become clearer, perhaps, if I compare it with Felix's position now. You treat him in the same way too—indeed, you employ one particularly dreadful method: if you think he does something messy when he eats, it's not enough for you to say, as you did to me, 'what a pig!' but you also add 'a real Hermann!' or 'just like your father'. Now perhaps—one can't say more than 'perhaps'—that doesn't do Felix any fundamental harm, for to him you are just a grandfather, a particularly important one, of course, but still not everything, as you were for me. Besides, Felix has a placid character, to some extent already mature; he might perhaps be taken aback by a voice of thunder, but not in the long run definitively affected. But above all he is with you fairly infrequently, and he is of course subject to other influences. To him you are more of a dear old curiosity from whom he can pick and choose what he wants to take for himself. But you were not a curiosity to me; I couldn't pick and choose; I had to take the lot.

And I had to take it without being able to protest, for it is impossible from the outset to talk calmly with you about any matter you don't agree with or don't initiate; your overbearing temperament won't allow it. In the last few years you have explained this by the nervous condition of your heart. I'm not sure that you have ever been fundamentally different; at most your nervous heart has been a tactic to exercise your power all the more strictly, for the thought of it is bound to stifle the last breath of argument in the other person. This is not, of course, a criticism, only a statement of fact. 'You just can't talk to her—she'll leap at you straight away,' is what you usually say, but in reality she doesn't leap at you at all to begin with; you confuse the subject under discussion with the person; the subject leaps out at you and you make up your mind about it at once without listening to the person; any argument after that can only irritate you further, never convince you. Then all one gets to hear from you is: 'Do what you like; as far as I'm concerned you're quite free; you're an adult now; I've no advice to give you'—and all spoken with the terrible hoarse undertone of anger and total condemnation. And if I tremble at it today less than I did in childhood, it is only because the child's exclusive feeling of guilt has given way to an insight into the helplessness we both share.

The impossibility of calm communication between us had a further, very natural, consequence: I lost the ability to speak. I probably wouldn't have been a great speaker even under other circumstances, but I would still have mastered ordinary, fluent, human speech. But from early on you forbade me words. Your threat: 'Not a word of contradiction!' and the raised hand that came with it have attended me ever since. In your presence I developed—you are, once it concerns your own affairs, an excellent speaker—a halting, stammering manner of speaking; even that was still too much for you; in the end I remained silent, at first perhaps from defiance, then because in your presence I could neither think nor speak. And because you were my true mentor, that went on to affect every aspect of my life. It is a curious mistake altogether if you believe I never obeyed you. 'Always anti' is truly not my life's principle towards you, as you believe, and as you accuse me. On the contrary, if I had followed you less, you would certainly be more content with me. Instead, all the measures you took in bringing me up hit the mark exactly; I didn't escape a single move; as I am now, I am the outcome (that is, of course, apart from my fundamental disposition and the influence my life has had on me) of my upbringing by you and my docility. That this outcome nevertheless distresses you—indeed, that unconsciously you refuse to acknowledge it to be the outcome of my upbringing—is because your hand and my raw material were so alien to each other. 'Not a word of contradiction!' you would say, meaning to silence the counter-forces in me that were offensive to you; but the effect of this was too strong for me; I was too docile; I fell completely silent; crept away from you, and only dared stir when I was so far away that your authority could no longer reach me, at least not directly. But you stood in the way, and once again everything seemed to you to be 'anti', whereas it was only the obvious consequence of your strength and my weakness.

The extremely effective and never-failing—at least towards me—rhetorical tactics you employed in bringing me up were: loud abuse, threats, irony, cruel laughter, and—curiously—self-pity.

I don't recall that you swore at me in expressly bad language. In any case, it wasn't necessary: you had so many other methods. Besides, I was surrounded by so many words of abuse flying about in conversation at home, and especially in the shop, that as a small boy I was sometimes almost stunned by them, and had no reason not to refer them to myself as well, for the people you were telling off were certainly no worse than I, and you were no more dissatisfied with them than you were with me. Here again your baffling unawareness and unassailability. You would shout abuse without a second thought about what you were doing—indeed, you condemned bad language in others, and forbade it.

You would reinforce the abuse with threats, which were certainly meant for me. I was terrified by remarks like this, for example: 'I'll tear you into little bits—like a fish!' although of course I knew that nothing worse would follow (as a small child, though, I did not know), but it tallied closely with my idea of your power that you should be capable even of that. It was terrible too when you would run shouting round the table to catch me, obviously not meaning to, but acting as if you did, and in the end Mother would pretend to rescue me. Once again it seemed to the child that he remained alive only thanks to your mercy, and he continued to carry his life as your undeserved gift. This is where your threats about the consequences of disobedience belong. If I started to do something that displeased you and you threatened me with failure, I was so much in awe of your opinion that failure, perhaps even if only much later, was inevitable. I lost confidence in doing anything for myself. I was unsettled, full of doubts. The older I got, the more evidence you could hold against me as proof of my uselessness; in some sense, gradually, you actually came to be right in the end. Again, I am wary of asserting that I became like that only because of you; you only reinforced what was already there, but you reinforced it so strongly because simply in relation to me you were very powerful, and used all your power to do so.

You had a particular confidence in an upbringing through irony. It was also perfectly in keeping with your superiority over me. A warning from you usually took this form: 'Can't you do such and such? You're sure it's not too much for you? Of course, you haven't the time, have you?' and the like. And every question of that sort accompanied by a mean laugh and a mean face. To some extent the child was already punished before he knew he had done anything wrong. And those reproofs were so infuriating: when one was treated as a third person, not worth addressing in anger directly, when pro forma you might be speaking to Mother, but actually to me, for I was sitting there too—for example: 'We can't have that from the young master,' and the like. (This game met its counterstroke at the time, for if Mother was there, I wouldn't dare ask you anything directly, and later, when it had become a habit, I wouldn't have dreamt of doing so. It was much less dangerous for the child to put questions about you to Mother sitting next to you; then he would ask her: 'How is Father?'—in this way insuring himself against sudden alarms.) There were of course also instances where one was in full agreement with the grossest irony, that is, when it was aimed at someone else, at Elli, for example, for I was on bad terms with her for years. It was a feast of gloating and ill-will for me when at almost every meal you would refer to her: 'She has to sit ten metres away from the table, the girl's so huge,' and when, spiteful in your armchair, you tried to mimic her, exaggerating without the least trace of kindness or humour but as her bitter enemy, as she sat there so utterly repugnant to you. How frequently this and things like it had to be repeated; how little in reality you achieved by it. I believe this was because your expenditure of rage and malice did not seem to be in proper proportion to the issue itself; one did not have the feeling that your rage was engendered by this trifle of sitting too far from the table, but was present from the start in all its entirety and only took this particular thing as the chance occasion to lash out. As one was convinced that some occasion would be found anyway, one didn't bother much; one was also becoming blunted by the constant threats. One wasn't going to get a hiding—gradually that became almost certain. One became a surly, inattentive, insubordinate child, always bent on flight, mostly inwardly. So you suffered; so we suffered. From your point of view you were quite right when you used to say so bitterly, with the clenched teeth and throaty laugh that gave the child his first idea of hell (as you did recently over a letter from Constantinople): 'What a crew!'

It seemed to be quite out of keeping with this attitude to your children when you were openly sorry for yourself for all to see—which happened quite often. I confess, as a child (certainly later) I had no feeling for this at all, and couldn't understand how you could possibly expect to find any sympathy. You were so like a giant in every respect, how could compassion, let alone help, from us matter to you? Surely you were bound to scorn help from us, as you had scorned us so often. So I didn't believe your lamentations, and looked for some hidden motive behind them. Only later I understood that you really did suffer on account of your children, but at the time, when under different circumstances your complaints might have met with a child's open and spontaneous mind ready to help in any way, to me they could only be yet another all-too-obvious method of child-rearing and child-humiliating—in itself not very powerful, but with the harmful side-effect that the child became accustomed to taking lightly the very things he should be taking seriously.

Fortunately, though, there were also exceptions to this, mostly when you suffered silently, when the power of love and kindness overcame everything that stood in their way, and moved me directly. That was rarely, it is true, but it was wonderful. Such as midday in those hot summers when I used to see you taking a nap in the shop after lunch, your elbows resting on the desk; or those Sundays, when you would arrive exhausted, to join us on our summer holiday; or the time when Mother was seriously ill, and you clung to the bookcase shaking with tears; or during my last illness when you came to me softly in Ottla's room. But you stayed in the doorway, only craning your neck to see me in bed, and out of consideration just waved a greeting to me with your hand. At such times one lay down and wept for happiness, and one is weeping again now, writing about it.

You also have a particularly beautiful way of smiling, not often seen—quiet, pleased, and approving—that can make the one it is meant for utterly happy. I can't recall that in my childhood it fell expressly to my share, but it might well have happened, for why should you have refused it to me then, when I still seemed innocent to you, and was still your great hope? In any case, even such impressions of kindness in the long run only succeeded in increasing my sense of guilt and making the world still more incomprehensible to me.

Rather, I would cling to what was tangible and ever-present. So as to assert myself against you just a little, and partly also from a kind of revenge, I soon began to observe and collect and exaggerate ridiculous little traits I noticed in you. For example, how you were so easily dazzled by persons of higher rank, most of them only ostensibly so, for instance some imperial councillor* or such, and would go on talking about them (on the other hand, things like that also hurt me: that you, my father, needed such empty reassurances of your worth, and boasted of them). Or I observed your liking for indecent remarks, which you made as loudly as possible, laughing at them as if you had said something particularly fine, whereas it was only a banal little indecency (at the same time, though, it was yet another expression of your vitality, putting me to shame). Naturally, there were plenty of such observations; I was happy with them; there was a chance for me to whisper and snigger. You noticed it sometimes, and it annoyed you; you thought it was malice, disrespect, but believe me, to me it was nothing less than a means of self-preservation—quite useless, incidentally. They were jokes of the kind made about gods and kings, jokes that are not only compatible with the deepest respect, but even belong to it.

Besides, as our positions in relation to each other were alike, you too attempted a kind of defensive counteraction. You always pointed out what an easy life I had, and how well I was actually treated.

That is correct, but I don't believe that under the circumstances prevailing it was of any fundamental use to me.

It is true that Mother was infinitely good to me, but to me it was all in relation to you, and so, as a relation, not a good one. Without being conscious of her role, Mother played the part of beater in the hunt. Where your style of upbringing might, on some unlikely occasion, have set me on my own two feet by generating defiance, dislike, or even hatred in me, Mother cancelled that out by being kind, by talking reasonably (in the confusions of childhood she was the epitome of reason), by interceding for me, and once more I was driven back into your circle, which otherwise I might have broken out of—to your advantage and mine. Or the situation was such that there was no real reconciliation, and Mother would only protect me from you covertly, give me something covertly, give me permission for something—and then in your eyes I was once again the underground creature, the deceiver conscious of his guilt whose nullity only meant that he could only get what he thought he had a right to by sneaking byways. Naturally, I then developed the habit of taking these paths to seek out what even in my own view I had no right to. Once again that increased my sense of guilt.

It is also true that you hardly ever really beat me. But for me, the way you shouted, the way your face turned red, the way you undid your braces in such haste and laid them on the back of the chair in readiness was almost worse. It is as if someone is to be hanged. If he is really hanged, then he is dead and it's all over. But if he has to share in all the preparations for his hanging, and only when the noose is dangling in front of his face learns of his reprieve, it is possible that he will suffer from it all his life long. And what is more, out of those many occasions when it was your clearly expressed opinion that I deserved a hiding but by your mercy only just escaped it, there built up once again only a great sense of guilt. From every side I came to feel guilty towards you.

For years you criticized me (alone or in front of other people—you had no sense of how humiliating this was—your children's concerns were always public affairs) because, thanks to your hard work, I lived without hardship, in peace, warmth, and plenty. I am thinking of remarks which must have literally made furrows in my brain, such as: 'When I was seven I had to push the cart through the villages.' 'We were glad if we had potatoes.' 'For years I had open sores on my legs because of the poor winter clothing.' 'When I was only a little lad I had to go to Pisek to work in the shop.' 'I got nothing at all from home, not even in the army; I was sending money home.' 'But all the same, all the same, my father was always my father. Who is there who understands that today! What do children know about it! Nobody has been through all that! Does any child understand that today?' Under different circumstances, tales like that could have been an excellent means of bringing up children; they could have given them the spur and strength to survive the same hardships and privations their father had gone through. But that is not what you wanted at all, for, simply as the result of your labours, the situation had changed. The opportunity to make a mark as you had done didn't exist. The only way to create such an opportunity would have required violence and upheaval, would have required one to break away from home (assuming that one had the resolution and the energy to do so, and that Mother for her part would not have worked against it by other means). But you didn't want all that at all. You called it ingratitude, folly, disobedience, treachery, madness. So while on the one hand you tempted us towards it by your example and your stories and by putting us to shame, on the other hand you forbade it in the strictest possible way. Otherwise, for example, leaving the incidental circumstances aside, you ought actually to have been delighted at Ottla's Zürau adventure.* She wanted to settle in the country—which you had come from; she wanted work and hardship—as you had had them; she didn't want just to enjoy the fruits of your labour—like you, who had also been independent of your father. Were these intentions so dreadful? So far from your example and your teaching? Well and good, Ottla's intentions came to grief in the end; perhaps they became rather absurd, carried out with too much sound and fury; she was not considerate enough to her parents. But was she alone to blame, and not also the circumstances, and above all the fact that you were so estranged from her? Was she any less estranged from you in the shop (as you yourself tried to persuade her later) than she was afterwards in Zürau? And wouldn't you have surely had the authority to make something very good out of this venture (assuming that you could have brought yourself to do it) by offering encouragement and advice and keeping an eye on it, perhaps even just by tolerating it?

Following such experiences, you used to say in bitter jest that we had it too easy. But in a certain sense, this jest is nothing of the kind.

What you had to struggle for, we received as a present from your hand. But the struggle for life in the world outside, which was open to you from the start and which in time of course we too were not spared, was something we ourselves had to fight for much later, with a child's strength, in our adult years. I am not saying that on that account our situation is really more unfavourable than yours was; rather, it is probably on a par with it (though that doesn't take in a comparison of our fundamental natures), only we have the disadvantage that we cannot flaunt our difficulties, nor use them to humiliate anyone as you have done with yours. Nor am I denying that it might have been possible for me to have enjoyed the fruits of your labours and their great success in the right way, helped them to prosper and carried them on—to your pleasure. But our estrangement stood in the way. I was able to enjoy what you gave, but only with shame, lassitude, weakness, and a sense of guilt. That is why I could only be grateful to you for everything as a beggar is, but not through my actions.

Outwardly, the most immediate result of this entire upbringing was that I fled from everything that even remotely reminded me of you. First of all the business. In itself I should have enjoyed it, especially in childhood, in the days when it was a shop on the street: it was so lively, lit up in the evenings, there was plenty to see, plenty to hear, one could help now and again, draw attention to oneself, above all admire your splendid talents as a salesman, how you sold things, how you treated people, made jokes, indefatigable; in doubtful cases quick with the right decision; and then the way you packed things up, or opened a box—it was a spectacle worth watching, and all in all it was certainly not the worst place for a child to learn. But gradually, as you came to terrify me on all sides and you and the shop became one and the same to me, the shop too became a place where I was no longer at ease. Things that at first I had taken for granted tormented me, filled me with shame, especially your treatment of the staff. I don't know, perhaps it was like that in most businesses (in my time at the Assicurazioni Generali,* for example, it really was very similar; I explained to the director there why I was giving in my notice, not entirely truthfully, but not entirely falsely either: I couldn't bear the cursing and swearing—which hadn't affected me directly, by the way—as I was already too painfully sensitive to it from home), though as a child I wasn't concerned with the other businesses.

But I heard you and saw you in the shop shouting abuse and raging in a way that, so I thought at the time, occurred nowhere else in the whole world. And not only shouting abuse—other kinds of tyranny. How, for example, with a flick of your hand you would throw down from the counter goods you didn't want to have mixed up with others—only the blindness of your rage was some small excuse—and the shop assistant had to pick them up. Or the phrase you constantly used about one assistant who was consumptive: 'He can go and snuff it, the measly dog.' You would call the staff 'paid enemies', and they were, too, but long before they had become so, you seemed to me to be their 'paying enemy'. That was also where I learned the great lesson that you could be unjust: if it had been to me, I wouldn't have noticed it so quickly, for too great a sense of guilt had already built up in me, acknowledging that you were in the right. But in my childish opinion—later modified slightly, but not all that much—these people were strangers, who worked for us after all, and so on that account were obliged to live in constant fear of you. Of course I was exaggerating here, for the simple reason that I assumed without question that you had the same terrifying effect upon them as you had on me. If that had been the case, they would really have been unable to live; but as they were mature adults, mostly with excellent nerves, they easily shook off your abuse, and in the end it did you more harm than them. But for me it made the shop unbearable; it reminded me too much of my relationship to you: quite apart from your interest in it as the owner, and quite apart from your domineering nature, simply as a businessman you were so much better than everyone who had ever been apprenticed to you that nothing anyone managed to achieve could satisfy you. Similarly, you were bound to be for ever dissatisfied with me too. That is why I belonged, of necessity, on the side of the employees—and also because, in my timidity I couldn't conceive how one could hurl such abuse at someone outside the family; and so, in my timidity, I wanted to put things right between the employees, who were, I thought, so terribly angry and upset, and you and our family, just for the sake of my own security. It needed more than ordinary polite behaviour towards them for that, not even a more retiring manner; rather, I had to be humble, not be the first to offer a greeting, but if possible avoid their return greeting. And even if, insignificant as I was, I had licked their feet down below, still it would never have made up for the way you, as their master, hammered away at them from above. This relationship to my fellow-men, which began for me here, continued in its effect beyond the shop and into the future (there is something similar, though not nearly as dangerous or far-reaching as in my case, in Ottla's prefer-ence for the company of poor people, for example, or for sitting in the company of the maidservants, which annoys you so much, and the like). In the end I was almost afraid of the shop, and in any case it had ceased to be my concern long before I entered the Gymnasium,* which took me still further away from it. Also, it seemed to me to be utterly beyond my capabilities, for, as you said, it wore down even yours. You tried then (I am touched by it today, and ashamed) to make my dislike of the business and what you had built up a little sweeter for yourself by declaring that I lacked any business sense, that my head was full of higher ideas. Mother of course was happy with this explanation, which you forced out of yourself, and in my vanity and neediness I allowed myself to be influenced by it too. But if it had been really or even mainly these 'higher ideas' that turned me away from the shop (which now, but only now, I honestly and actu-ally hate), they would have had to be expressed in some other way than by letting me coast gently and timorously through Gymnasium and law studies until I ended up behind a bureaucrat's desk.

If I was to escape from you, I also had to escape from the family, even from Mother. True, it was always possible to find refuge with her, but only in relation to you. She loved you too much, and was too loyal and devoted to you, for her to be able for any length of time to act as an independent spiritual or intellectual power in the child's struggle. In any case, the child's instinct was a true one, for as the years went by, Mother became more and more closely bound to you. Although with respect to herself she always, within the narrowest limits, preserved her own independence delicately and tenderly and without ever fundamentally hurting your feelings, nevertheless, as the years went by, more in her feelings than her understanding, she would blindly adopt your judgements and verdicts on the children more and more fully, particularly in Ottla's—admittedly difficult—case. Of course, one must never forget how agonizing and utterly wearing Mother's position in the family was. She had toiled away in the shop, run the household, shared all the family illnesses twice over, but the crown of it all was what she suffered in her position as mediator between us and you. You have always been loving and considerate towards her, but in this respect you spared her just as little as we spared her. Ruthlessly we hammered at her, you from your side, we from ours. It was a diversion; we meant no harm; we were thinking only of the war that you were waging with us and we with you—and she was the battleground where we rampaged. And it was not a good contribution to a child's upbringing either, the way you made her suffer—you were not to blame, of course—on our account. It even gave us an apparent justification for our own otherwise quite unjusti-fiable behaviour towards her. What she had to put up with from us on account of you and from you on account of us, quite apart from those instances where you were right, because she did spoil us, even though sometimes her 'spoiling' us may itself have been a silent, unconscious demonstration against your system. Of course, Mother could not have borne it all if she had not been able to draw strength and endurance from her love for us all, and her happiness in that love.

My sisters were only partly on my side. The one who was happiest in her relations with you was Valli. She was the closest to Mother, and like her she bowed to your will without much difficulty or dam-age. But you also accepted her more kindly, because she reminded you of Mother, although there was little of the Kafka in her. But perhaps that is just what suited you: where there were no Kafka traits, even you could not demand them of her; also, with Valli you didn't have the feeling you had with the rest of us that something was being lost which would have to be rescued by force. In any case, you never had any particular love for the Kafka qualities as far as they showed in the women. Valli's relationship to you might perhaps have been even warmer if the rest of us hadn't rather upset it.

Elli is the sole example of someone who broke out of your circle with almost total success. In her childhood she was the one from whom I would have least expected it. She was such a slow, lethargic, timorous, ill-tempered, guilt-ridden, subservient, malicious, lazy, greedy, tight-fisted child that I could scarcely look at her, let alone talk to her, she reminded me so much of myself, she too a captive under the same spell of our upbringing. Her avarice in particular I found abominable, for I had it even worse, if that is possible. Avarice is one of the most reliable symptoms of profound unhappi-ness; I was so uncertain of everything that in fact I possessed only what I was holding in my hands or in my mouth, or at least was on the way there, and that is just what Elli, who was in a similar plight, most enjoyed taking away from me. But all that changed when, while she was still quite young—that is the most important thing—she went away from home, married, had children, became light-hearted, carefree, brave, generous, unselfish, full of hope. It is almost incredible how you haven't noticed this change in her, and haven't in any case appreciated it as much as it deserves, you are so blinded by the rancour you have always felt, and still feel, unchanged, towards her, only that now your rancour applies far less to the present Elli, as she no longer lives with us, and besides, your love for Felix and your regard for Karl have made it less important. Only Gerti* has to pay for it sometimes.

As for Ottla, I hardly dare write about her, for I know if I do I shall put at risk all the effect this letter is meant to have on you. Under ordinary circumstances—that is, as long as she isn't in particular distress or danger—all you feel for her is hatred. You have admitted to me yourself that in your opinion she causes you grief and worry again and again on purpose, and while you are grieving on her account she is pleased and happy. What a monstrous estrangement, greater than between you and me, must have come between you and Ottla for such a monstrous misunderstanding to be possible. She is so far away from you that you hardly see her any longer, but put a phantom in the place where you think she is. I grant you, she gave you a particularly hard time. I don't entirely understand her very complicated situation, but in any case here was something like a kind of Löwy equipped with the finest Kafka weapons. Between you and me there was no actual conflict; I was soon finished off; what remained was flight, bitterness, grief, inner conflict. But you two were always poised for battle, always at the ready, always full of energy. A sight as magnificent as it was desolate. You were certainly very close to each other at first, for even today, of the four of us Ottla most clearly represents the marriage between you and Mother, and the strengths that were united in it. I don't know what robbed you of the concord between father and child; I'm inclined to believe that the development was very similar to my case. On your side your tyrannical nature, on her side the defiance, touchiness, sense of justice, unquiet spirit of the Löwys, and all that supported by the awareness that she had the vigour of the Kafkas. I may have influenced her too, though hardly from any initiative of my own, but by the mere fact of my being. Anyway, she came as the last arrival into ready-made power-relationships, and could form her own judgement on the basis of the mass of evidence awaiting her. I can even imagine that for a while her nature was undecided as to whose breast she should fling herself upon, yours, or your enemies'; obviously you missed an opportunity then, and rebuffed her; but if it had been at all possible, you would have made a splendidly complementary couple. True, it would have lost me an ally, but the sight of the pair of you would have compensated me richly for that; and you too would have been transformed—much to my advantage—by the immeasurable happiness of finding complete contentment in at least one of your children. But today that is only a dream. Ottla has no contact with her father and has to find her own way alone, like me. And to the extent that she has more confidence, self-assurance, good health, recklessness in comparison with me, she is in your eyes that much more wicked and treacherous than I am. That I can understand: from your point of view she cannot be otherwise. Indeed, she too is capable of seeing herself through your eyes, of having compassion for your sorrow, of being—not in despair, despair is my part—but very sad. Granted, you often see us together, apparently contradicting this, whispering and laughing, and you hear yourself mentioned. You have the impression of brazen conspirators. Strange conspirators. You *are* one of the main subjects of our conversations, as you have been the subject of our thoughts, but it is truly not to dream up plots against you that we sit together, but with the utmost effort, with fun, gravity, love, anger, defiance, resentment, submission, sense of guilt, with all the powers of head and heart, it is to discuss together in every detail, from every side, on all occasions near and far, this terrible trial hanging fire between us and you, in which you constantly claim to be judge when you are, at least for the most part (I am leaving the door open to all the errors I might of course be subject to), one of the parties and just as weak and blinded as we are.

For the situation as a whole, Irma* provides an instructive example of the effects of your training. On the one hand she came from outside, and was already an adult when she entered your business; she had to deal with you mainly as her employer, so she was only partly exposed to your influence and already of an age when she was able to resist it. On the other hand though, she was also a blood-relative and respected you as her father's brother, so you had much more power over her than the mere power of an employer. Nevertheless, this girl, who despite her frail body was so competent, clever, hard-working, modest, reliable, selfless, and loyal, who loved you as her uncle and admired you as her employer, who held her own in other jobs before and later, was for you not a very good clerk. She was of course close to being in the same position towards you as your children—and naturally we pushed her into it too; and so great was the power of your nature to bend others, Irma included, that she became forgetful and careless (though only towards you, and, I hope, without the deeper suffering a child might go through), developing a black humour and even a little defiance, as far as she was at all capable of it—and this by no means takes into account that she was not well, and in other ways not very happy either, and burdened with a wretched domestic life. For me, what your relation to her suggested so richly was summed up in that remark of yours, which for us became classic: it was near-blasphemous, but it demonstrated your unawareness of your treatment of people: 'The dear departed has left me a filthy mess.'

I could describe further circles of your influence and our struggle against it, but I would be entering uncertain ground, and would have to make things up; besides, it has been the case for years that the further away you are from business and family, the more kindly, amenable, considerate, sympathetic (I mean outwardly too) you become, just like a sovereign, for instance, when he is outside the borders of his country and has no reason to be tyrannical all the time, but can mix affably with even the lowliest folk. In fact, on those group photographs from Franzensbad you always stood tall and cheerful among those surly little people, looking like a king on his travels. Your children, too, might certainly have benefited from this, only they would have needed to be capable of recognizing it while they were still children, which was impossible, and I for one would not have had to dwell constantly within the, so to speak, innermost, harshest, and most constricting circle of your influence, as in reality I did.

This made me lose not only family feeling, as you say—on the contrary, I did have a feeling for family, though it was mainly negative, an inner (of course never-to-be-ended) attempt to break away from you. But my relations with people outside the family suffered from your influence even more, if that is possible. You are quite mistaken if you believe I do everything for other people from affection and loyalty, and from coldness and deceit nothing for you and the family. I repeat for the tenth time: I would probably have been a shy and timid person under any circumstances, but from there it is still a long, dark way to the place I have actually arrived at. [Until now* there is relatively little in this letter I have kept back on purpose, but now and later I shall be compelled to withhold (from you and from myself) what is still too difficult for me to admit. I say this so that, if the overall picture were to become blurred, you should not believe it is due to lack of evidence: it is rather that evidence is there which would make the picture unbearably stark. It is not easy to find the right mean.] Anyway, it is enough here to recall the point I made earlier. In your presence I lost my self-confidence, and exchanged it instead for a boundless sense of guilt. (With this boundlessness in mind, I once wrote of someone, rightly: 'He was afraid the shame would live on after him.'*) I could not suddenly transform myself into another person when I was with other people; rather, I felt an even deeper sense of guilt towards them, for as I have already said, in sharing the responsibility, I was obliged to make good the wrongs you had done them in the shop. Besides, you had some objection to make against everyone I had to do with, openly or behind their back, and I had to apologize to them for that too. The mistrust you sought to instil in me in business and family towards most people (name me one person in my childhood in any way important to me that you didn't criticize root and branch at least once), which, oddly, didn't weigh on you at all (simply, you were strong enough to bear it, and anyway, perhaps this was in reality just a mark of the ruler), this mistrust—which for me as a small boy I found nowhere confirmed in my own eyes, for all around I could see only people of unattainable excellence—turned into mistrust of myself and constant anxiety towards everyone else. So they were certainly not a place where I could escape from you. You deceived yourself in this way perhaps because you didn't actually have any knowledge of my relations with other people, and assumed suspiciously and jealously (am I denying that you are fond of me?) that I am bound to compensate elsewhere for what is missing in my life in the family, for it would surely be impossible that I should lead my life outside it in the same way. By the way, in this respect, in my childhood at least, I still had a certain consolation in my very mistrust of my own judgement; I would say to myself: 'Surely you're exaggerating, like all young people, feeling trivialities too much as huge exceptions.' This consolation is something that later, as my knowledge of the world increased, I have lost almost entirely.

I found just as little escape from you in Judaism. This could have been a place where escape might have been thinkable; or better, it might have been thinkable that we two could have found each other in Judaism, or that we might even have started out from it as one. But what sort of Judaism was it that I got from you! Over the years, I have taken something like three different positions towards it.

As a child, in agreement with you, I reproached myself because I didn't go to temple often enough, didn't observe the fast days, etc. I believed I was doing some wrong, not to myself but to you, and was consumed by a sense of guilt—which of course was always lying in wait.

Later, as I grew older, I couldn't understand how, with the utter nothing of Judaism you had at your disposal, you could reproach me for not making an effort (out of reverence, as you put it) to practise a similar nothing. And as far as I could see, it really was a nothing, a joke, not even a joke. You went to temple on four days in the year, and you were closer, at the very least, to the indifferent members there than to the ones who took it seriously; you got through the prayers patiently, as a formality; sometimes I was astonished that you were able to turn up the passage in the prayer-book that was just being recited; for the rest, as long as I was actually in the temple (that was the main thing) I was allowed to hang around where I wanted. So I yawned and dozed through hour after hour (the only time I was as bored later, I believe, was in dancing-class) and tried to find as much enjoyment as I could in the few little diversions there were, such as when the Ark* was opened, which always reminded me of the shooting-range at the fair, where if you shot a bull's-eye the door to a cupboard would also open, only there something interesting would always come out, and here it was always the same old headless dolls.* And besides, I was also very frightened there, not only of the numbers of people one came close to—that went without saying—but also because you once mentioned casually that I too might be called up to read from the Torah. For years I trembled at the prospect. But otherwise I was not essentially disturbed in my boredom, at the most by my bar-mitzvah*—though that required only ridiculous rote-learning, and so led only to a ridiculous examination success; and then by small, insignificant incidents involving you, such as when you were called to read from the Torah and came through what I felt was a purely social occasion very well, or when you stayed behind in the temple for the Service for the Dead and I was sent away. For a long time, obviously because I was sent away and in the absence of any deeper understanding, this roused in me the scarcely conscious sense that something indecent was going on. That is how it was in temple; at home it was even more meagre, and was limited to the first evening of Passover,* which more and more turned into a performance accompanied by fits of laughter, under the influence, it's true, of the children as we were growing up. (Why did you have to fall in with this influence? Because you brought it about.) So that was the raw material of the faith that was passed on to me, added to it at best your hand pointing out 'Fuchs the millionaire's sons', who attended temple with their father on the High Holy Days. How one could do anything better with this stuff than rid oneself of it as fast as possible I had no idea; getting rid of it seemed to me itself to be the most reverent act of all.

Still later, though, I took a different view again, and came to understand how you could believe that in this respect too I was wickedly betraying you. From your little, ghetto-like village community you really had brought something of Judaism with you still; it wasn't much, and it got lost bit by bit in the city, and in the army; nevertheless, the impressions and memories from your youth were just enough to sustain a sort of Jewish life, particularly as you didn't need a great deal of that kind of support, but came from sturdy stock and by nature could scarcely be shaken by religious doubts—as long as they were not mixed up too much with doubts about society. Fundamentally, the faith guiding your life consisted in your belief in the absolute rightness of the opinions held by a certain class of Jewish society, and so, actually, as these opinions were a part of your being, in your belief in yourself. Even in this there was still enough of Judaism, but as a tradition to be handed down further, it was too little for the child: it trickled away even as you were passing it on. Partly, these were impressions of your youth that could not be passed on anyway; partly, you were too frightening a personality. Also, it was impossible to get a child too sharp-eyed with fear to understand that the handful of nullities that you practised in the name of Judaism with an indifference appropriate to their nullity could hold any higher meaning. For you they held a meaning as small mementoes from earlier days, and that is why you wanted to pass them on to me, but for you too they no longer held any intrinsic meaning, so you could only do it by persuasion or threat; on the one hand this couldn't possibly succeed, and on the other, as you simply didn't acknowledge the weakness of your position, it was bound to make you angry with me for my apparent obstinacy.

The whole thing is not an isolated phenomenon, of course; the circumstances are similar for a large part of this transitional generation of Jews who migrated from the countryside, which was still relatively devout, to the cities. That took place of itself; only it simply added to our relationship, which already had sore spots in plenty, one more that was painful enough. On the other hand, on this issue too you have to believe, as I do, that you are not to blame, but you should explain that absence of blame in terms of your nature and the historical conditions, and not merely by external circumstances, so you ought not, for instance, to declare that you had too much other work and worry to be able to devote yourself to such things. This is how you habitually twist your undoubted blamelessness into an unjust reproach against others. That is an argument that is easy to refute in every case, including this one. After all, what was at stake was not any item of instruction you should have given your children, but an exemplary life. If your Judaism had been stronger, your example would have been more compelling, that is obvious, and again, it is not a criticism, only an attempt at fending off criticism from you. You have recently been reading Franklin's recollections* of his youth. I did give them to you intentionally—not, as you ironically remarked, because of a small passage on vegetarianism*— but because of an account of the relations between the writer and his father as described there, and between the writer and his son, expressed so naturally in this memoir he wrote for his son. I won't point out any particular passages here.

Your attitude in recent years, when it seemed to you that I was becoming more interested in things Jewish, has given a certain retrospective confirmation to my view of your Judaism. As you have always from the start shown a dislike for all my activities, and particularly for the nature of my interests, you showed it here too. But over and above that, one might have expected that in this case you would make a small exception. After all, it was Judaism of your Judaism that was stirring here, and with it the possibility of a new relationship between us. I don't deny that if you had shown any interest in these questions, it would have been the very thing to make them suspect in my eyes. I certainly wouldn't dream of declaring that in this respect I am somehow better than you. But it wasn't even put to that test. Because I was the mediator, Judaism became abominable to you, Judaic scriptures unreadable; they 'disgusted you'. This might mean that only the Judaism you had shown me in my childhood was the one true kind, and that there was nothing beyond it. But surely it was scarcely thinkable that you should insist on that. But if so, your 'disgust' (apart from the fact that it was not aimed in the first place at Judaism, but at me) could only mean that unconsciously you acknowledged the weakness of your Judaism and of my Jewish upbringing, had absolutely no wish to be reminded of it, and responded to any reminder with open hatred. Besides, your negative appreciation of my newly acquired Judaism was very exaggerated; in the first place, my Judaism carried your curse within it, and in the second, for it to develop fully, one's fundamental relationship to one's fellow-men was crucial—and so, in my case, fatal.

You were closer to the mark with your dislike of my writing and of what, unbeknown to you, was connected with it. Here I had in fact escaped from you some little way by my own efforts, even if it did rather remind me of the worm whose tail had been trampled by a foot, but tears itself free and drags itself aside with its front. I was relatively safe; I was able to breathe again; for once, the dislike which of course you promptly felt for my writing too was actually welcome. My vanity, my ambition, certainly suffered from your acknowledgement of my books, which became legendary among us: 'Put it on the table by my bed!' (mostly you were playing cards when a book arrived), but fundamentally that suited me very well, not only out of rebellious ill-will, not only out of pleasure at fresh confirmation of my view of our relationship, but deep down, because to me those words sounded something like: 'Now you are free!' Of course it was an illusion. I was not free, or at best not yet free. My writing was about you, indeed, I poured out my complaints there only because I couldn't pour them out on your breast. It was a deliberately long-drawn-out parting from you, only that although it was you who forced me into it, it took the direction I determined. But how little it all was! Indeed, it is only worth mentioning it at all because it happened in my life—elsewhere it would have been hardly noticeable—and also because it dominated my life: in childhood as a presentiment, later as a hope, and still later often as despair, and it dictated—in your shape again, it seems—my few little decisions.

For example, my choice of profession. You certainly gave me complete freedom here, in your magnanimous and even, in this respect, tolerant fashion. Though in doing so, you were also following the way the Jewish middle class generally treat their sons, which was the standard you took—or at least you were following their value-judgements. Ultimately, it was also affected by one of your misunderstandings concerning my personality. Out of paternal pride, ignorance of my true nature, and inferences you drew from my delicate health, you have always regarded me as particularly diligent. As I child, in your opinion, I persevered at my lessons, and later I persevered at my writing. That is not in the remotest bit true. With far less exaggeration one might say rather that I learned very little, and nothing with any effort; given a middling memory and a fair intelligence, something has stuck, so it is not so very remarkable after all. At any rate, the total sum of my knowledge and particularly of its basis is utterly pitiful in comparison with the expenditure of time and money in an outwardly untroubled and stable life, and in particular in comparison with almost all the people I know. It is pitiful, but to me understandable. Ever since I have been able to think, I have had such deep anxieties about asserting my intellectual existence that everything else was a matter of indifference to me. Jewish Gymnasium-boys of our class and kind are slightly odd; one finds the most unlikely types among them, but I have nowhere else come upon my cold, scarcely disguised, ineradicable, infantile-helpless, near-ridiculous, deadly complacent indifference, the mark of a self-sufficient, but coldly imaginative child; in any case it was my only defence against having my nerves ruined by fear and a sense of guilt. Only my own anxieties absorbed me, though in the most various ways. Such as anxiety about my health. It began unremarkably; now and again some little alarm over my digestion, hair falling out, round shoulders, and so on; this intensified in countless gradual stages, and finally it ended with a real illness. What was it all about? It was not really an illness of the body. But as there was nothing I could be sure of, and as I needed some fresh confirmation of my existence from every moment, and there was nothing I could call my own true, undoubted, sole possession, determined by me and me alone, in truth a disinherited son, it was natural that I should become unsure of the thing closest to me, my own body. I shot up, but couldn't cope with my height, the burden was too heavy; my shoulders stooped; I scarcely dared move, let alone do gymnastics; I remained weak; in amazement I regarded everything that still functioned as a miracle—my good digestion, for instance. That was enough to lose it. And so the way was open to all kinds of hypochondria, until at last, under the superhuman strain of my wanting to marry (I'll come to that later) blood issued from my lung—the part played by the flat in the Schönbornpalais* may have been enough, of course—though I needed the flat only because I believed I needed it for my writing, so that too belongs to my present theme. So it didn't all come from overwork, as you always imagine. There were years when I spent more time lazing on the sofa in the best of health than you have done in your entire life, including every one of your illnesses. When I dashed away from you, looking busy, it was mostly to lie down in my room. The total amount of work I get through in the office (where laziness is admittedly not very noticeable, and anyway was kept within bounds by my timidity) as well as at home is tiny, and if you had an overview of it all you would be horrified. It is probably not in my disposition to be at all lazy, but there was nothing for me to do. In the place where I lived, I was rejected, written off, kept down, and though I put my utmost efforts into escaping, that was not work, for it was a matter of something impossible which, apart from small exceptions, was beyond my powers to attain.

So this was the state I was in when I received the freedom to choose my profession. But was I actually still capable of making use of such freedom at all? Did I still have the confidence in myself to get as far as a real profession? My self-esteem was far more dependent on you than on anything else, success in the outside world, for instance. That gave me strength for the moment, nothing more, but on the other side, your weight was always stronger, dragging me down. I would never get through the first class in elementary school, I thought—but I managed it; I even got a prize. But I would certainly fail the entrance exam to the Gymnasium—no, I didn't. But now I'll certainly fail the first class in the Gymnasium—no, I didn't, and went on managing it. But this didn't give me confidence; on the contrary, I was always convinced—and to me the dismissive expression on your face was virtual proof of it—that the more I succeeded, the worse it was bound to end. In my mind's eye I often saw how the terrible assembly of schoolmasters (the Gymnasium is only the most concentrated example—but it was the same everywhere around me) would gather in conclave when I had got through the first class—that is, in the second class; and when I had got through that, in the third class, and so on, to enquire how, in this unique and scandalous case, I, the most incompetent and certainly the most ignorant of pupils, had managed to sneak up into this class—which, now that general attention had been drawn to me, would naturally spew me out, to the rejoicing of all just men now freed of this nightmare. It is not easy for a child to live with such notions. Under these circumstances, what did I care about my lessons? Who was able to strike a spark of interest from me? The lessons, and not only the lessons but everything around me at this crucial age, interested me rather in the way a bank fraudster who is still in his job and trembling at the possibility of discovery is interested in the current little transactions he still has to perform for the bank as its employee. It was all so small, so remote, in comparison with the main thing. This went on until my school-leaving exam, which I really did pass, partly just by cheating, and then it stopped. Now I was free. If I had managed to remain absorbed only in myself despite the pressures of the Gymnasium, how much more so now, when I was free. So there was no actual freedom in my choice of profession; for I knew that, compared with the main thing, it would all become just as indifferent to me as every subject at school had been, so it was a matter of finding a profession which, without hurting my vanity or my ambition too much, would most readily accommodate this indifference. So Law was the obvious thing. Small attempts in the opposite direction, out of vanity, or hope, such as two weeks of studying chemistry, or a half-year of German, only reinforced that fundamental conviction. So I studied Law. This meant that for a few months before the exams, to the ruination of my nerves, I nourished my mind on sawdust, which had already been chewed by a thousand jaws before me anyway. But in some sense that was just to my taste, just as in some sense the Gymnasium earlier and my position as an official later were, for it was all in perfect accord with my plight. Anyway, in this respect I showed astonishing foresight; as a small child I had presentiments enough regarding my studies and my profession. I didn't expect any deliverance by that route; there I had long ago given up.

But I showed no foresight at all with regard to the significance and the possibility of a marriage for myself. This, the greatest terror of my life till then, came upon me almost entirely without warning. The child had been such a slow developer; externally, these things were too remote from him; now and again it became necessary to think about them; but there was no way of knowing that this was where a permanent and decisive ordeal, the bitterest even, was being made ready. But these attempts at marriage were in reality my greatest and most hopeful attempts to escape you—though then of course their failure too was correspondingly great.

I am afraid, because I fail in everything that has to do with it, that I shall never succeed in making my attempts at marriage comprehensible to you. And yet the success of this entire letter depends on it, for on the one hand what positive forces I had at my disposal were concentrated in these attempts, while on the other, all the negative forces I have been describing as the outcome of my upbringing at your hands—the weakness, the lack of self-confidence, the sense of guilt—were also gathering almost frenziedly here, and literally drawing a cordon between me and marriage. My explanation will also be difficult to make because I have been thinking it through and raking over it all here for so many days and nights that now even I am confused at the sight of it. The only thing that makes an explanation easier is what I consider your total misunderstanding of the matter; to put such total misunderstanding right just a little does not seem excessively difficult.

First of all, you place the failure of my attempts at marrying as one in a series of my other failures; fundamentally, I would not object to that, provided you accept my previous explanation for those failures. It does in fact belong among them, only you underestimate the importance of the matter to me, and you underestimate it to such a degree that when we talk about it we are actually talking about quite different things. I would dare to say that nothing that has happened to you in your entire life was as important to you as my attempts at marriage were for me. I don't mean that you haven't experienced anything as important. On the contrary, your life has been much richer, more full, more troubled than mine, but that is the very reason why nothing like this has happened to you. It is as if one person has five shallow steps to climb up, and the second only one, but that step is as high as all the other five together; the first won't take just the five in his stride, but hundreds and thousands more besides; he will have led a great and strenuous life, but none of the steps he has mounted will have held such significance for him as that first high step will have had for the second, who finds it impossible to climb even with all his strength, and is unable to get up it, nor of course get beyond it.

To marry, to found a family, to accept all the children that may arrive, to support them in this uncertain world and even give them a little guidance—that, I am convinced, is the utmost a man can accomplish. That so many apparently manage it with ease is not evidence to the contrary, for in the first place not many do in fact manage it, and in the second, those few mostly don't 'do' anything—they simply let it happen. Admittedly, that is not the 'utmost' I have in mind, but it is still something very great and very honourable (particularly as 'doing' and 'happening' are not to be sharply distinguished from each other). And ultimately it is not a question of this 'utmost' at all, but of a distant but decent approximation to it; after all, it is not essential to fly right into the centre of the sun, but it *is* to creep to some clean little corner on the earth where the sun sometimes shines and one can warm oneself a little.

What kind of preparation did I have for this? As bad as can be. That is clear from what I have said up to this point. But as far as there is such a thing as a direct preparation of an individual for it, or a direct acquisition of the basic requirements, you did not intervene very much from outside. And it cannot be otherwise, for the crucial factors here are the general sexual mores of class, nation, and the time. All the same, you did intervene here too, not very much—for this kind of intervention can only be on the basis of strong reciprocal trust, and at the crucial time that had long been lost to both of us—and not very happily, either, for of course our needs were quite different; what excites me is bound to leave you hardly touched, and vice versa; what is innocence in you may be guilt in me, and vice versa; what has no consequences for you may be the lid on my coffin.

I remember taking a stroll one evening with you and Mother—it was on the Josefsplatz, near what is now the Provincial Bank, and I began to show off stupidly, talking superciliously, arrogantly, coolly (that was bogus), coldly (that was genuine), stammering, as I mostly did when I was talking to you, about these interesting matters. I complained that you had left me uninformed, that it had been down to my schoolfellows to put me in the picture, and that I had been running great risks (I was telling bare-faced lies, after my fashion, to show how daring I was, for, being so timid, I had no more precise idea what these 'great risks' might be, beyond the usual sins of the bed that city children are prone to); and I finished by suggesting that now, fortunately, I knew it all, had no need of further advice, and everything was fine. I had in any case begun talking about these things mainly because it gave me pleasure at least to talk about them, and then out of curiosity too, and also, lastly, to take revenge on you both somehow for something. You took it very simply, in accordance with your nature; you only said more or less that you could give me some advice on how to do these things without risk. Perhaps that kind of answer was just what I wanted to draw from you; it was certainly in keeping with the prurience of a child overfed on meat and good things, physically inactive, forever concerned with himself—but all the same, my surface modesty was so offended, or I thought it must be so offended, that against my will I couldn't talk to you about it any longer, and arrogantly broke off the conversation.

It is not easy to judge the answer you gave then; on the one hand there is something shatteringly frank, primeval as it were, about it; on the other hand, as far as the message itself is concerned, it is very modern and casual. I don't know how old I was at the time, certainly not much older than sixteen. For a boy like that, though, it was a very curious answer, and it is a sign of the distance between the two of us that it was actually the first direct lesson in life that I had from you. But its true meaning, which already sank in even at the time, though I became half-conscious of it only much later, was this: what you were advising me to do was in your opinion and certainly in mine at the time really the filthiest thing there was. It was a minor matter that you were being careful my body didn't bring home any of the filth; that was only to protect yourself, your house. The main thing was rather that you remained apart from your advice, a married man, unspotted, high above these things; this was probably because the married state too seemed indecent to me, and so it was impossible for me to apply what I had heard in general about marriage to my parents. This made you still more spotless, raised you still higher.

The thought that perhaps before your marriage you could have given yourself similar advice was totally unthinkable to me. Thus it was that not a trace of earthly stain clung to you. And you were the one who with a few frank words was thrusting me down into this filth, as if it were my destiny. So since the world consisted only of you and me—an idea that seemed quite obvious to me—then the purity of the world came to an end with you, and on account of your advice the filth began with me. In itself it was incomprehensible that you should pass such a sentence on me; only my old guilt and the deepest contempt on your part could explain it. And so I was once again shaken in my deepest being—severely too.

Perhaps this incident reveals most clearly how neither of us is to blame. A. gives B. some frank advice, in keeping with his view of life; it is not very pretty, but still quite usual today in town, perhaps preventing injury to health. This advice is no support to B. morally, but there is no reason why he shouldn't be able to work his way out of harm in the course of the years; besides, he doesn't have to follow the advice at all, and in any case, the advice on its own is not an occasion for B.'s entire world to fall apart. And yet something of this kind does happen—but only because you are A. and I am B.

That neither of us is to blame is something I can also see particularly clearly in broader terms, because a similar collision between us took place again some twenty years later under quite different circumstances. As something that actually happened it was horrifying, though in itself much less damaging—for was there anything in me at thirty-six that could still be damaged? I am referring to a little remark you made on one of those frenzied few days after I had told you of my last intention to marry, when you spoke your mind. You said to me something like: 'She'd probably chosen some fancy blouse to wear—these Jewish girls in Prague know how—and of course you promptly decided to marry her. As soon as possible, in a week, tomorrow, today. I don't understand you. You're a grown man; you've been around town, and the only thing you can think of doing is straight away to marry the next girl that happens to come along. Aren't there any other possibilities available? If you're afraid, I'll come with you myself.' You said more than that, and said it more explicitly, but I don't remember the details any longer; perhaps my eyes were misting over; I was almost more interested in Mother, and how, though she was completely of one mind with you, all the same she picked something up from the table and went out of the room with it.

You have probably never humiliated me more deeply with your words, nor shown your contempt more clearly. When you spoke to me in a similar vein twenty years ago, with your eyes one might perhaps have been able to see something even like respect in them for the precocious city boy, who in your opinion could already be introduced to life in this way, without beating about the bush. Today, this consideration could only make your contempt the greater, for the boy who was just taking his first steps in life has remained stuck there, and today seems to you to be the richer by not a single experience, but only the more pathetic by twenty years. My choice of a girl means nothing at all to you. You have always (unconsciously) held down my strength of purpose, and now you believed (unconsciously) you knew what it was worth. You knew nothing of my attempts at escape in other directions, so you couldn't know anything about the course of my thoughts that had led me to this attempt to marry; you had to try to guess at it, and you guessed in line with your overall judgement of me in the coarsest, most disgusting, most ludicrous way. And you didn't hesitate for a moment to tell me as much, in just the same style. To you, the wrong you did me then was as nothing in comparison to the wrong which, in your opinion, I would be committing against your name by this marriage.

I know that with regard to my attempts to marry* you have plenty of answers to give me—and you have done so, too: how you couldn't have much respect for my decision when I'd already twice broken off my engagement to F. and then twice taken it up again; when I had dragged you and Mother off uselessly to Berlin for the engagement, etc. All that is true—but how did it get to that point?

The fundamental idea behind both marriage attempts was quite proper: to set up house and become independent. An idea that is congenial to you, after all, only in reality it then works out like the children's game, where one child holds another's hand, even squeezes it tight, and at the same time cries: 'Off you go, off you go then! Why aren't you going?' Though in our case it is more complicated, for you have always meant that 'Off you go!' sincerely, while without knowing it but just as sincerely, simply by virtue of your nature, you have always held me back—or rather, held me down.

Both girls—by chance, it's true—were still extraordinarily well chosen. Yet another sign of your total misunderstanding that you can believe that I, the timid, the hesitant, the mistrustful, should decide to get married all of a sudden, carried away by some blouse. Rather, they might both have turned into sensible arranged marriages, if this means that day and night, the first time for years, the second time for months, all my powers of thinking were bent on the plan.

Neither girl disappointed me—only I disappointed them both. My opinion of them is exactly the same today as it was at the time I wanted to marry them.

Nor is it true, as you think, that in my second attempt I disregarded the experiences of the first, in other words that I was not being serious. The two cases were simply quite different—indeed, the very experiences of the first were able to give me hope for the second, which had far better prospects altogether. I don't want to go into details here.

So why have I not married? There were certain impediments, as there are everywhere, but after all, life is made up of accepting such impediments. The essential impediment, though, which has nothing to do with specific cases, is that mentally and spiritually I am obviously incapable of marrying. The outward signs are that from the moment I decide to marry, I can't sleep; day and night my head is burning; it is a life no longer; I waver to and fro in desperation. It is not actually my worries that cause this, though it's true, it is in keeping with my melancholy and pernickety nature to be accompanied by countless worries. But these are not the decisive factors; they do, like worms, finish off the work on the corpse, but the really decisive cause afflicting me is something else. It is the general pressure of fear, weakness, and self-contempt.

I will try to explain more specifically. It is here, in the attempt to marry, that two apparent opposites in my relationship to you clash more forcibly than anywhere else. Marriage is assuredly the pledge of complete self-liberation and independence. I would then have a family—in my opinion the highest attainment one can reach—that is, it is also the highest that you have attained. Then I would be your peer; all the old and ever-new disgrace would be merely history. This would certainly be like a fairy-tale—but that is just where it is suspect. It is too much; so much is unattainable. It is as if someone were imprisoned, and had the intention not only to escape, which might perhaps be achievable, but also and at the same time rebuild his prison as a pleasure palace for himself. But if he escapes he cannot rebuild, and if he rebuilds he cannot escape. Caught in this peculiar and unhappy relationship to you, if I am to become independent I have to do something that has no possible connection with you whatever; marrying is the highest there is, and offers the most honourable kind of independence, but at the same time it also has the closest connection with you. That is why trying to get out and beyond it has its share of madness, and every attempt is punished with something very close to it.

It is this close connection itself of course that also partly attracts me to marrying. I imagine the parity that would then arise between us, which you would be able to understand better than anyone else, as being so beautiful simply because I could then be a free, grateful, guiltless, honest son, and you an untroubled, untyrannical, compassionate, contented father. But to bring that about, everything that has happened would have to be undone, that is, we ourselves would have to be obliterated.

But as we are, marriage is barred to me because it is simply your very own province. I sometimes imagine the map of the world unrolled, and you stretched out across it. And then it seems as if the only regions fit for me to live in were either those you do not cover or those lying beyond your reach. And in keeping with the image I have of your magnitude, these regions are few and rather bleak—and marriage in particular is not among them.

This comparison alone is evidence that I certainly do not mean that you drove me from marriage by your example, more or less as you did from the business. On the contrary—in spite of any remote similarities. In your marriage I had before me one that was exemplary in many respects, exemplary in faithfulness, mutual support, number of children; and even when the children grew up and disturbed your peace more and more, your marriage remained essentially untouched by it. It was perhaps on this model that I formed my high idea of marriage; the ineffectiveness of my desire for matrimony was simply due to other causes. These lay in your relationship to your children—which of course is what this entire letter is about.

There is a view that the fear of marriage is sometimes due to a dread that the children would later repay one's own sins against the parents in the same coin. That doesn't mean very much in my case,

I believe, for after all my sense of guilt has its origin in you, and is also too deeply aware that it is a unique case—indeed, this feeling of uniqueness is part of its agony: any repetition is unimaginable. Anyway, I must say that I would find such a mute, dull, dry, obsessed son quite intolerable, and, if nothing else were possible, I would almost certainly run away from him, emigrate, as you never meant to do until I intended to marry. So I might have been partly influenced by that too in my unfitness for marriage.

But a more important factor there is my anxiety for myself. To be understood like this: I have already suggested that in my writing and the things connected to it I have made small attempts at independence, attempts at flight, with the smallest success. They are hardly going to lead anywhere—I have a great deal of evidence for that. Nevertheless it is my responsibility to watch over them—or rather, that is what my life consists in: in preventing any danger it is in my power to avert—even the possibility of such a danger—from approaching them. Marriage is the possibility of such a danger; true, it is also the possibility of the greatest support, but it is enough for me that it is the possibility of such a danger. What would I do if it were a danger after all! How could I go on living in a marriage and sense this danger, unprovable perhaps, but in any case undeniable! Faced with this, it is true I am capable of wavering, but the final outcome is certain: I must do without it. The proverb of the bird in the hand and the two in the bush applies here only in the remotest degree. In my hand I have nothing: in the bush, everything there is. But even so—for this is how the conditions of my struggle and the needs of my life decide it—I am bound to choose the nothing. Similarly, I was bound to choose the profession I did.

But the most important impediment to marriage was my ingrained conviction that to maintain, let alone to guide, a family necessarily requires all those things I have acknowledged in you, that is, all of them together, the good and the bad, as they are organically united in you. I mean strength and contempt for the other, good health and a certain excess, readiness of speech and unapproachability, self-confidence and dissatisfaction with everyone else, superiority over the world and tyranny, knowledge of human nature and mistrust of most human beings, and then again qualities without any drawbacks to them such as hard work, stamina, quick wits, fearlessness. In comparison, I had almost nothing, or very little, of all these, and was it with this I wanted to risk marrying, when at the same time I could see that even you had to struggle hard in your marriage, and with your children even failed? Of course I didn't expressly ask myself this question, and I didn't expressly answer it, otherwise common sense would have dealt with the matter and pointed to other men who are not like you (to name one near at hand who is very different from you: Uncle Richard*), and in spite of that have still married, and at least haven't gone to pieces under it—which is already a great deal, and would have been more than enough for me. But I simply didn't ask this question, for it had been my life from childhood on. I wasn't examining myself simply in respect of marriage, but in respect of every little thing; and in respect of every little thing you convinced me by example and by upbringing, just as I have been trying to describe it, of my unfitness. And what was true for every little thing, and put you in the right, was of course bound to be true of the greatest thing: marriage. Until my attempts at marrying, I had grown up rather like a businessman who, for all his worries and foreboding, does not keep strict accounts, living from one day to the next. He makes a few small profits, which are so rare that he is constantly nursing them, exaggerating them in his imagination, but otherwise he makes only daily losses. Everything is entered, but never balanced. Now comes the time when he is compelled to balance the books, that is, my attempt to marry. And with the huge sums that have to be reckoned with then, it is as if the smallest profit had never been, and everything was one single great debt owing. And now marry, without going mad!

So ends my life with you up until now, and such are the prospects it bears within it for the future.

You might, if you view the reasons I have given for my fear of you, reply: 'You maintain I am making things easy for myself when I explain my relationship to you simply by putting the blame on you. But for my part, I believe that in spite of all your apparent efforts, you are at least making it no harder for yourself, indeed far more to your advantage. In the first place you too disclaim any guilt or responsibility on your part—so in that respect we are proceeding in the same way. But whereas I then ascribe the sole guilt to you as frankly as I mean it, you try to be "too clever for your own good" and at the same time "too caring for your own good" and absolve me of all guilt too. Of course, you are only seemingly successful in this (and you're not aiming for more than that, are you?), and it emerges between the lines, in spite of all your "fine phrases" about nature and contraries and helplessness, that really I have been the aggressor, while everything you have done was only self-defence. So by your bad faith you might have achieved enough to satisfy you by now, for you have proved three things: first that you are innocent, secondly that I am guilty, and thirdly that out of sheer magnanimity you are not only prepared to forgive me, but also—which is both more and less—on top of that even prove and even want to believe yourself that I, though it is contrary to the truth, am innocent too. That should already be enough to satisfy you, but it is not enough for you yet. For you have got it into your head to try to live off me to the last drop. I grant, we fight each other, but there are two kinds of fighting. The chivalrous combat, where two independent adversaries measure their strength against each other; each stands for himself, wins for himself, loses for himself. And the battle of the vermin who not only bites but straight away also sucks blood to stay alive. That is the real professional soldier and that is what you are. You are unfit for life; but to make yourself easy in that state, without a care or self-reproach, you prove that I have robbed you of all your fitness for life and put it in my pocket. Why worry now that you are unfit for life—I'm responsible. As for you, you can stretch out comfortably, and allow yourself to be carried along in life, in body and mind, by me. An example: when you wanted to marry recently, at the same time—you have admitted as much in this letter, haven't you?—you did not want to marry. But, so that you didn't have to make the effort, you wanted me to help you on your way to not marrying, by forbidding it on account of the "disgrace" the union would be to my name. But that never occurred to me for a moment. First, I never wanted to be "an impediment to your happiness" in this or in anything else, and secondly, I never want to hear such an accusation from a child of mine. But has overcoming my own wishes and leaving the marriage up to you done any good? Not in the least. My dislike of the marriage wouldn't have prevented it—on the contrary, it would have been one more incentive to you to marry the girl, for of course it would then make your "attempt at escape", as you put it, complete. And my permission for your marriage hasn't prevented your accusations, for you have just proved, haven't you? that in any case it is my fault that you haven't married. Fundamentally, though, all you have proved to me in this as in everything else is that every one of my accusations was justified, and that amongst them one especially justified accusation is missing, and that is the accusation of bad faith, false humility, and a capacity for blood-sucking. If I am not much mistaken, you are still sucking my blood with this very letter.'

To which I reply that in the first place this interpolation, which can also be partly turned against you, doesn't come from you, but from me. Not even your great mistrust of others is as great as my mistrust of myself, instilled as it was by you. I do not deny that your intervention has a certain justification, for it does contribute something new to characterizing our relationship. Of course, in reality things cannot fit together as neatly as the evidence I give in my letter—life is more than a Chinese puzzle—but all the same, with the adjustment arising from this intervention, an adjustment I am neither able nor willing to work out in detail, still, something in my view so much more nearly approaching the truth is reached that it may give us both a little peace, and make living and dying easier.

Franz.

EXPLANATORY NOTES

MEDITATION

5 *fools*: perhaps recalling the German proverb 'Children and fools speak the truth'.

8 *A. . . . C.'s company*: Kafka's manuscript identifies A. as his friend the Yiddish actor Isaak Löwy, B. as his sister (presumably Ottla, the sister to whom he was closest), and C. as Max Brod.

9 *fashions*: the businessman is evidently in the same line as Kafka's father, who dealt in fancy goods such as umbrellas and clothing accessories such as scarves, ribbons, gloves, and fans. See Mark Anderson, *Kafka's Clothes: Ornament and Aestheticism in the Habsburg Fin de Siècle* (Oxford: Clarendon Press, 1992).

10 *rob him*: Kafka often imagines small businesses as precarious and vulnerable to robbery: cf. the 'empty, plundered shop' Georg imagines in *The Judgement* (p. 26).

THE JUDGEMENT

19 *Georg Bendemann*: Kafka commented, with an air of surprise, in a letter to Felice Bauer (2 June 1913): 'And now look, Georg has as many letters as Franz, "Bendemann" consists of Bende and Mann, Bende has as many letters as Kafka and the two vowels are in the same position, "Mann" is presumably a compassionate attempt to strengthen this poor "Bende" for his struggles.'

St Petersburg: has been interpreted as 'Peter's city' (i.e. Rome), and thus as initiating the pattern of Christian allusions in the story.

colony: the friend, presumably a native speaker of German, has failed to establish contact with the large community of emigrants from German-speaking countries living permanently or temporarily in St Petersburg.

20 *political situation in Russia*: insecurity following the abortive 1905 revolution.

21 *Frieda Brandenfeld*: the initials are also those of Felice Bauer, to whom the story is dedicated. 'Brandenfeld' may have been suggested by 'Brandenburg', the province surrounding Berlin, where Felice lived. Kafka noted that the suffix *feld* (= field) might have been suggested by *Bauer*, which means 'farmer' (letter, 2 June 1913).

well-to-do family: Kafka's manuscript shows that he originally considered making Frieda Brandenfeld the daughter of a well-to-do factory-owner, jeweller, or cinema-owner—the last a sign of Kafka's interest in new media.

21 *we're both of us to blame for that*: Kafka leaves it ambiguous whether 'we' means Georg and his fiancée, or Georg and his friend.

22 *giant*: cf. the stature of the father in *The Metamorphosis*, where Gregor is 'amazed at the gigantic size of his boot-soles' (p. 58). Kafka's father was a big man, and Kafka, in a letter to Felice of 20–1 January 1913, describes his father's family as 'strong giants'.

23 *our dear mother*: this curious expression implies that Georg's father thinks of his late wife as his mother as well as Georg's.

24 *to deny him to you at least twice*: perhaps alluding to Peter's threefold denial of Jesus (Mark 14).

25 *Russian revolution*: that of 1905, in which the priest Father Gapon played a prominent part. Here the priest appears to be inciting a crowd to violence.

26 *a son after my own heart*: cf. 1 Samuel 13: 14: 'the Lord hath sought him a man after his own heart'; quoted also at Acts 13: 22.

plundered shop: here Kafka's manuscript has the deleted sentence: 'A trampling mob went past', possibly suggesting an anti-Semitic riot.

27 *what if he were to fall*: ambiguously suggesting both concern and malice.

28 *really—but more really*: a literally nonsensical expression.

death by drowning!: perhaps recalling the punishment visited on the Egyptians, who, pursuing the fleeing Israelites led by Moses, were drowned in the Red Sea (Exodus 14: 28).

He still held on: Georg's position suspended from the railings may recall that of Jesus on the cross, anticipated in the cleaning-woman's cry.

THE METAMORPHOSIS

29 *vermin*: Kafka's word 'Ungeziefer' suggests a 'pest' or 'vermin', but no specific creature. The details of Gregor's body do not correspond to any insect, and do not cohere: if his belly is so domed, how do his small legs reach the ground?

a lady: the pin-up recalls Sacher-Masoch's *Venus in Furs* and the fashions of 1912, when, as fashion magazines show, furs were particularly popular. See also the Introduction, p. xxiii.

30 *little white dots*: perhaps the traces of a nocturnal ejaculation?

It would make him fall off his desk: a veiled wish for his employer's death; cf. *The Judgement*, p. 27.

31 *spineless*: a Freudian slip, since as an insect Gregor lacks a spine, though he does not yet consciously know it.

fist: this motif will recur significantly throughout the story: see p. 39.

34 *leaving his bed*: the awkward syntax expresses the illogicality of the thought: Gregor thinks that his non-appearance at the station ought to be interpreted as showing his devotion to his work.

39 *reserve*: Gregor has done a spell of compulsory military service.

41 *deliverance*: this word, repeated on p. 43, introduces a faint suggestion of liberation.

46 *out of tact*: this is Gregor's interpretation; the reader will easily think of a different one.

47 *cries to the saints*: the first of several indications that the family are Catholics.

49 *Christmas Eve*: the story begins in autumn or early winter, with appropriately dismal weather, and ends in spring.

50 *Charlottenstrasse*: a name presumably chosen for its ordinariness.

58 *uniform*: the father has assumed the attributes of masculinity—soldierly bearing and uniform, etc.—that Gregor himself had during his military service (cf. p. 39).

59 *nailed fast*: possibly a hint of Jesus being nailed to the cross.

memorial in his flesh: Cf. 2 Corinthians 12: 7: 'there was given me a thorn in the flesh, the messenger of Satan to buffet me, lest I should be exalted beyond measure'.

63 *run to and fro*: Kafka's manuscript says, in a deleted phrase, that Gregor 'was crouching on the lady's portrait, as he had often done recently', a further sign of the importance for him of the picture of the lady in furs.

IN THE PENAL COLONY

75 *enquiring traveller*: the original term, 'Forschungsreisender', has no precise equivalent: it suggests neither an explorer nor a scientist, but somebody travelling in order to inform himself. A well-known contemporary prototype was the criminal lawyer Robert Heindl, who in 1909–10 visited penal settlements in New Caledonia, the Andaman Islands, and China at the request of the German government, and published his findings as *Meine Reise zu den Strafkolonien* (1912). Kafka almost certainly knew this book.

77 *French*: recalling the French penal colony on Devil's Island, off the coast of South America.

83 *script*: this may suggest Holy Scripture, especially as the officer regards it with reverence.

98 *teahouse*: suggests an Oriental setting, as in Mirbeau's *The Torture Garden* (*Le Jardin des supplices*). See Introduction, p. xxix.

LETTER TO HIS FATHER

100 *Schelesen*: (Železná), a resort where Kafka and Brod stayed in a hotel in November 1919.

temple: the normal colloquial term for 'synagogue' used by Kafka and his contemporaries.

100 *Franzensbad*: (Františkovy Lázně), a spa and popular holiday resort in Czechoslovakia, where Hermann and Julie Kafka stayed in the summer of 1919.

factory: in December 1911 Karl Hermann, the husband of Kafka's sister Elli, founded an asbestos factory, employing twenty-five workers. Kafka, officially a sleeping partner, was constantly reproached by his parents for taking too little interest in the factory. The factory was not profitable; it ceased production when the war broke out, and was wound up in 1917.

wilfulness: Kafka's youngest sister Ottla, an independent-minded young woman, had a long relationship with a Gentile bank employee, Josef David, whom she married in July 1920. She helped reluctantly in her father's shop, and wanted to learn farm management. In 1917 she got her chance: the family placed her in charge of a run-down farm which her brother-in-law Karl Hermann had bought near his home town, Zürau (Siřem). In 1919 she began studying at an agricultural college at Friedland (Frýdlant) in northern Bohemia. Her parents disapproved of her seeking a profession; also, while her two sisters had accepted husbands found for them by marriage-brokers, Ottla had formed her own relationship, and with a Gentile who was relatively poor.

recent intention to marry: in September 1919 Kafka became engaged to a 28-year-old businesswoman from Prague, Julie Wohryzek (1891–1944), but the engagement was terminated two months later when the couple's hopes of finding an affordable flat were dashed.

101 *too old for that*: in November 1919 Kafka was 36, his father 67.

Robert Kafka: the son of Hermann Kafka's brother Philipp; a lawyer in Prague. Kafka admired his physical vitality.

Karl Hermann: a businessman who had married Kafka's sister Elli in 1910. He was energetic, extravagant, and keen on sometimes imprudent business ventures.

102 *Uncle Philipp . . . Ludwig . . . Heinrich*: Hermann Kafka's three brothers, all dead by the time this letter was written.

Valli: Kafka's second sister Valerie.

103 *Felix*: Felix Hermann, son of Kafka's sister Elli and her husband Karl; born in 1911.

pawlatsche: a wooden balcony at the back of the house.

104 *Pepa*: Josef David, soon to be the husband of Kafka's sister Ottla.

105 *meschugge*: 'crazy'.

106 *Löwy*: the Yiddish actor Isaak Löwy or Jitskhok Levi (no relation to Kafka's mother) who belonged to the theatre troupe from Lemberg in Galicia which performed in Prague's Café Savoy in 1911–12; Kafka attended many of these performances, wrote about them enthusiastically in his diary, and formed a close friendship with Löwy.

vermin: the word used here, 'Ungeziefer', is also used to describe the transformed Gregor Samsa at the beginning of *The Metamorphosis* (see note to p. 129). According to Kafka's diary for 3 November 1911, his father said of Löwy: 'If you go to bed with dogs, you rise with bedbugs.'

112 *imperial councillor*: a title awarded to high-ranking civil servants, roughly equivalent to a British knighthood.

114 *Zürau adventure*: Ottla's management of the farm at Zürau (see above, note to p. 100). The farm proved unsustainable because late in the war it was impossible to obtain seed-corn and animal fodder; Karl Hermann and Ottla agreed to abandon it in August 1918.

115 *Assicurazioni Generali*: a private insurance company with its head office in Trieste; Kafka worked in its Prague branch from October 1907 to July 1908.

117 *Gymnasium*: grammar-school; Kafka attended the humanist Gymnasium, where Latin and Greek were central to the curriculum, in the Old Town of Prague, from 1893 to 1901.

119 *Gerti*: second child of Karl and Elli Hermann, born in 1912.

120 *Irma*: Irma Kafka, daughter of Kafka's uncle Heinrich; after the deaths of both her parents she helped alongside Ottla in Hermann Kafka's shop, and was Ottla's closest female friend. She died, probably of Spanish flu, in May 1919.

122 *Until now* . . . : the square brackets are in Kafka's original text.

He was afraid . . . him: Kafka is quoting (from memory) the last sentence of *The Trial*: 'It seemed as if his shame would live on after him.'

123 *Ark*: a cupboard at the eastern end of the synagogue, covered by a curtain, and containing the sacred scrolls on which the Torah (i.e. the Pentateuch, the first five books of the Bible, containing the Law) is written. During a service a number of people are called up to read a portion of the Torah, though normally each is required only to recite a benediction before and after the reading, which is chanted by a specially qualified person.

headless dolls: Kafka's disrespectful description of the scrolls on which the Law (Torah) was written, and which were kept in the Ark of the Covenant (see Exodus 25: 10–22) and reverentially displayed.

bar-mitzvah: literally 'son of commandment', the adult status attained by a Jewish boy at the age of 13; this transition may be marked by ceremonies, in which the boy is called up to read from the Torah (or, as with Kafka, to recite a portion which he has previously learned by heart).

124 *Passover*: the spring festival commemorating the Jews' exodus from Egypt, in which God killed all the first-born sons of the Egyptians but 'passed over' the Jewish households (Exod. 12: 23). The first night of Passover is marked by a festive family meal (*Seder*) in which rituals celebrating the exodus are performed.

125 *Franklin's recollections*: the autobiography of the American scientist and politician Benjamin Franklin (1706–90); Kafka gave his father a Czech translation.

vegetarianism: Kafka was a committed vegetarian and a devotee of the burgeoning movement for *Naturheilkunde*, which sought to cultivate a healthy body through gymnastics, diet, and comfortable clothing; such interests struck his father as eccentric.

128 *Schönbornpalais*: an eighteenth-century mansion in Prague, where in March 1917 Kafka rented a two-room flat.

134 *my attempts to marry*: Kafka is referring to his two engagements, the first to Felice Bauer ('F.') in 1914, and the second to Julie Wohryzek in 1919–20. See Chronology.

138 *Uncle Richard*: Kafka's maternal uncle Richard Löwy, a small business-man who dealt in children's and workers' clothing, was married with four children.

American Literature

British and Irish Literature

Children's Literature

Classics and Ancient Literature

Colonial Literature

Eastern Literature

European Literature

Gothic Literature

History

Medieval Literature

Oxford English Drama

Poetry

Philosophy

Politics

Religion

The Oxford Shakespeare

A complete list of Oxford World's Classics, including Authors in Context, Oxford English Drama, and the Oxford Shakespeare, is available in the UK from the Marketing Services Department, Oxford University Press, Great Clarendon Street, Oxford OX2 6DP, or visit the website at www.oup.com/uk/worldsclassics.

In the USA, visit www.oup.com/us/owc for a complete title list.

Oxford World's Classics are available from all good bookshops. In case of difficulty, customers in the UK should contact Oxford University Press Bookshop, 116 High Street, Oxford OX1 4BR.

	Late Victorian Gothic Tales
JANE AUSTEN	Emma
	Mansfield Park
	Persuasion
	Pride and Prejudice
	Selected Letters
	Sense and Sensibility
MRS BEETON	Book of Household Management
MARY ELIZABETH BRADDON	Lady Audley's Secret
ANNE BRONTË	The Tenant of Wildfell Hall
CHARLOTTE BRONTË	Jane Eyre
	Shirley
	Villette
EMILY BRONTË	Wuthering Heights
ROBERT BROWNING	The Major Works
JOHN CLARE	The Major Works
SAMUEL TAYLOR COLERIDGE	The Major Works
WILKIE COLLINS	The Moonstone
	No Name
	The Woman in White
CHARLES DARWIN	The Origin of Species
THOMAS DE QUINCEY	The Confessions of an English Opium-Eater
	On Murder
CHARLES DICKENS	The Adventures of Oliver Twist
	Barnaby Rudge
	Bleak House
	David Copperfield
	Great Expectations
	Nicholas Nickleby
	The Old Curiosity Shop
	Our Mutual Friend
	The Pickwick Papers